FENG SHUI +

CHARLOTTE NIGHTINGALE

風
水

Forthcoming books by Pam Ferderbar

The Further Exploits of Charlotte Nightingale

#Charlottemoment:
A Collection of Horrifyingly Embarrassing and Ridiculous Mishaps

Mo's Indian

FENG SHUI +
CHARLOTTE
NIGHTINGALE

PAM FERDERBAR

Henschel
HAUS
publishing, inc.
MILWAUKEE, WISCONSIN

Cover design by Deborah Tyszka.
Cover photography by Pam Perderbar
Author photo by Tom Ferderbar

Published by
HenschelHAUS Publishing, Inc.
www.henschelHAUSbooks.com

Paperback ISBN: 978159598-385-5
Hardcover ISBN: 978159598-398-5
E-ISBN: 978159598-386-2
Audio book ISBN: 978159598-387-9

Publisher's Cataloging-In-Publication Data
(Prepared by The Donohue Group, Inc.)

Ferderbar, Pam.
Feng shui + Charlotte Nightingale / Pam Ferderbar.
pages ; cm
Issued also as an ebook and an audiobook.
ISBN: 978-1-59598-398-5 (hardcover)
ISBN: 978-1-59598-385-5 (paperback)
1. Women--Fiction. 2. Feng shui--Fiction. 3. Fortune--Fiction. 4. Attitude
change--Fiction. 5. Humorous stories, American. I. Title. II. Title: Feng shui and
Charlotte Nightingale
PS3606.E74 F46 2015
813/.6   2015933656

For Aunt Gracie,
my inspiration

風
水

CHAPTER ONE

Charlotte Nightingale was plain like oatmeal is plain. Not crunchy and wearing Birkenstocks like granola, nor as delicate as a good piece of whitefish.

Joey Lozzi, who at his insistence went as "Frank," might have (with a bit of class and two nickels to rub together) passed for a young Sinatra. However, on most days, his thrift shop suits smelled of mothballs and the pockets were empty.

The dull thud of an empty bottle hitting the carpet seemed to trigger Charlotte's clock radio. Stuck between stations, it blasted a cacophony of L.A.'s top Latino talk radio and an infomercial concerning toenail fungus. Charlotte opened her eyes in the hope that something might have changed, but her life, her man, and her room were just as they were left the night before. The bedside table remained dusted with cigarette ashes Joey never seemed to quite deposit in the ashtray. Cigarette butts floated in an ice bucket that Joey insisted accompany his bottle of Jack Daniel's and a chipped crystal tumbler he kept with him at all times.

The thin veneer of Charlotte's dresser remained curled and peeling where the years and inferior glue had left their mark. Shreds of nylon hose hung like cobwebs over drawers that overflowed with odd socks, bra straps, and scraps of paper. The surface of her dresser was a jumble of books, handbags with broken straps, mate- less earrings, magazines, matchbooks, sewing projects that she never quite got to, an empty tape dispenser, and a dusty bouquet she caught at a cousin's wedding.

The bandleader had asked all the single women to line up for the big toss and although she loathed such corny displays, Charlotte capitulated after her ribs were nearly cracked by Mom's aggressive elbow. Charlotte leapt up, straight out of her seat, upsetting her chair with a loud crash. The bouquet hit her square in the face, producing a black eye and an allergic reaction to calla lilies that caused her lips to swell like a grouper.

A protrusion in the bed beside Charlotte stirred. "Be a good dame for chrissakes and turn off that noise," spoke the lump that was Joey. Charlotte reached over and banged the clock radio into submission, then sat up, startled, as she was every morning, by her own reflection in the dresser mirror facing the bed.

She pulled Joey's wrinkled white dress shirt closely around her and got up. Navigating the floor, which was strewn with odd shoes, heaps of clothing, books, and the empty liquor bottle, Charlotte stubbed her big toe on the leg of a chair. She hopped on one foot and attempted to tug loose a bra from the tangled mess in the drawer.

"Frank needs some sugar," Joey said, puckering up. He lit a cigarette and smiled rakishly. "Is that my shirt?" He squinted at Charlotte. "Hey, I have to wear that today!"

She looked back for a moment, and then gave the bra another tug, whereupon the strap broke loose and the undergarment was jettisoned deep into the drawer. She extricated a jog bra, its elastic long since its prime, and a pair of stretched-out knee socks, and turned to him.

"Do you have an interview today, Joey?" Charlotte was as hopeful as possible, given the response of which she was resignedly certain.

"How many times I gotta tell ya, Baby?" He flicked cigarette ashes onto the nightstand some distance from the ashtray. "Now get over here and give Frank a smooch."

"Frank," she said flatly, taking a seat on the edge of the bed. "You promised you were going to look for a job today."

He dropped his cigarette butt into the murky ice bucket. "I think it's gonna rain," he growled playfully, tugging her shirt.

Rolling her eyes, she pulled the garment tightly around her, lifted the hat off his toe, and plopped it on his head. "You said you were going to look for a job."

Charlotte got up, missed the treacherous chair leg, and disappeared into the closet while Joey adjusted his hat and lit another cigarette.

"You know I work at night, Baby," he said, and then blew a smoke ring.

From within the bowels of the closet, she countered unenthusiastically, "You don't actually work at all, Frank."

He swung his legs out of bed. "What did you say?"

"Nothing."

She emerged from the closet with a terrific assortment of mismatched skirts, pants, sweaters, and shirts that she scattered across the bed. "What should I wear?"

He picked up a plaid skirt with the hem falling down. "What goes with what?"

She took the skirt from him and dug into the pile, where she pulled loose a floral blouse and a cardigan without a single color in common with the other two garments. "There. This goes together," she said, questioning her own judgment.

He looked at the bizarre ensemble, raised his eyebrow, and smiled. "You look good in anything, Baby."

Not entirely convinced, but running out of time, she dashed out of the room. "Staple the hem for me, would you? I'm late."

He sat down on the bed, puffed his cigarette and glanced around the room. "Stapler," he mused, exhaling.

Charlotte closed the bathroom door behind her and pulled a string that turned on a flickering light over a stained porcelain sink. She frowned at her reflection in the medicine cabinet mirror. She felt that her eyes were set a little too closely, her nose curved slightly to one side, and her mouth lacked character. It wasn't the look of a fashion model, or even a woman in an erectile dysfunction commercial. Those women leaned more toward the glamorous. Charlotte's looks were perfectly suited to a librarian—her dream job. Looking down the barrel of another day at her current crappy job, she moaned quietly as she pulled off the shirt and opened the bathroom door. Joey was sitting on the bed, smoking. She hung the shirt on the outside doorknob.

"Stapler, Frank. Stapler."

She closed the bathroom door and reached into the tub to turn on the hot water. Waiting for it to heat, Charlotte slid the medicine cabinet mirror over and took out her toothbrush and the Mentadent, which felt heart-sinkingly light in her hands. Expectantly holding her toothbrush under the nozzle of the plastic dispenser, she pushed on the head to no avail.

Taking a deep breath, Charlotte braced the contraption against her thigh and pushed on it until the oval-shaped bottom was embedded in her flesh, then slapped the toothpaste gadget on the chipped edge of the sink and heaved on it with the heel of her hand. The Mentadent dispenser was unyielding, but the sink was not. It jerked a few inches from the wall, revealing the black abyss between apartments. She grabbed a dingy towel and stuffed it into the hole before sucking the last molecules of minty dreck out of the Menta-dent nozzle. She stepped into the tub, flung the mildewed shower curtain closed and pulled the lever for the shower.

Snatching the Herbal Essence from a rusted wire shower caddy, only to discover it was empty, Charlotte nonetheless was determined to wash her hair. She unscrewed the cap and held it under the showerhead adding enough water to dilute the coagulated gunk stuck to the bottle's innards. The milky suds that eventually plopped onto her scalp did little more than coat her hair in a thin film—and provide an enormous annoyance—when the shower cut off mid-stream. She stepped out of the tub, put on a shabby chenille bathrobe, opened the bathroom door, and groped for the outside knob. The knob was bare. Joey's shirt was gone.

A narrow hallway ran the length of Charlotte's apartment, leading to a cramped living room, traversed overhead by heavy beams that the previous tenants—Druids, Charlotte supposed—had painted black. A small closet, built without permits by said Druids, jutted into the room at a bizarre angle. The combination of architec-tural abomination and the mismatched furniture shoved against the walls, gave the space the appearance of a waiting room at a free clinic in Uzbekistan. What the apartment lacked in visual appeal, however, was overcompensated for by a sheer volume of books—amassed along the walls, wedged between chairs, towering from every surface and arranged in strict accordance with the Dewey Decimal System.

Charlotte marched to a tall stack of classics under the room's singular window. Carefully setting aside the top three books, she reached for the fourth and flipped it open. *"To my darling Jemma,"* the inscription read. *"Happy Wednesday. With all my love, Brian."* Jaw clenched, Charlotte's hand quickly scoured the pages. In desperation, she shook the book upside down—empty. She resented Jemma and

Brian and their damned happy days of the week, but mostly it irked her that people would mar a perfectly good book with such banal sentiment. *They should invent a library prison for people like that,* she posited. Then she thought about what had been taken from the book and her stomach seized with anxiety.

"Joey, you asshole," she muttered to herself, plopping onto the sofa, one leg of which had been replaced by three *Plumbing for Dummies* editions, thick as phone books.

"Hey, you're a smart broad. You don't need to use that kind of language, Baby." Joey sauntered out of the kitchen, swirling Jack Daniel's over the melting ice in his crystal tumbler. He tossed back half the drink and grinned cockeyed at Charlotte.

She stood to face him and her knees went weak. He was a louse all right, but he was a sexy louse. "The rent money's gone. I thought you left." The words poofed into thin air and lost their gravity even as they came out of her mouth.

"What happened to your hair?" He stared at the hard crust forming atop her head and took a sip of his cocktail before setting it on a volume of Keats. "I wouldn't just take your dough and blow. You really know how to hit a guy where it hurts." He tripped over a wilted potted plant in the foyer and opened the front door. "I'll pay you back tomorrow."

He was gone.

"It's the rent money. I gotta have it," she pleaded to no one, wiping a ring of condensation from the cover of the poetry book with the sleeve of her bathrobe. Shoulders slumping, scratching an itchy scalp, Charlotte shuffled into the kitchen with Joey's glass.

The avocado green stove, harvest gold fridge, and flecked yellow linoleum floor had, in the decades since they were first installed, taken on a grimy patina. Charlotte walked through the dreary room and out the sliding aluminum doors to the balcony, which overlooked Spanky's, a hugely popular fetish and sex toyshop across the street. Ever since S&M had gone mainstream the shop did booming business at all hours of the day and night.

She pulled a quilted blue moving blanket off a group of five-gallon water jugs, and in spite of a seemingly apparent lack of muscles, she effortlessly picked up one of the heavy bottles and hoisted it onto the seat of an old canvas director's chair with the words "Hair & Make-Up" stitched across its back. In one synchronized movement she dropped to her knees, ripped the red rubber seal off the bottle, ducked beneath the torrent of cold water and rinsed her hair.

It would have appeared that she had managed rather gracefully to pull off this peculiar bathing ritual had it not been for her neglect in bringing a towel to the party. When nothing was left in the bottle Charlotte blindly groped for the towel, knowing she had forgotten it. As icy water soaked her bathrobe and pooled around her kneeling figure, she squeezed as much liquid as possible from her dripping hair.

Life at the Emperor's Kitchen restaurant in L.A.'s Chinatown began the same way every morning. Old Man Kwan hosed down the sidewalk in front of the establishment and cursed the people who had deposited chewing gum and cigarette butts on his property. Years of practice taught him exactly how to position the hose at his hip, crooked thumb pressed over the mouth just so, giving him maximum water pressure and trajectory.

"Yeeeeha!" he screeched as he made a direct hit on a boy with a purple Mohawk whizzing by on a $500 Tony Hawk skateboard. "Yeeeehoooey!" he squawked while dousing another boy, drenching the kid's Laker jersey.

A battered white Toyota pulled up at the curb, and the old man made a grand gesture of looking at his bare wrist as though it displayed a watch. "You are late," he said flatly as his son stepped out from behind the wheel.

Known simply as Kwan, the young man looked nothing like his father. Standing erect, dressed casually in faded jeans and white T-shirt, and sporting a long silky black ponytail, Kwan was tall, lean and muscular. With high, well-defined cheekbones, deep brown eyes and a full, expressive mouth, Kwan was simply beautiful.

He had slept well the night before, but as he did every single workday, he felt exhausted the instant he got to the restaurant. Sighing, he picked up a cigarette butt his dad had missed.

"I get here the same time every day," Kwan said, placing the cigarette in a Folgers coffee can on the sidewalk.

"Watch your tone," the old man admonished, narrowing his eyes. He toyed with the idea of turning the hose on his son, then thought better of it as a gang of schoolchildren came his way, lugging Sponge Bob backpacks and Spiderman lunch boxes. His thumb twitched over the nozzle of the hose.

"Dad! Don't you dare!"

The old man's shoulders slumped with disappointment as he trudged to the spigot, turned off the water, and coiled the hose. "They could walk on the other side of the street," he griped.

A pimped red Honda with an Indy-sized spoiler screeched to a stop a fraction of an inch behind Kwan's Toyota, vibrating with the BOOM BOOM BOOM of West Coast gangsta rap. The old man lunged for the spigot. Kwan blocked him.

"I'll finish up here. Go on inside, Dad."

"No-good-nik," the old man hissed, glaring at the Honda.

"Is that Russian? Kwan asked.

"I picked it up playing chess at the park with Vladimir Efimov," Kwan's father explained, then added, "...when I'm not busy working to support my family and bring a better way of life for my children than I had in Yangtze Province where we didn't have shoes or..."

Kwan cut him off. "Yes, yes, I know. It was uphill to the people's re-education center. It was uphill back home to the commune. It was all uphill."

Kwan Senior grumbled and shuffled his way into the restaurant. The Honda's driver watched the old man disappear before getting out of the car.

"Dog," the young man exclaimed with a South Central inflection although he was Chinese, and originally from the O.C.

"Shit, Dragon Breath is off the chain." Harold Yee, Kwan's best friend since first grade, was a squat young man wearing baggy jeans slung well below his butt and a Sean John polo shirt big enough to house the entire Ming Dynasty. He ran his hands over his shaved head. "Let's hit the beach."

Kwan glanced at the door to the restaurant. "Yeah, right."

Traffic on the street had backed up due to a rusty Jetta stalled at the light. A piece of plaid fabric fluttered from the bottom of the driver's door. The car lurched forward and stalled a second time, forcing a trailing Mercedes to jam to a screeching halt. Horns blared and fists shook. Charlotte Nightingale could only slump behind her Jetta's wheel.

"Yo," Harold said, looking at Charlotte. "Check it out."

"She's a customer." Kwan took a step off the curb in Charlotte's direction. "Maybe I can help..."

Harold grabbed him by the sleeve. "No!"

Kwan pulled his arm away. "What?"

Wiping an invisible smudge from the passenger door of the Honda with the tail of his shirt, Harold shook his head.

"*Shar chi*," he said solemnly. "She's got the poison arrows on her ass, man."

Kwan rolled his eyes. "Not that again."

Harold was a skimmer. He could flip through a book on nuclear fission, or Feng Shui, and pick up enough catch phrases to sound knowledgeable as long as the person with whom he was speaking had no actual knowledge of the subject. In the event the person knew a little something about the topic, Harold looked like a boob, which was a constant source of irritation to Kwan. Nonetheless, they had been friends since childhood and Harold just wouldn't go away. Kwan had always worked in the family's restaurant and Harold prevailed upon Kwan to get him a job there as well—a constant source of aggravation to Old Man Kwan, who viewed Harold as a parasite rather than an employee.

Charlotte bent forward and banged her head on the Jetta's steering wheel.

"Straight up. She probably has to crawl into that hoopty through the window. She's a hot mess," Harold said. "Look, her dress is hanging out the door. Come on, open your eyes. You're the Feng Shui master, and she's a disaster!" Harold beamed. "Who says Chinese don't flow?"

"I am a student, not a master," Kwan said, and for good measure windmill-kicked Harold who then fell to the ground with a thud. That was the other reason they remained friends; both were ardent martial arts enthusiasts, although like everything else Harold had only a perfunctory command of the various martial arts disciplines and absolutely no skill. He picked himself up and attempted to throw a right hook that Kwan ducked, nearly causing Harold a dislocated shoulder.

The Jetta whined pathetically when Charlotte tried to restart it. Just as the engine caught and the car jerked forward, an elderly woman pulling a cart laden with grocery bags entered the opposite crosswalk. To avoid running the woman over Charlotte hit the brakes and once again the Jetta died—this time in the intersection. The old woman shook her fist at Charlotte as total gridlock ensued.

Harold pushed Kwan toward the restaurant. "Come on, let's get goin' before your old man passes a stone." He chuckled. "And I am flowin'!"

Hoping to perform a disappearing act, Charlotte sank ever deeper into her seat.

風
水

CHAPTER TWO

For most at the car dealership, hope dangled before them like the cardboard evergreen deodorizers that hung from the rearview mirrors of the back lot's used cars. The new car salespeople were eternally optimistic that the next person through the door would be the ideal customer, providing them with an opportunity to sell at full manufacturer's suggested retail price. The men and women who sold Previously Owned Vehicles lived each day as if it were their last on the used car lot, and tomorrow their first in the glamorous environs of New Car Sales.

Even the mighty men of the service department contemplated the perfect customer. She would be the kind of pretty woman who would readily accept even the direst engine prognosis with a wink, a smile, and a throaty, "Thanks, guys. You're the best. Keep the car as long as you want."

It was the eternal hope of the mechanics and service manager that this ideal customer would return a month later to reclaim her finely tuned auto, swing her curvy hips over to the cashier's window, and that would be that. They didn't care that at the cashier's window the lovely creature would peruse her bill and simultaneously emerge from her feminine chrysalis a screaming shrew. Hope had never paid a visit to the cashier's window. Behind that scratched Plexiglas and as far from hope's doorstep as one could be, Charlotte Nightingale was not at her post, and on the customer side of the bulletproof barrier an angry mob was forming.

When Charlotte swung her Jetta onto the blacktop of Eebner Brothers Lincoln-Mercury City of Glendale, the new and used car salespeople alike did their utmost to divert the attention of the "live ones" in the showroom and on the lot. Oblivious to—or perhaps because of the contempt with which her coworkers regarded both Charlotte's car and her mere presence among them—she floored it the last few feet to her designated parking spot behind the service department.

The engine of the decrepit heap died as she coasted into a thicket of brambles littered with barrels of dirty engine oil, leaky batteries and oozing cans of viscous pink fluid. With some difficulty, she pushed open the driver's door against the dense foliage brushing the side of her car. She stumbled away from the Jetta as a substantial purple thistle snagged her sock. A skull and crossbones warning label on an overturned fifty-gallon drum seemed to mock her. The skull appeared to judge Charlotte as she struggled to make her way to the back door.

"I want my frickin' keys!" a man in a stiff white collar shouted as Charlotte entered the building. He waved a long yellow form in the air and took another step toward her. "And you can take this invoice and shove it up your keester!" The priest was furious, and no one in the dissatisfied group of Eebner City's customers seemed to disagree. They drew nearer.

"You have to talk to the service manager about the bill. I'm just the cashier," Charlotte said calmly, but was already taking evasive action and had nearly reached the door marked *Authorized Personnel Only* when the mob broke apart and a surly man with a shaved head blocked her path.

"My car's been in here practically a month—to replace a fan belt—and my bill looks like the national deficit. I haven't seen or heard from the service manager in three weeks!" He slapped a yellow invoice into Charlotte's hand, put his hands on his hips and narrowed his eyes to steely slits.

Charlotte sighed, fixed her gaze in the distance, and then waved the paper in the air as if showing it to someone who could help. In the instant it took the malcontents to turn their heads and realize it had all been a ruse, she was safely through the *Authorized Personnel Only* door and taking her seat behind the Plexiglas shield of the cashier's window.

"Who's next?" she asked the unruly group, each of whom was opening a pocketbook, wallet, or checkbook in preparation of paying an exorbitant bill in order to reclaim the keys to their vehicles. Whether it was the bulletproof glass that lent an aura of authority to Charlotte, or simply because she was presently incapable of being physically accosted, the customers were quietly resigned to the situation, and she took their checks, credit cards and cash without a hint of malice.

Even the priest relented when she told him that Eebner policy required he produce two forms of identification and a retinal scan with his check. One by one, other customers stepped up to the window, grudgingly paid their ridiculous debts and then quietly slunk away.

Finally, the space in front of the cashier's window cleared and Charlotte stood to stretch her legs. A chunky woman in her late fifties, wearing too much make-up and too-tight clothing appeared on the other side of the Plexiglas, clacking lollipop red gel nails on the shield. Charlotte stared at the bizarre woman through the Plexi and wondered whether the thick plastic had distorted her own image. The woman rolled her eyes and disappeared only to resurface on Charlotte's side of the glass. As she stood in the doorway to

Charlotte's cubicle, Charlotte decided that the thick plastic had been kind to the woman, providing a sort of "romantic filter" like in old movies when they smeared Vaseline on the lens in order to make Doris Day look youthful and wrinkle-free.

"Ready for lunch?" The woman pursed her collagen-injected lips and impatiently tapped a white leatherette high heel. "There's a big clearance sale at the beauty supply store in Cerritos."

"Cerritos?" Charlotte was incredulous. She covered her mouth and sneezed. The woman's perfume was as sickeningly sweet as the Piña Colada car fresheners they sold in the dealership's accessory department. "That's an hour away."

"Not in the Eco-Boost Navigator, it ain't," the older woman replied as they walked out of the cashier's cubicle, each dubiously appraising the other. "That look is all wrong for you, Charlotte."

Any time this particular co-worker deigned to speak with Charlotte it included the exact same critique of Charlotte's wardrobe choice, regardless of what she was wearing.

"Can I borrow your stapler for a minute?" Charlotte asked, ignoring the woman's commentary, as she always did.

"I'm not even gonna ask what for. I've gotta pee. I'll meet you in back." She clattered down the hall in her cheap, scuffed-up pumps.

Charlotte was within a few feet of the woman's desk, decorated with trolls, an array of plush bunnies, a ceramic planter in the shape of a Corvette and a brass plaque that read *New Car Sales Associate,* when a man in tan Sansabelt slacks and white loafers tapped her on the shoulder.

"Charlotte?" he asked, as if uncertain of her true identity. She turned to face him and as he recognized the limp hair and weird outfit, he was at once reassured *and* let down. She wondered whether the wearing of white shoes was a prerequisite to selling new cars. "I need you to work tonight. I can pay some overtime. The rest you can add to your point pool," he informed her.

"I'm not in the point pool, Mr. Stanton. I have no hope of promotion here at Eebner Brothers Lincoln-Mercury City."

Don Stanton, Eebner City's general manager, shrugged. "I need you to inflate the balloons for tomorrow's gigantic price roll-back event. The Mexicans'll be busy washing the vehicles on the lot. I need someone to blow up the balloons. I could pay a college kid seven bucks an hour to do what you do. Do you want to keep your job or what?"

"You pay me seven bucks an hour and I have a college degree." She was circumspect and merely stating a fact.

"What are you, a smart ass?" He stared at her for a moment. "What kind of degree do you have?"

"English Lit, but once I've paid off my undergrad student loans I plan to complete my Master of Library Science."

He blinked several times as if he felt a stye coming on. "You'll have to pick up balloons and helium at the party store. Get a company credit card from Phyllis before she leaves for lunch. I suggest you finish your paperwork and get your ass over to the party store. Pronto. I want a lot of balloons. People love the balloons."

And he was gone.

Charlotte heard the persistent and unmistakable honking of the twin turbo V-6, eco-friendly goliath, behind the wheel of which Phyllis Schlotzky impatiently awaited her arrival so that they could careen through lunch at the beauty supply store closeout sale.

She grabbed an alligator stapler from Phyllis's desk and applied it to her skirt. When she had stapled half the fallen hem, the infernal reptile would staple no more. It was decidedly and completely clenched on the plaid fabric and impossible to extricate. As the honking outside doubled in frequency, Charlotte hurried through the dealership holding the stapler and the hem of her skirt as she went.

Phyllis powered down the passenger window as Charlotte approached. "Hurry up!" she barked. "Everything will be picked over!"

When Charlotte leaned in through the open window, the stapler banged against the opalescent finish of the SUV. "Hey! I signed the car out!" Phyllis screeched.

Charlotte looked down the side of the car and rubbed the scratched surface with her sleeve. "I can't go. I have to work…" She was nearly decapitated as Phyllis hit the gas and peeled out of the lot. Charlotte stood in the wake of the behemoth auto, shouting after Phyllis, "I need the company credit card to buy balloons!" But Phyllis was already a blur on the road to the beauty supply store and Charlotte was merely a speed bump.

By nine o'clock in the evening, even the car washers were long gone. Charlotte tethered one last neon-colored balloon to a mile-long line of balloons anchored to the bumper of a Grenoble Green Continental. Eebner City, awash in the eerie glow of orange sodium vapor lights, blanketed by arch after arch of balloons, might have been mistaken for a child's birthday party on Mars. There were so many balloons, in fact, that it was difficult to actually see a car without batting aside the colorful orbs floating over the lot.

Charlotte picked up two of the ten helium tanks she had emptied during the evening and lugged them across the pavement, bobbing and weaving to avoid the prolific little blimps covering the car lot. By the time she had loaded the last of the depleted tanks into the trunk of her car, she was exhausted and barely had the strength to open the door against the hearty weeds that had seemed to reproduce in the course of just one day. She fell into the driver's seat and pulled the door shut. She put the key in the ignition and turned it…a sickly grinding sound emerged from the engine, followed by silence. One more attempt and total silence.

"Shit!"

She banged on the steering wheel with the heel of her hand, and then went in search of jumper cables. Trudging through the toxic waste dump, she stumbled against a big drum of used motor oil, catching herself just short of falling. When she finally made her way to the service department, her hands were so slick with black oil that she could not turn the knob, so she rang the buzzer with her nose. She waited what she felt was a polite length of time before ringing again. Eventually, Charlotte was convinced no one remained within the service department. With a lump forming in her throat and a quivering lip, she pushed a strand of hair off her face, subsequently smearing a thick black trail of grease across her cheek and the bridge of her nose. Standing alone in the dark, covered with grime, and having no plan for getting home, it seemed the imperfect end to a perfectly typical day.

She cautiously approached a bus stop where a person covered with newspapers was sleeping on the bench. Clutching her handbag tightly to her chest, she stood beneath the streetlight and looked up the road in the hope that a bus, any bus, was forthcoming. It was one of the few times all day that Charlotte had felt the slightest twinge of hope. Upon seeing that the street was completely desolate she reminded herself that it really didn't pay to hope for much of anything. As the newspapers rustled she wished she hadn't fallen asleep during the newscast that gave tips on how to avoid becoming a victim.

"You can park it right here next to me," the homeless man offered, carefully folding up a cache of papers to clear a spot for Charlotte.

She furtively glanced up and down the street. However, she and the wild-haired man were the only creatures stirring. "I'm okay, thanks," she said, stepping off the curb, ostensibly preparing to board a bus that hadn't materialized. "The bus is coming."

He looked up the empty street and shook his head. "The twenty -seven don't run by here no more. Not since last year when that old lady was macheteed to death." Charlotte blanched. "It was a dirty shame, too. She was a nice old girl," he said softly.

Knowing that she would be defenseless against a machete attack, Charlotte sat down. "I don't suppose you know where I can catch a bus to Hollywood?" She slumped against the seat.

"Whereabouts in Hollywood?" he inquired politely. "I used to live there."

"Off Vine, near Hollywood Boulevard."

"That's right where I lived." He slapped his leg. "Right in front of Frederick's!"

"Small world," she said, slightly annoyed.

"That's not a safe area anymore." He wrinkled his forehead paternally. "You're better off right here in Glendale. Better class of streets."

"Where old ladies get hacked to bits?" She stood up. There was a gaping hole in her skirt where she had had to cut the stapler from the hem and the axle grease on her face glistened in the light from the streetlight.

"You look like you'd clean up real nice," he said sympathetically. "What's your story?"

One of Charlotte's problems, she suddenly realized, was that she didn't have a story, and the man's question antagonized her to no end. "Do you know where I can catch the bus or not?" The thought of being put out of her misery with a swift blow from a dull machete was somehow comforting.

He sniffed indignantly, stretched out, and began unfolding sheets of newspaper over himself. "Hey, Lady Gaga, go fuck yourself."

風
水

Charlotte's head swam as she walked down the deserted boulevard. Here she was, an educated young woman and by some accounts, certainly on better days however, not half bad looking. She had a boyfriend, such as he was, a job, such as it was, likewise the apartment, and, Charlotte was further disheartened to realize, a car that she could no longer count among her blessings, such as they were. She wondered what had become of her life, and then had difficulty remembering if it had ever been any other way.

The early days, she recalled, were ordinary enough. Dad worked while Mom stayed at home with Charlotte and her younger sister, Charlene. Dad frequently worked late so they could afford to send the girls to Catholic school. Mom had big fights with Dad when he came home very late...some mornings. Charlotte came to understand this, years later, when her father ran off with a manicurist. He returned after just three days, tail between his legs, and Charlotte's mother welcomed him back into the fold with the kind of zeal a Mississippi warden has for an escaped inmate's return.

Charlotte spotted a bus in the distance and ran for it. The driver saw her coming and waited. As she approached, he scrutinized her dirty face and torn clothes and quickly whooshed the door shut. When Charlotte rapped on the glass, he opened the door a centimeter.

"Do you have the fare?" he asked skeptically.

Charlotte reached into her bag, took out her wallet, and extracted a couple of dollars. The driver opened the door. Charlotte deposited her money in the box and took a seat on the otherwise empty bus. The driver watched her in the rearview mirror as he pulled away from the curb.

"This bus only runs 'til midnight tonight. You'll hardly get your money's worth." His voice smacked of pity.

"I get off at Hollywood and Vine," she said, plastering a fake smile on her face. "If you'll be good enough to let me out there, I will feel as though I got more than my money's worth, thank you." She tried to appear pleasant and non-homeless.

He waved indifferently. "At least you don't stink."

Charlotte thought of the man at the bus stop and wished she had been nicer. She looked out of the window and traced the indecipherable scribing etched into the glass with her finger. She thought about the thousands of balloons she had inflated for the gigantic price rollback event. Would she be castigated for having selected the wrong colors, or for under-inflating or over-inflating them?

As she pictured the gas-filled airheads bobbing up and down without a care in the world, Charlotte's thoughts suddenly turned to her sister, Charlene. If it weren't for the fact that Charlotte had been there during Mrs. Nightingale's pregnancy, and present in the hospital waiting room with Dad when the blessed birth took place, she would have sworn that Charlene could not possibly have sprung from the same womb.

Charlene was prone to good luck and had flawless features, none having been taken from either parent, whereas Charlotte considered her own face to be a combination of the worst between them. In addition, the younger Nightingale was popular, a trait shared by no one in the entire extended Nightingale clan. Charlotte spent her childhood sequestered in closets, corners, under tables, and in the garage—anywhere she could read a book in peace—while Charlene pranced about, blonde ponytail swinging, long tanned limbs effortlessly transporting her from party to party, compliment to compliment, game to game.

Possessing an innate sense of entitlement, Charlene would bound into Charlotte's room and select whichever of Charlotte's dolls had the longest, prettiest hair and then proceed to cut it all off in a made-up game of hair salon. If she and her friends wanted to play hospital it was Charlotte's clothes they'd shred and cover in ketchup so that Charlene could play nurse to whichever cute boy acted as doctor. The only possessions Charlene had no use for were Charlotte's books. While it was plain that Charlene had a lot going for her physically and socially, a sharp intellect was not among her virtues. She still considered *Teen Vogue* a very good book. Nonetheless, it was understood that any hope of success, grandchildren, and happiness ought to be pinned on the younger of the Nightingale offspring. Charlotte's money was on Charlene as well.

By the time Charlotte reached her building, it was nearly midnight. She let herself into the drab lobby and headed for a tarnished bank of brass mailboxes. She unlocked her slot and grabbed a spate of junk mail and past-due bills in pink envelopes.

Why not red? she asked herself. *Or something dire, like black?* Pink was rosy, a deceptively cheery choice for mail that scolded you when opened. Rifling through the letters, she used her elbow to press the elevator call button. When the doors slid open, she stepped inside. Clenching the mail in her teeth, she used her free hand to push the button for her floor. As the doors began to close, a man's hand reached in and hit the bumper.

The door receded as Kwan stepped in holding a brown paper bag. When he saw that the button for the fourth floor was lit, he grimaced. "The number four is unlucky."

"You say that every time I see you," Charlotte said, forcing a smile. She had recently read a study in the *New England Journal of Medicine* that said the mere act of smiling released pheromones that decreased stress and created a feeling of happiness. Aware that her upper lip was now stuck to her teeth, surely giving her the expression of an angry badger, Charlotte questioned the veracity of the finding.

Kwan reached into the paper bag and extracted a napkin, with which he wiped oil from her cheek. She looked at the black smudge on the napkin, ran her tongue over her teeth and sighed. "It's been one of those days." *Yup, the science is flawed,* she told herself, making a mental note to write a letter to the *New England Journal of Medicine.*

Kwan nodded sympathetically and handed her a flyer. "New menu." The doors opened at the third floor, and he stepped out. "You ordering tonight?"

Charlotte began to tell him, "I'm broke, besides…" but the doors closed between them. "I have a piece of fish I have to cook before it spoils," she informed no one as she disembarked on the unlucky fourth floor. She opened the door to her apartment and flipped on a dim overhead light in the foyer.

Grocery bags stuffed with newspapers and magazines that she never quite got around to recycling lined the walls of the narrow space that led into her apartment. Behind the bags, covered in an inch of dust, an old mirror was propped against the wall—another project Charlotte meant to undertake if and when she could remember to buy a hammer and nails. The plant Joey had tripped over on his way out had finally expired and dropped a little pile of dried leaves around it. She tossed her keys onto a credenza cluttered with trinkets, mementos and junk, then tripped over the dead plant and subsequently kicked it and the spilled dirt to the side.

As if she were headed to the dentist's chair for an unanesthetized root canal, Charlotte shuffled in on feet made of lead. It was the same every day. Exhausted, she dropped into a chair to regroup. She knew she should bring some order to the place, but the notion only depressed her. *Where to start?* She asked herself. It was overwhelming, like taking the first step in a million-mile journey, or having a gallon of Caramel Biscuit and Cream Häagen Dazs in the freezer and thirty pounds to lose by the weekend. Further disheartened, she realized she'd never write a letter to the New England Journal of Medicine. She took a deep breath, got up, and walked across the living room.

She stared out of the room's only window, hypnotized by a flashing neon sign over a seedy bar across the street. Open. Open. Open. When the "n" suddenly went dark, she dropped her bag onto the sofa and sat down. Next to the couch, on a side table strewn with magazines, books and some broken pottery Charlotte meant to fix one day, the telephone answering machine also flashed hypnotically. She blinked in unison with the machine until the phone rang and startled her out of her trance.

She picked up the phone. "Hello?" she said tentatively. Perhaps she had only dreamed the phone was ringing.

"Hello, Mother," she groaned upon hearing the caller's voice, disappointed that it hadn't been a dream. "No, I just got in. I was just going to listen to my messages."

"Well, then, I don't have to repeat myself," said Charlotte's mother, a lilting Southern accent giving everything she uttered a sweetly acrid flavor, like honey on burning rubber. "Dad said to remind you to bring a date, but if you plan on bringing that... *imposter*, hmph. It would be best if you came alone."

"Impersonator, Mom. He's a Frank Sinat..."

Ignoring Charlotte, Mother continued, "And of course I would understand completely if you didn't want to come at all." Charlotte could hear her dad in the background, but what he was saying was unclear. Her mother resumed, sighing a long-suffering sigh, "Haaaaaah. Just wear something terrific. Your father wants you to come. Dr. Belmont will be here. Please look *nice*." Her mother said "nice" the way a serial killer might say "fava beans and chianti," sending a shiver down Charlotte's spine.

Click. Mother hung up.

Charlotte pressed the play button on her answering machine, walked into the kitchen, and opened the refrigerator to retrieve a small parcel wrapped in white paper. Meanwhile, the machine informed her that there were six new messages. The first, a jarring missive from her landlord, detailed his resentment that the water cascading over the balcony every morning had drowned his cactuses.

"I prefer cacti," Charlotte muttered, while turning on the oven. She yanked a chipped Corningware casserole off a shelf, banged it on the counter next to the sink, and unwrapped the white parcel. As Charlotte was nearly KO'd by the stench of rotten fish, the machine played its next message.

Charlotte was seized by the gag reflex as her mother disclosed that the younger sibling had finally been asked to marry a certain

Dr. Belmont. Charlotte used the slimy butcher paper to stuff the odious seafood into the garbage disposal. On the machine, while her mother chirped with the news that Dr. Belmont was a plastic surgeon in Beverly Hills, no less, Charlotte flipped the switch for the disposal and turned on the tap. Water dripped out in such pathetic droplets that it did nothing to prevent the mulched pieces of putrid haddock from flying out of the drain and sticking to everything against which it splat.

Mrs. Nightingale wrapped up her message by telling Charlotte that the ring given the younger Nightingale girl was a rock the size of New Hampshire; actually it was a rock the size of New Hampshire flanked by two equally gigantic states along the Eastern seaboard cut in sizzling baguette configurations, and could Charlotte paleeeeze wear something *nice* to dinner on Friday.

With globs of spoiled seafood stuck to her hair and clothes, Charlotte was tempted to stick her hand in the In-Sink-Erator just so she could go to the hospital where they might give her something for the pain. However, realizing the folly of this line of thinking (given her slim chance of making any plan work), she turned off the grinding apparatus.

The answering machine warned her of another message, and although she sensed any further messages were likely to be equally upsetting, she was powerless to move, just like in the recurring dream Charlotte had in which someone driving a dusty Arizona Beige Mercury Villager with a golf ball-sized dent under the passenger side review mirror (suspiciously similar to the family minivan of her childhood) was trying to run her down in the street, and if she could only get one foot on the curb she'd be safe, but her shoes had suddenly become made of concrete. Charlotte stood before the sink as Joey told her answering machine that he was called out of town for a few days and would have to repay the clams he borrowed upon his return. Charlotte became aware that her mouth was open in the silent scream that accompanied the minivan nightmare. She snapped her jaw shut.

At that point, the answering machine went haywire and once again informed Charlotte that she had six new messages, and then it repeated the second message—her mother's triumphant bulletin concerning the impending nuptials between Charlene and the Beverly Hills doctor.

Charlotte touched the oven. It was cold. She wished half-heartedly that the gas company had not cut off her service. It looked kind of comfortable inside—a place for quiet reflection away from Mother's giddy news flash. Charlotte kicked the stove and stomped into the living room, where she stabbed at the buttons of the answering machine to no avail. As she ripped the electrical cord from the socket, the machine droned out the words, "Doc-torrrr-Bel -mont-will-be-therrrrrre."

Charlotte noticed the Emperor's Kitchen menu sticking out of her purse. While scanning the menu, she picked up the phone and dialed.

"Hello? Anyone there? Hello? Hello?"

"What?" It was Old Man Kwan, and he sounded put off.

"Uh, I'd like an order of Emperor's cashew chicken for one delivered to six-fifteen…"

"No have. New menu."

Charlotte turned the menu over. "Yes, I can see that you don't have Emperor's cashew chicken on your new menu, but I've ordered it so many times that I…"

Click. He hung up.

Charlotte put the phone down, flicked a piece of haddock off her sweater, and headed for the shower. She pulled the string for the bathroom light and caught a glimpse of her reflection in the mirror. She had seen a lot of bad-hair, bad-face, and bad-outfit days in her time, but this took the cake.

Bits of rotten fish stuck to the axle grease on her nose and forehead, causing a wave of nausea to wash over her. More stinky little globs hung from her hair like bait Christmas ornaments. Her sweater and blouse were equally revolting. She reached into the tub, turned on the water, and peeled off her stinking clothes.

By the time she had slipped out of the baggy jog bra and pulled off her droopy knee socks, steam was emanating from the tub. For the first time all day, her spirits were elevated. She pulled the lever for the shower and hot water sprayed out with delicious force. She put one foot inside the tub, and then quickly retreated. The Herbal Essence bottle was empty. This time she was going in prepared. She dug around in all the dribs and drabs of junk under the sink until she found a tiny, half-filled bottle of hotel shampoo. She swung the cabinet door shut and stepped into the steaming shower.

Luxuriating in the thick suds produced by the hotel shampoo, she began washing off the fish bits and oil and bad luck the day had deposited on her. She closed her eyes and breathed in the heady scent of gardenia.

Just before the birth of Charlotte's younger sister, the Nightingales took their first and last family vacation. Mom had nagged Dad to death to book a room inside Grand Canyon National Park before it was too late, but he wanted to wait until the rates dropped. Assured by Mrs. Nightingale that the rates would not drop in the middle of the summer, Mr. Nightingale finally called every lodge in the Park, which were by then completely booked. They went to the Grand Canyon anyway, spending twenty minutes at the South Rim before driving 375 miles to a motel with a vacancy in Nevada.

Another family had checked in at the same time. They also had a little girl, who informed Charlotte from a splintered teeter-totter on a dusty patch of dead grass behind the Sleep Cheap Motel, "This place is a piss hole."

That family went on two vacations every year and usually stayed in nice places with bellmen and room service—and gardenia-scented shampoos. The little girl was kind, as Charlotte recalled, and had given Charlotte one such delightful amenity as a gift. Charlotte had immediately retreated to her family's room and washed her hair, trying to imagine what it must be like to go on a vacation every single year. She used only half the bottle, wanting to save the rest until someday she stayed somewhere nice with free toiletries. All these years later, she remained impressed. The shampoo still smelled good.

With her hair in a foamy lather, Charlotte scooped the suds into her hands and slathered her body with luscious cleansing bubbles. All was finally right with the world—until the pipes creaked, groaned, and sputtered. She wiped the soap from her eyes and looked up to see the showerhead pitifully dripping its last drop.

She tore open the shower curtain. Light glinted off Joey's vintage straightedge razor, which had been left open on the back of the toilet. Charlotte glanced at a disposable Lady Schick stuck to the side of the tub by its ancient, gummy, safety strip, and figured now was as good a time as any to shave her legs, and there would be less carnage with Joey's sharpened blade. Plus, if her hand were to slip in the vicinity of her wrist…

After calculating the distance from tub to toilet, versus the odds of slipping en route and breaking some bone or other that would not result in shaving or death, but which would cause her to lie helplessly for days before being discovered comatose, and eventually placed on permanent life support, Charlotte considered passing on both ideas. But yet...

She gingerly stepped out of the tub and carefully reached for the razor when the doorbell rang. Ignoring it, she snatched up Joey's razor. The doorbell rang again. She set the blade back on the toilet, and then decided to set it on the tub's edge where it would be handy.

Charlotte pulled her bathrobe around her soapy body and walked out of the bathroom, gobs of shampoo plopping onto the floor in her wake. The bell rang again as she put her eye to the security hole. Kwan stood on the other side staring straight ahead.

She opened the door.

"Hello, 4-D," he said, shaking a brown paper bag. "Emperor's cashew chicken. Fourteen-fifty, plus tip."

"You don't have Emperor's cashew chicken anymore," she repeated from an earlier conversation.

"Hey, 4-D. You wanted Emperor's cashew chicken, you got it. Fourteen-fifty. Plus tip." He vigorously shook the brown sack.

Normally resigned to events of this nature, Charlotte had finally reached her limit. "Look, Mister...?"

"Kwan. Just Kwan."

"Charlotte. Nightingale. Hi. I did not order that food because I was told you no longer offered it, i.e., it's not mine." She crossed her arms emphatically over her bosom.

He shifted from one foot to the other. "If you'd just get the money, you could finish your shower and..."

Something about the soapy rivulets running down her face touched him. He opened the bag, took out a napkin, and wiped soap from her cheek. A puddle expanded on the floor where the bubbles slid down her legs and melted, creating a small cesspool when it reached the decaying leaves and detritus of the dead fern kicked over by Joey.

Glancing into the living room, and then at the unruly hodge-podge of junk cluttering the foyer, Kwan's skin began to crawl. "Fourteen-fifty," he said anxiously. "I've got other deliveries to make."

She nodded stupidly and turned away. "Wait here. I'll be right back." There was no fight left in her. Charlotte went to her bag on the sofa, fished around, and came up with four dollars. "I thought Emperor's cashew chicken was seven-fifty," she said, plunging her hands deeper into the purse in search of loose change at the bottom.

"New menu. Ten-fifty." He set the food on the chair next to the credenza, the only free space available.

She counted a handful of quarters, dimes, nickels, and pennies. "But it's not even on the menu. Anyway, that makes it ten-fifty then."

He studied the Pez dispensers, knick-knacks, seashells, and animal figurines jumbled on the entryway table. "There's a minimum charge for delivery, twelve-fifty." He blew dust off a porcelain horse.

She dumped the entire contents of her pocketbook onto the sofa and found a few more coins and a leaky pen.

"Then it's twelve-fifty," she said, and so far had accumulated six dollars and twelve cents. She used a ratty tissue to wipe ink off her fingers.

"The delivery charge is two bucks. Also new. My dad said..." He stopped to pick up a small wooden duck. "Is this a Mandarin duck?" He ran his thumb back and forth across its smooth surface.

Charlotte checked under the sofa cushions for change. "I thought they were Canada geese. There's another one somewhere. I got them at a flea market." She found a few pennies and the remote from the television. "I'll be right back," she said mindlessly, heading toward the bedroom.

She went into her closet and searched various jacket pockets until she had unearthed another handful of coins and two crumpled one-dollar bills. Making the mental calculations that told her she was still several dollars short, without the tip, Charlotte reached for a purse dangling from a shelf high above the hanging clothes. She grabbed the strap, but the handbag was caught. She gave it a good tug whereupon the entire clothes rod and the shelf above it collapsed onto Charlotte.

Several dusty, balled-up napkins lay on the floor at Kwan's feet as he replaced the last freshly cleaned knick-knack on the sideboard. He gathered up the used napkins and stuffed them into one of the recycling bags, where he spotted the missing duck.

Kwan picked it up and compared it to the other one. "These are Mandarin ducks," he said quietly. "Not geese." He wiped off the bird carving and set it with its mate.

Charlotte clawed her way out of the pile of clothes and emerged victorious, the elusive purse clenched in her hand. She sat down on the bed and dumped everything into her lap.

Kwan wiped up the mess from the dead plant, deposited it and the lifeless fern into a bag stuffed with empty plastic bags, and placed the recycling and garbage outside the door, intending to take it out when he left. He pushed the table into a more symmetrical position in the foyer, then got on his knees and exhaled on the dusty mirror leaning against the wall, polishing it with his sleeve before setting it on the tabletop.

Charlotte excavated lipsticks with missing caps, opened tampons, and an assortment of unwrapped hard candies with hair and tissue stuck to them, but in terms of money, came up empty-handed. By this time, the suds on her body had dried, and she alternately scratched and whimpered.

A jolt ran down Kwan's spine as he walked into the living room and observed the ugly beams overhead and the absolute shambles down below, but he resisted the impulse to flee and instead unplugged a lamp tucked behind the sofa.

He set it on the entryway table, located an outlet in which to plug it, and he turned it on. Immediately, the alcove became more inviting. Returning to the living area, he sighed. It was overwhelming. For a fleeting moment, he knew exactly how Charlotte must feel each time she set foot in the room. *No wonder she's a wreck*, he told himself.

Something outside the apartment emitted a thick, metallic clunking like a child banging on a pot with its lid. Curious, Kwan went to the window.

Out of sheer frustration, Charlotte put her head in her hands and noticed that the polish on her toes was chipped. She added a touch-up to the long mental to-do list of things she knew she'd never do. The nail polish would eventually grow out and that would be that.

Staring down at her toes, she glimpsed the corner of a photograph peeking out from under the bed. She swept her hand behind the dust ruffle and came up with a Polaroid. Her mouth fell open. It was a photo of Joey receiving a blowjob from a buxom blonde wearing nothing but a hot pink thong and tall Lucite heels. Charlotte closed her eyes. *A stripper,* she thought. *How original.* Her eyes popped open and she looked around the room, and again at the picture, certain it had been taken right where she currently sat.

Kwan dangled halfway out of the window trying to get hold of a metal wind chime hanging from the fire escape; its tubes tangled in the wrought iron railing. Taking a deep breath, he extended his reach until he was able to nab the chimes, then he pulled himself back into the room. He untangled the mess and held each cylinder to his eye, blowing the gunk and debris from those that were clogged, so that chi could flow through them unimpeded.

He carried a chair to the center of the living room, climbed up onto it and hung the wind chime from a bulb-less light fixture in the ceiling. When he flicked the tubes, they played a delicate song. *The wind chime itself offsets the negative energy caused by the heavy beams, which shoot poison arrows of bad luck in every direction*, he thought. *This ought to do the trick.*

Charlotte raised her chin and stood up. She crossed the bedroom and dropped the offending Polaroid over the wastebasket, where it hit the rim and fell on the floor. Looking down, it seemed like Joey was looking up, smiling, but she knew that his satisfied expression had nothing to do with her. Then another thought crossed her mind and her lip began to quiver. *Who had taken the picture?*

Rubbing her eyes with the back of her hand, she bent to pick up the photo and deposit it once and for all in the trash when something in the wastebasket caught her eye. She reached in and extracted a crumpled twenty-dollar bill from a pile of tissues and old papers. She smoothed out the money and smiled bravely.

Who said the fourth floor was unlucky?

Later that night, as a cockroach climbed down a chopstick sticking out of a carton of Emperor's cashew chicken, Charlotte slept through the newscast that related the story of a beauty supply store owner in Cerritos who had been slain earlier in the day by an unidentified female customer. Witnesses reported seeing the woman, allegedly angered by the poor quality of products that remained for sale, grab a pair of Tweezerman tweezers and stab the shop's owner in the neck. In the live coverage at the scene, recorded earlier, one shaken shopper gave her account of the events as they had unfolded.

"Well, we never saw it coming, that's for sure. One minute she was stuffing powder puffs in her basket and the next she was screaming something about the damned shampoo. Can I say that? Damn, on TV?" The woman looked into the camera, unsure.

A pretty Latin-American/Asian-American/African-American/ Native-American/Inuit reporter originally from Sheboygan urged the woman to continue.

"Anyway, she was yelling something about the hair care products, you know? She went wild at that point and when Lydia, that's the gal who owns, I mean who owned, the shop argued with her, the crazy bitch stuck Lydia with them tweezers and kept sticking her, too, until poor Lydia stopped screaming."

She wiped away a tear and looked nervously into the camera. "Was it okay to say bitch on TV?"

CHAPTER THREE

Joey crouched next to a Dumpster outside the Polynesian Palace as he waited to meet a friend who worked there. The friend was an entertainer and Joey had hoped to borrow a few bucks from her. The reek of rotting garbage and urine in the alley emboldened Joey to step away from the giant trash bin. As he stood to stretch his legs, the back door swung open—placing Joey face to face with an outraged man.

"I'm gonna kill you!" the man yelled, grabbing Joey by the lapels, and then slamming him against the side of the brick building.

"I didn't touch her," Joey eked out despite the chokehold the man had on him. "I swear!"

The man hauled off and decked Joey, who slid down the bricks and slumped to the pavement. He swatted Joey's fedora off his head and stomped on it.

"Hey, not the lid!" Joey cried. "It's part of my image!"

Shaking his head, the man kicked Joey's hat across the pavement. "My niece is a piece of work, I'll give you that," he said, "but she's my brother's kid, and you don't mess with my family. Are we clear, asshole?"

Joey's eye was swelling. "Like I never met her."

"Good." The man turned to walk away, and then he stopped. "She says you're some kind of singer. I hate that rap shit."

"They compare me to 'Old Blue Eyes' actually." In spite of the goose egg forming over his eye, Joey puffed up his chest. "You looking for a singer?"

Regarding Joey like he was Kanye West in a leather skirt, the man snapped, "It's a strip club, you moron. Get lost." He walked into the bar and closed the door behind him. Joey rubbed his jaw and tried to unmash his hat.

The Polynesian Palace was a hole-in-the-wall strip joint frequented by hardcore alkies and those boozers only a few drinks shy of full-blown dipsomania. Ammonia pellets vaporizing in the urinals competed with the stench of stale beer and the cheap perfume the strippers liberally spritzed on their bodies in order to mask the horrible odors around them. Most patrons needed a drink or two just to keep their breakfasts down.

Sig Macaroni walked through the back room, past the "dressing room," a cubbyhole with a full-length plastic mirror so bendy and warped it might have been borrowed from a funhouse at a circus, and into the main room, with its small stage and requisite pole.

A bored girl in pasties and a G-string sat on the edge of the stage eating a Vienna Red Hot. She looked up. "Hey, Uncle Sig. Did you see Frank out there? He's late." She licked mustard off her fingers.

"Frank my ass. Frank was a class act. Frank had talent. Frank was...he was..." A vein sprouted across Sig's forehead. "He was Frank-goddamn-Sinatra, for chrissakes! That jackass out there is a piece of shit two-bit..."

She stood up. "Frankie's out there?" she asked excitedly.

He grabbed her by the shoulders and shook her, causing the right pasty to detach and fall to the sticky floor. "I bet his name's not even Frank!" He looked away as she bent down to retrieve the tiny suction cup and tassel. "You deserve better than that loser!"

She stuck the nipplewear back on. "Yeah, sure. Have you looked around here lately?" Old men without teeth were gumming pretzels and pickled eggs while older women wearing bad wigs and their daughter's clothes guzzled the cocktails purchased for them by the old men.

"Your father wanted you to go to vocational school, but you wanted a career in entertainment. Don't complain to me if it's not all champagne and caviar."

She pouted. "I'm going to get an Oscar some day."

"You'll be lucky to get a buck from some guy named Oscar. Now get to work."

The Polynesian Palace was probably the only strip club in L.A. where the patrons were more interested in dollar shots than stuffing dollar bills into a girl's G-string.

The young stripper looked around. "They're mostly passed out. The guy at table three may be dead. He hasn't moved in an hour. What is it you want me to do?"

Sig sighed. "Go clean the bathrooms. I told your dad I'd give you a job. I'm not running a goddamn charity." He grabbed a shiny, black *Members Only* jacket off the back of a chair and walked out the front door of the club.

At the same moment, Joey crept in through the back. Heading past the dressing room, he caught a glimpse of himself and cringed. His shiner, distorted by the wonky mirror and looking to be the size of a Ford F-150, stared back at him like a cyclotic extraterrestrial.

"Frankie," the girl cooed, slinking Joey's way. Gloria Macaroni had a soft spot for directionless losers, and Joey was no exception. His pitiful appearance touched something in the young woman. "I wanna go to the mall," she said.

"Do you see I have just had the shit knocked out of me by some angry relative of yours?" His eye had turned black, blue, and a malevolent yellow.

She shrugged. "Doesn't look so bad."

He dropped into a peeling Naugahyde booth. "Maybe get me a drink? With ice."

"Okay," Miss Macaroni said, heading to the bar. "There's a shoe sale at Nordstrom's."

"What's wrong with the ones you're wearing," he asked.

"Seriously." Gloria rolled her eyes as she spit onto a napkin and wiped a smudge off the five-inch Lucite heel of her left shoe. "You have got to get a job. I need new shoes."

Joey leaned back and closed his eyes. He didn't understand why things had suddenly gone to shit. No matter how little work he did, or how infrequently he looked for a little work, somehow he always managed to land on his feet.

Before Charlotte "helped him out" there had been Margaret, a sweet if hapless ex-nun. Before Sister Margaret there was a young woman with a dozen cats, and so it went. He brought a little color into their otherwise drab lives.

In exchange, often unwittingly, they loaned him whatever money he found in their unattended purses. And cookie jars. And underwear drawers. It seemed only fair to have a girl on the side, like Gloria, from whom he could take comfort, find a little excitement, and occasionally borrow ten bucks, which was usually in the form of damp, crumpled singles.

Gloria returned with his drink. He pressed the glass to his temple and looked at her. Even in the pasties, thong, and lap-dance footwear, she looked innocent and trusting.

He touched his nose to indicate the gravity of what he was about to tell her. "This bird is cooked, Baby. I'm a real Clyde."

She blinked several times, unsure. "What does that mean?"

"You're a great dame, but I gotta blow, Baby." He playfully knocked her jaw.

"You're dumping me, aren't you? I can't believe it."

"Dumper, dumpee. We don't have to put a label on it, Baby."

Scrunching her mouth to one side, she looked up at the stained ceiling tiles and rolled her eyes. "What a load of crap. Why don't you just say it? You don't want to go out with a stripper." She lowered her head, ashamed.

"What? I love strippers!" Joey protested. "Really. It's not that."

"You got another girl?"

Contrary to his instincts and for reasons beyond his comprehension, he answered "yes."

Tears immediately flowed down Gloria's cheeks. "How could you?"

Joey basically got the fact that he was a shmuck. What he didn't get was why he suddenly found himself fessing up to it. "I thought you and me were just having a few laughs, Baby. I never said you were my girlfriend."

"Wow," she said, wiping her face with the back of her hands. "I can't believe you're telling me this."

"Me either."

She slapped him across the cheek, taking care to avoid the bruised area around his eye. "I had to do that," she said apologetically. He nodded. It seemed right to him, too. "This girl. She's special, Frankie?"

"I didn't realize it 'til just this minute." He got up and adjusted his hat as best he could, considering it had been stomped into the ground.

"My sister's in town again," she said, with an inflection that was meant to entice.

He headed for the door and winked at her with his good eye. "So long, Baby. Name's Joey, by the way."

風
水

CHAPTER FOUR

There is no Chapter Four.

(It's the death number, if you believe that sort of thing.)

風
水

CHAPTER FIVE

Charlotte opened her eyes and ran her hand over the empty spot beside her in the bed. She sat up and wiped the sleep from her eyes and looked around. Dust covered every surface. Joey's cigarette butts bobbed in the ice bucket, and her books and clothes were strewn around the room. She shuddered to think how she would find anything suitable to wear now that her closet, with its fallen rod, was a mangled heap of clothes and junk. Lying back on the bed, watching rivulets of rain run down the dirty window, Charlotte fell fast asleep.

When she awoke again, it was clear that she was going to be very late for work. She jumped out of bed, raced to the closet, and stared hopelessly at the mess.

Burrowing into the huge pile of clothes on the floor, she pulled out a pair of ancient pink bellbottoms, a ruffled paisley shirt and a shiny fuchsia jacket from an old tracksuit. She briefly looked at the items in her hands, shrugged, and bolted into the bathroom.

One glance in the mirror revealed the crunchy branches of hair set in place by the dried shampoo from the night before. She turned on the shower, and as it was heating, dashed into the kitchen to grab a box of baking soda. The bathroom was filled with steam upon her return and immediately Charlotte leapt in, daring to hope that there might be sufficient hot water, but reasonably sure she would be disappointed.

As the hot water revived the shampoo, she scrubbed her head until all the suds were rinsed out, had run the length of her body, and were swirling down the drain. At that, the water ceased to flow, but a victorious Miss Nightingale stood proudly in the tub—she had cheated fate by employing a two-pronged hygiene system. Soap up, day one. Rinse off, day two. She was finally clean.

Stepping out of the tub, she wrapped her hair in a towel, sprinkled baking soda into the palm of her hand, and mashed it into her toothbrush. She turned on the sink's water. Out it dribbled in fat, albeit infrequent drops, but nonetheless, it was enough to fulfill the tooth-brushing process. She pulled the towel off her head, pitched it into the tub and ran a comb through her hair. Somehow her hair seemed thicker, but this was the first time in months it was free of shampoo residue.

She wiped her mouth with a hand towel and dropped it into the sink before forcing on the pants, now somewhat tighter than when they had last been worn. As she pulled up the zipper, something cut into her hip. Barely able to squeeze her hand inside the pocket, she managed to extricate a wadded-up flier from the Roosevelt High School Freshman Cavalcade of 2006, themed "A Tribute to 1979." A fleeting look at the bell-bottoms produced a small smile.

She put on the ruffled blouse, added the vivid magenta jacket, and inspected the combination in the mirror. Her damp straight hair framed a singularly pale face that almost vanished in the bright colors of the clothes. She opened the small cabinet beneath the sink and pulled out a clear plastic shoebox filled with cosmetic samples, mostly with missing caps and lids, and searched until she found one lipstick intact. She twisted the base of the tube until it produced a pulpy head of frosty pink, which she pressed against her mouth. The ancient cosmetic disintegrated on contact, forcing her to smooth the little clots into her lips with her finger. It wasn't what she would have hoped, had hope been an option, but it was the best Charlotte could do and she was late for work. She placed the make-up on the back of the toilet and ran into the living room, grabbed her purse, scooped its contents off the sofa and raced out the door.

Once outside, Charlotte was pleasantly surprised that the rain had abated and had given way to a gloriously sunny southern California day. Facing the empty carport, Charlotte now recalled with a heaving sigh, her car was still at Eebner City.

Suddenly an unwanted visitor appeared—a very excited and corpulent man in a colorful muumuu.

"Murderer!" he screamed.

"What?" She backed away.

"You're intentionally destroying property! You are killing my cactuses!"

"I wouldn't have to rinse my hair on the balcony if the plumbing worked, Mr. Shirley," Charlotte said politely as she took a big step to the side. She tried to move past him, but he was huge and in spite of his unwieldy size, rather agile in blocking her.

"Maybe I'd fix the plumbing if you paid the rent!" He rattled a set of worry beads in her face.

"I had the rent. I mean, I have the rent, but I told you I wasn't going to give it to you until you fixed the plumbing." She stood still, then faked right, but was thwarted by his deft maneuvering.

"There's nothing wrong with the plumbing," he growled. "Nobody else has complained." He took a menacing step toward her. "I want you out! You can consider this your notice to pay rent or quit. You have three days."

"Isn't that supposed to be in writing?" she asked. "I have rights, too, you know."

"You have the right to move out! You are nothing but trouble, Nightingale. I never liked you."

"I told you why I was withholding the rent. You can't just kick me out on a whim." She found a voice that was both steady and sure. "I think I'll call the Building and Safety Inspectors and see what they have to say about the plumbing."

Mr. Shirley flinched as if stung by a wasp and miraculously moved his huge body aside.

"Although cactuses is acceptable, the preferred plural form of cactus is cacti." She brushed past him on her way out.

He gathered up the hem of his bright frock and followed her to the sidewalk. "This isn't over by a long shot! You'd better have that money by Monday morning or I'm gonna make your life a living hell!"

"Take a number," she said flatly. When she turned the corner, her cheeks were flushed and she felt a little woozy. She bent over and took a few deep breaths before continuing to the bus stop. Almost immediately the bus arrived and Charlotte got on, still feeling the adrenaline surge from her run-in with Mr. Shirley.

She dropped her money into the box and was disheartened to see that the only unoccupied seat on the entire bus was beside the priest who had tongue-lashed her only twenty-four hours earlier.

"Hello," she said timidly, bracing for the tirade that was sure to ensue, but the priest looked at the pretty girl with the nice hair and colorful clothes, and smiled pleasantly.

"Good morning, young lady," he chirped, clearly misidentifying her as someone with whom he was not angry.

She forced a small, uncertain smile.

"Gosh, you look familiar," he said, studying her face, "but for the life of me, I can't place from where."

Trying to avoid him, she turned away and wished he would disembark anywhere other than at her stop. Each time the bus did stop, she rose partially out of her seat, ever hopeful that the man would get off before recognizing her. She suddenly felt a great fondness for the scratched piece of thick Plexiglas that usually separated her from the Eebner customer, but the bus crawled along, mired in rush-hour traffic, and Charlotte had no choice but to sit and wait.

When they arrived at her stop, sure enough, both she and the priest rose at the exact same moment and a look of recognition swept over the clergyman's face that would have turned Joan of Arc's blood to ice water. Charlotte was in the stairwell in a heartbeat, with the priest hot on her heels.

"You! The lying heathen from Eebner City!"

More than a few of the passengers were nearly startled out of their seats. He turned to them and said he had been ripped off, and Charlotte was the one who did the ripping. They glared at her. She looked at the bus driver, imploring him with her eyes to open the door, but he, too, was waiting for her to answer the charges.

"OPEN THE GODFORSAKEN DOOR BEFORE I KICK IT OPEN!" The driver's hand flew to the silver lever. The door whooshed open, and Charlotte stepped off. She waited at the curb for the priest, but he mumbled something to the driver about getting off at the next stop. The door closed, and Charlotte watched the shocked faces of the passengers in the window seats as the bus pulled into traffic. She lifted her chin and walked away.

The first thing she saw when she was within a block of the dealership were the trillions—surely they had multiplied in the night—of balloons that obscured the Eebner Brothers Lincoln-Mercury City signage, the driveway, and even the cars. Charlotte immediately recognized the problem and was quick with an excuse when the Eebners, Ed and Abe, and Don Stanton rushed toward her.

"It was dark," she explained to the fuming trio, then addressed Stanton directly, "and you said you wanted a lot of balloons. People love the balloons. Your exact words."

Stanton was ready to explode right out of his tan Sansabelts, but Ed Eebner put his arm around Stanton's shoulder to calm him, and the other Eebner stepped forward.

"You stupid idiot!" Abe hooted. "No one can even see our sign!"

She had only ever seen pictures of the actual Eebners. "Are you Abe Eebner or Ed?"

Convinced she was the stupid idiot he imagined, Abe hopped up and down, swinging his arms in the direction of the balloon convention blanketing his precious dealership. "An Eebner's an Eebner! And you no longer work for either!" Then he turned his fury on Stanton. "And you're fired, too!"

Ed quickly withdrew the comfort of his arm from Stanton's shoulder.

Charlotte did digest the fact that she was fired, but it seemed not to penetrate as deeply as she might have expected. As a matter of fact, she didn't feel badly at all. "I have some vacation coming, and my paycheck from the last two weeks," she told them, and added, "plus you owe me for the balloons and helium."

They flew into a rage. "You're out of your mind if you think you're getting one more dime out of us! You can just turn around and get the hell out of here right now, you moron!"

Stanton had hoped that Charlotte would quietly comply so that he could talk some sense into the Eebner brothers about his own termination.

"I don't think so," Charlotte said, planting her feet in the middle of the driveway to square off with the irate siblings.

"Abe!" Ed squawked. "Call the police!"

Don Stanton stared in disbelief at the belligerent Charlotte Nightingale, who was literally standing between him and his job. "Oh, for chrissake, Charlotte," he pleaded, "Walk away."

She stood her ground. "Let them come. I'll personally show them the toxic waste dump behind the service department."

The Eebners smiled evilly. "Do you think we are so stupid or just lucky that the environmental people have overlooked our situation? Show the police, go ahead," Abe snarled.

"That's right, we've been paying off those asshole bureaucrats for years," Ed threw in for good measure, in response to which Abe punched him hard on the arm.

"Shut the hell up, you blabbermouth," Abe said. "I am surrounded by idiots."

Sirens wailing, a police cruiser and an unmarked car screeched to a halt in front of Eebner City. Two uniformed officers and a detective leapt from their respective autos.

"That was fast," Don Stanton said, shocked.

The detective approached the group standing in the driveway. "Who's in charge here?"

Abe stuck his chest out and took a step forward. "I'm Abe Eebner, and that's my brother Ed."

Drawing on everything he had learned from watching police shows on television, Ed spoke up, the voice of authority. "What we have here is a disgruntled former employee."

The detective produced a notebook and a pen. "You'd have to be pretty upset to commit that kind of crime. I'll need just a bit of information from you and we can get out of your hair."

"I knew it!" Ed said, turning to his brother. "I told you she was bad news."

"What about it?" The detective was all business. "Details."

Abe and Ed gestured to the sea of balloons covering the lot. "She's insane!"

"I don't know much about balloons, but I can tell you, off the record of course, that she had to be a little loony to stab that poor woman to death," the detective confided.

The Eebners and Don Stanton looked at Charlotte, agape, and then each took a step back and away from her.

Don sucked in his breath and exhaled through his teeth. "Jeez," he said, keeping an eye on Charlotte, "I wouldn't have thought she had it in her."

Abe shoved Charlotte toward the detective. "So why isn't she under arrest? I don't want some murdering nincompoop on my lot."

"Whoa there, pal," the detective warned. "Where I come from, that kind of thing can be construed as assault."

"What are you talking about?" Abe flinched incredulously. "You said yourself she was nuts!"

The detective took a step toward Abe. "You have any identification on you, Mr. Eebner? Half the people in L.A. are mentally incompetent. You don't go around assaulting all of them, do you?" Abe pulled his driver's license from his wallet and handed it over. The detective copied down the information.

"I am asking you again, why isn't she under arrest?" Abe's voice had become shrill. He gestured toward Charlotte with a sweaty hand.

The detective handed back the driver's license and frowned. "She is."

"Then take her away!" Abe gave Charlotte another good shove, whereupon she tripped and fell at the detective's feet. In a blur, the uniformed officers rushed the scene, cuffing Abe and reading him his rights.

The detective helped Charlotte to her feet. "You can press charges if you like. We were all witness to the assault."

Ed could take no more and tried to wrest his brother from the uniformed officer's hold. When the officer pushed him back, Ed swung at the cop and knocked his hat off, at which point, he was immediately handcuffed as well.

Don Stanton wanted no part in this business and attempted to quietly slink away.

"Where do you think you're going?" an officer asked, pulling Stanton back by the collar.

"I didn't think you needed me, plus we've got customers on the lot and we're a little light on salespeople today," Stanton said hopefully.

"I imagine so, with Miss Schlotzky in custody, and all." The detective turned his full attention to Stanton. "You're a co-worker, then?"

"Phyllis Schlotzky?" Stanton asked incredulously.

The gigantic price rollback sale was in full swing and several curious customers had gathered around, chomping free hot dogs and drinking soda out of flimsy paper cups.

The Eebners furtively looked at the customers, who were looking at the Eebners and not at the new cars. Several patrons angrily batted balloons out of their faces, and a few used pocket-knives, toothpicks and other sharp objects to puncture the annoying spheres.

"What is the meaning of this?" Abe demanded to know.

The uniformed officers flanked the brothers. "Take them to the station," the detective ordered. "We can question them there after we process the assault paperwork." The Eebners, under great protest, were led away.

Don Stanton was in shock. "What's this about Phyllis, I mean, Miss Schlotzky?"

The detective narrowed his eyes. "You were close to the perp?"

More customers had gathered around. Stanton didn't know where he stood. Should he try to get the customers back into the swing of things, or not? If he was truly fired, then screw the Eebners, but if those things were said in the heat of the moment, he should at least try to move some cars. He was perplexed.

"Were you close to the accused or not?" The lawman was rapidly losing patience. Stanton stood with his hands searching out the pockets of his Sansabelt slacks, unable to speak.

Charlotte stepped forward. "He was banging her, officer." The detective noted this in his book while Stanton stared helplessly at Charlotte. "I'm just the cashier, or I was the cashier 'til I got fired just a few minutes ago because I threatened to go to the authorities about the toxic waste dump out back."

She looked over the detective's shoulder as he took it all down. "You wouldn't think in this day and age you could get away with that kind of thing, but the Eebners have been paying somebody off. Seriously, you should see it. Battery acid, used oil, transmission fluid, you name it. It's all just dumped out back."

The detective jotted down every word.

"I didn't really know Phyllis Schlotzky very well, but we were supposed to go to the beauty supply store yesterday at lunch," Charlotte concluded.

The detective raised an eyebrow. "Did she go on her own?"

"Oh, yeah. She nearly ran me over trying to get there before all the good stuff was picked over."

"That fits with what Ms. Schlotzky told us, all right," he said, handing her his card. "Please call me if you can think of anything else." He gave her a quick once-over and smiled appreciatively. "I'll be in touch if I need anything further." He turned to Stanton. "You'll be coming with us."

"What? I didn't do anything," Stanton gurgled.

"You were intimate with her, sir. We need to ask you some questions." Stanton was pulled, lead-footed, to an unmarked car. Abe and Ed sat in the back of a police cruiser, watching as their customers ate free hot dogs, drank free sodas and stabbed at the irritating balloons getting between them and the vehicles.

As Charlotte headed down the driveway, Abe hollered at her through the partially open window of the squad, "You terrorist! Get rid of those balloons! Look at the customers!" His right eye began to twitch as his face turned the color of a fertile baboon's ass. Charlotte looked at the Eebners, helplessly locked in the back of the police car, and she waved.

The detective pushed Stanton, virtually comatose, into the backseat of his car. Charlotte looked at all the people milling around, wandering among the balloons, and saw the burly man with the shaved head who had been nasty to her the day before, popping balloons with a shiny stiletto knife.

"Excuse me, sir. May I please borrow that for a moment?" she asked courteously. He sized her up, curious, and handed over the blade. She turned to the Eebners, their noses pressed to the squad's windows.

"She's got a knife!" Ed screamed as Charlotte took a step toward the police car. The officer behind the wheel was talking to his girlfriend on his cell phone and gestured for Ed to be quiet.

"Do something!" Abe yowled, wherein the cop reached back and tasered him.

Charlotte waved at the Eebners, and then she disappeared into the sea of balloons with the shiny knife. As the police vehicles pulled away, the Eebners shook their fists in her direction. Stanton, suffering from an acute anxiety attack, eyes watering, put his head between his knees to avoid throwing up in the detective's car.

For a brief instant, the lot went silent. Then thousands and thousands of balloons began to rise. Charlotte stood beneath them as they effortlessly drifted past her, upward, into the heavens. She nudged one or two as they floated by on their way to the sky, liberated, and wished them a fond farewell.

For the first time in forever, Charlotte Nightingale was filled with exhilaration and hope. Framed by the brightly colored balloons, she raised her face to the sun, stretched out her arms, and closed her eyes in bliss.

風
水

CHAPTER SIX

Sunshine filtered through a skylight in Kwan's downtown loft, producing an ethereal radiance that imbued the air with positivity and good fortune. Thirty feet below on a polished concrete floor, Kwan lay bent backwards over a giant redwood stump, a one-hundred-pound slab of granite balanced on his chest. After an hour, with sweat pouring off his body and his abdominal muscles on fire, he heaved the giant stone off of his chest.

He took a long drink of cool, green tea, sat on the floor in the lotus position, and attempted to meditate, but he couldn't empty his mind. Visions of Charlotte and her wreck of an apartment plagued him, preventing him from achieving nothingness. He carefully picked up a very old book with a fragile rendering of a dragon on the cover and began to read. Each time he'd turn a page, the book would cough up ancient dust.

Kwan studied an illustration of a pair of Mandarin ducks, tracing the graceful brush strokes with his finger. As Kwan closed the book, it spewed a fine powder into the atmosphere. The particles drifted up and into the light like a million tiny balloons. *I haven't thought of balloons since I was a child,* he thought as he placed the rare volume on a bookshelf especially reserved for it. As he headed for the shower, the sparkly flecks of dust floating up toward the skylight again distracted him, and he stubbed his big toe on the leg of a chair. *Zen, Zen, Zen,* he told himself as he hopped across the room.

He slid open a shoji screen that partitioned the bathroom from the living space and removed his clothes. He tossed his sweats into a wicker hamper and turned on the shower. The pale green tiles of the bathroom reminded him of a beautiful garden he had seen in another Feng Shui book, which he had taken with him to the home improvement store to match the tile colors exactly. No detail had been spared in creating harmony and good fortune in Kwan's living space. His entire life was predicated on the theory that a person could control the direction of his or her life by simply putting the things around them in order.

He stepped onto the shower floor's moss-colored ceramic tiles and at once realized he was going down. His legs flew out from under him as his full weight landed squarely on his butt, knocking the wind out of him. He sat in the stream of water for a few moments, trying to decipher how something so ridiculous could happen to him, a natural athlete, a martial arts master, and a generally lucky man.

He looked around to see whether an errant bar of soap might have been the culprit, but since he used only hemp shower gel, he knew the search would be fruitless. Rubbing his hand over the tiles, he checked to see whether perhaps they had become slimy over time, but being a fastidious housekeeper he knew mildew was not to blame. Something was amiss, but what?

He sat under the rain showerhead and looked around. An image popped into his head—that of Charlotte Nightingale, soap suds running down her face, scrounging for change in the bottom of her purse, her apartment a Feng Shui disaster area. He closed his eyes and tried to change the subject in his mind, but the picture of Charlotte was indelibly etched in his brain.

As he gingerly got up and massaged his bruised tailbone, Kwan reflected on what Harold had said about Charlotte's shar chi rubbing off on him. *Ridiculous*, he thought. More people die in their own showers than in car wrecks. After a lifetime of good luck and positive chi, the law of averages simply dictated that it was Kwan's turn to take a little spill. He survived; he didn't break his neck or get a concussion. It's all good, he confirmed. Could happen to anyone.

He reached for a thick terry bath sheet, neatly folded on a small, wooden stool beside the shower, and fell a second time. The towel tumbled into the shower, immediately becoming sodden. He scrambled quickly to his feet, figuring that if he was fast enough he could pretend the second mishap hadn't occurred.

As he picked up the sopping towel, it slipped from his hands, striking the tiled floor with a heavy THWAP; perhaps he should revisit the Feng Shui texts in the area of water and their implications. Perhaps something of which he was unaware was amiss in the bathroom. Perhaps the simple rearrangement of bamboo was all that was needed to restore order in the universe.

風
水

CHAPTER SEVEN

By the time the emancipated balloons were mere pinheads against the mid-morning sun, Charlotte's exhilaration had turned to dread; for the first time since college she was faced with unemployment. Without the job, she'd never be able to repay her student loans, and until she was out from under that debt, she couldn't secure another loan for graduate school. Charlotte's hopes of becoming a librarian seemed to float up and disappear just like the balloons. *Pop. Pop. Pop. There go my dreams*, she thought. *Par for the course.*

With the Eebners and Don Stanton out for the day, and given the manner in which she had been unceremoniously discharged, Charlotte knew she stood no chance of receiving a paycheck or reimbursement for the small fortune she had personally spent on balloons and helium.

Her wreck of a car was another matter entirely. She certainly didn't have the money to fix the old heap. Her only prospect was that the auto be buried so deeply in the mutant weeds that no one would notice she had disposed of it there for eternity. While picking up her personal belongings from her former cubicle, Charlotte decided to take a peek at the Jetta. If it were indeed concealed by the foliage, she would take her chances and leave it.

She crept in through the service department and slipped undetected into her tiny office. The shade was drawn over the cashier's window, and to avoid discovery, Charlotte groped her way through the darkness. The only object that actually belonged to her was a small rubber plant with yellowing leaves, wilted and shunted to one side of her desk. She picked it up and quietly opened the door for a covert departure—only to stumble into the midst of an angry caucus of customers bearing down on an auto mechanic.

When the man spotted Charlotte, and as she heard the unmistakable click of the *Authorized Personnel Only* door locking behind her, he wiped his hands on his grimy overalls and pointed to her.

"There's the person you want to talk to," he said with an ugly smirk. "She's the cashier."

Before Charlotte could protest that she was no longer the cashier, the angry mob broke toward her with her nemesis, the priest, leading the charge.

"You're not such a smarty when you're on this side of the bulletproof glass, are you?"

A few customers jeered like villagers with pitchforks in a Frankenstein movie.

"Look," she told them, "I don't work here anymore. You're just going to have to deal with the service manager and figure something out." They murmured their distrust as the mechanic slunk quietly away. Charlotte watched his stained overalls disappear behind the Authorized Personnel Only door. "I'm sorry. I can't help you," she said.

"Well, there's nobody around here to help us, and the Bible says God helps those who help themselves," the priest pontificated, as the mob closed in on Charlotte and her shriveled plant. "We've been ripped off, abused, and taken for fools, and I'm telling you right now, this is where the buck stops."

He folded his arms over his chest. All the men and women crossed their arms and took a stance for justice and retribution. As they fervently nodded in agreement with the priest, Charlotte found herself doing the same. Glowering, the preacher raised his hands dramatically over his head as if he were about to excise snakes or chase a spider off someone's head.

"What the hell are you agreeing for?" he snapped, but before she could answer, he rolled over her with his fiery oratory. "Oh, I see. This is some kind of hooey they teach you when you come to work here, isn't it? Sure, agree with the customer, go along with the customer, and say whatever you think the customer wants to hear." A thin layer of sweat was forming on his upper lip. "Then whammo, stick 'em!" he spat out the words. "'Tis the work of Satan!"

The pissed-off horde had been touched by the priest's delivery, and more than a few were reminded of a rousing sermon for which they had once managed to stay awake. They looked at Charlotte as though she were a succubus about to eat a litter of kittens.

"I'm not evil," she protested. "Just unlucky."

The churchman brought it home. "Then this is your unlucky day!"

Charlotte considered this for a moment and found it mildly amusing that he thought her unlucky days might be limited to this one. "Well, what do you intend to do?" the priest demanded.

Charlotte handed him the half-dead rubber plant, then turned on her heel. She was a few feet from the door marked Authorized Personnel Only when he grabbed her by the arm, simultaneously dropping the potted plant. It crashed to the floor between them. The room fell silent. Charlotte looked the priest in the eye and then glanced down at the lifeless remains of her little rubber tree. A low-watt smile began to form.

"Let's see. The dealership has been unresponsive to your complaints. You've gotten no satisfaction, right?" She spoke the truth, but her peculiar smile was disconcerting and more than a few customers wondered if Charlotte wasn't a crook, but rather just plain crazy.

"And, I don't lie," she stated firmly for the record. "They fired me this morning, and they also cheated me out of two paychecks and the three hundred bucks that came out of my pocket to pay for the balloons and helium."

An elderly man at the back of the group brightened. "The balloons were a nice touch," he acknowledged. The others glared at him.

Charlotte mouthed a thank you and continued. "The difference between you and me is that I have the key to unlock that door." She nodded over her shoulder to the heavy steel door. A few mechanics had wandered over to the window separating the service department from the cashier's area. They watched the scene with great interest.

"What are you saying?" the priest asked, his bravado deflating somewhat.

"The people who write the checks are gone. Given that all you people are here with complaints, I'd guess the service manager is gone, too. The general manager is at the police station answering questions about his affair with another of my former co-workers, and she's in jail for murder."

The crowd inhaled with a collective gasp.

A lady in the back raised her hand. "Did she kill a customer, Miss?"

"Well, could you blame her? You've accosted me and smashed my plant, and you've been making all kinds of threats."

The priest made the sign of the cross as the others looked down, ashamed.

"No, she didn't kill a customer, but that was pure luck. It could have been any one of you who set her off." People glanced at their neighbors, awash in guilt.

"So here's what I'm proposing," Charlotte continued. Their stricken expressions turned somewhat buoyant. "Let's decide among us what's fair. We'll go over your complaints and come up with a mutually satisfying compromise. Eebner Brothers Lincoln-Mercury City will make a fair profit for their efforts, and you will pay a fair amount for services rendered. Does that sound like a plan?"

The customers perked up.

"Now, I need to get into the cashier's cubicle because that's where your car keys are locked up. Anybody have a problem with that?" Nobody moved a muscle. "Great." She opened the Authorized Personnel Only door and was behind the cashier's window in a flash. She slapped open the shade.

"Who's first?" They pushed the priest forward. He reluctantly slid a yellow invoice into the aluminum tray beneath the Plexiglas.

"I thought they made this repair earlier in the week," she said.

"So they told me. Then my car made the same noise as before, and when I brought it back, they said it was something different. It's the exact same thing and now they want me to pay for the same repair twice, and I'm not even sure it's fixed this time."

Charlotte retrieved a copy of the previous invoice from the files in her desk and compared the two documents. "They've written down that it was two different problems, but it looks like they used the same parts to make the repairs both times. That is odd."

The priest whistled through his nose, relieved that someone was finally hearing his side of the story, but when Charlotte stood up and walked away, he turned to the woman behind him in line. "We're done for," he groused. "She's outta here."

A moment later, Charlotte reappeared and slid the priest's keys into the tray. He looked at her, unsure. "Well, take them," she said. He tentatively reached for the keys and then snatched them up before Charlotte might change her mind.

"No charge. Who's next?" She scooted her chair closer to the window.

The priest moved aside, and a woman in line behind him stepped up and nervously slid her paperwork over. "This is the first time I've brought my car in, and I think most of this stuff is supposed to be under warranty. I don't understand why I'm being billed for all the parts and labor."

"Do you have your original paperwork?" Charlotte inquired.

As the woman produced the four-inch-thick binder with the bill of sale from the purchase of her car, a man in line slapped his forehead and squawked, "It'll take her all day to sift through the goddamned paperwork! We're doomed!"

Ignoring the outburst, Charlotte slid the sales contract back to the female customer. "As far as I can tell, all your parts and most of the labor are covered under the warranty. You do have to pay for items five and nine."

"That's more like it." The woman opened her pocketbook. "Cash okay?" Charlotte nodded, and the woman pushed some money into the tray.

Charlotte counted five ten-dollar bills. "That'll be forty-seven fifty out of fifty." She opened her cash drawer, dismayed to discover that it was empty. It had either been pilfered or Don Stanton had failed to prepare it before he was carted off to jail. Her heart sank, and she feared the mob wasn't going to like this development one bit. "I don't have change," she said, waiting for the shit to hit the fan.

"Keep the change, honey. Put it against what they owe you," the woman told her.

A middle-aged man wearing an "I'm the Boss" T-shirt was pushed forward by his wife. "I think whoever can pay cash, should," he proposed. "If she's willing to help us, maybe we can help her recoup some of the dough these crooks owe her. If nobody's here to write checks or deal with us, then it's like the Father said. God helps those who help themselves." People started opening their wallets and handbags.

Charlotte grabbed a notepad and began a tally of what was hers and what belonged to the Eebners.

A young construction worker bellied up and smiled timidly. He stuffed a thick invoice into the tray. "I don't dispute the labor or parts, but every time I called to see if my car was ready, I was told to call back later when the service manager was in. It took three weeks before he finally took my call, and now I'm being charged storage."

Charlotte went over the paperwork. "Looks like your car was ready the day after you brought it in," she confirmed. "We'll just take off all the storage fees."

Happily bouncing on the balls of his feet, the man counted out three large bills and slid them over. After making change from the money given her by the last customer, Charlotte deducted the appropriate amount from the running total on her notepad.

The priest came up and rapped on the Plexiglas with his keys. "Thanks for everything. It's a shame you've been fired." He stepped aside so that the next person could be heard.

An elderly man with thick, snow-white hair and a confused expression handed Charlotte his paperwork. "Can't make heads or tails out of it. I just wanted somebody to explain it to me."

Charlotte held the yellow forms in her hands as the door to her cubicle flew open and the service manager stormed in and spun her chair around with dizzying force.

"What the hell do you think you're doing?" He showered her with spittle.

"There's the bastard now!" an elderly woman with a walker hollered. "That's the service manager!" A few people hissed.

The service manager grabbed the paid invoices, scanned them, and then tossed them into the air. He bore down on Charlotte as sheets of yellow paper fluttered down around them.

"Are you insane?!" Bellowing at the top of his lungs, bending over Charlotte's chair, he nearly touched noses with her. She flinched and tried to roll back, but one of the casters was stuck. "You can just go ahead and make all the changes you want, but every last dime you deduct from these bills is going to come out of your paycheck."

He snatched the invoice out of Charlotte's hands. "Let's see, the old man's bill is five hundred bucks. How much you gonna take off this one?" He rustled the papers in Charlotte's face.

"He simply wants to know what all this stuff is," she said, pushing his hand away. "He just wants an explanation."

"Explain this," he jeered. "He wanted his car fixed and we fixed it. End of story."

"What's this, then?" She pointed to an item near the bottom of the page.

He blinked a few times. "Are you blind? It's a carburetor."

"Look at the model number. It doesn't go with his make of car." He placed his hands on the arms of Charlotte's swivel chair and leaned in so closely she could count the pores on his bulbous nose.

"Are you questioning me?"

"It's not right," she countered. "It's not fair."

He stared at her, speechless, and then he turned and walked to the door.

"You're way out of your league," he said calmly. "Every penny you bilk this company out of is coming off your hide. You'll be working every weekend and night until you're a hundred. You'll die a lonely old woman, right here behind the cashier's window at Eebner Brothers Lincoln-Mercury City." He walked out and slammed the door.

The elderly gal pushed forward with her walker, the front legs of which were stuck into lime green tennis balls. "This is all our fault. We've really gotten you in dutch."

"Don't worry about it." Charlotte was unperturbed. "How many times can they fire me?"

The customers heaved a united sigh of relief, pleased that Charlotte had a positive attitude, hopeful that it would sustain until the last of them had received satisfaction. For her part, Charlotte felt terrific. It was the first time in as long as she could remember that she had taken the bull by the horns.

"Now, where were we?" She winked at the old man, a gesture she had never made before, but one that she made a mental note to practice more often. "Oh yeah, you were charged for parts that weren't used on your car." She happily scratched out the total at the bottom of the page, wrote a new figure over it, and pushed it back through the slot.

He triumphantly held the bill over his head. "Thank you, Miss. Thank you very much!" He pushed several hundred-dollar bills into the tray. She made change, and then she made the calculations that told her she was finally square with the company. She put the money in an envelope, dropped it into her handbag, and put the sheet of paper with the notations in another envelope. She sealed it and wrote the Eebner's names on it and stuck it in the cash drawer.

"Next," she said with a wink.

風
水

CHAPTER EIGHT

The lunch rush at Emperor's Kitchen was always hectic. Old Man Kwan ordered the kitchen and wait staff around with such interminable vigor that his employees were constantly tempted to murder him. Kwan worked twice as hard as anyone else just to keep the peace, while Harold provided the color commentary that made everyone homicidal.

"Shake your money-maker," he'd say to a frazzled waitress. "Think tips, tips, tips."

"Die now," she'd invariably reply with a sharpened chopstick in her apron pocket.

When the order came in for a delivery to the same building in which Charlotte lived, Kwan dropped everything to personally take care of it.

"Kwan," Harold said. "I'm the D-man today, but I just detailed my ride, so if you want to make the run…"

Kwan stood over the cook, urging him to hurry, and sounding so much like Old Man Kwan that the waitress quietly dropped her sharpened chopstick into the cook's pocket.

"Sorry," Kwan apologized. "I'm a little stressed today."

The cook looked at him. "You okay?"

"Yeah, Dog," Harold chimed in. "Mr. Tranquility. What up?" The cook filled cartons with steaming noodles, broccoli with mushrooms in black bean sauce, and Kung Pao chicken.

Kwan tucked in his shirt and smoothed his ponytail. A grin spread across Harold's face. "That's what I'm talkin' about. Who is she?"

"You're nuts." Kwan used a napkin to clean a spot on his sneaker. "The order's for a man named Shirley."

"No shit?" It seemed fishy to Harold. "You lyin', Dog?"

Kwan snatched the cartons of food the instant they were ready and quickly bagged them. "Where are the good fortune cookies?" he asked. "The ones we give special customers?" The cook pointed to a box in the corner labeled Super Lucky Fortune. Kwan grabbed a handful of super lucky fortune cookies and walked out.

"Whoa," Harold said to no one in particular. "Kwan is getting his freak on."

Old Man Kwan rushed into the kitchen and swatted Harold, the cook, a busboy, and two waitresses with one deft swipe of his bony hand. "What do I pay you for?"

The cook clutched the chopstick shiv in his pocket, and with his free hand, flipped a batch of bok choy in ginger sauce sizzling in a giant wok.

It was just after noon when Kwan rang the buzzer of apartment 3-D in Charlotte's building.

"About time," Mr. Shirley complained into the intercom. "If it's cold, I'm not paying," and with that, buzzed Kwan into the lobby.

Junk mail lay in heaps in front of the tarnished mailboxes. Discarded boxes, candy wrappers, soda cans and a pair of men's underpants littered a tiny seating area in the vestibule. Potted plants, long dead, stooped from their cracked plastic pots, which had been used as ashtrays to the point of overflowing. The floor around the plants was an inch thick with dusty brown leaves and cigarette butts.

Kwan located Charlotte's name on the mailboxes, set down the bag of food, and began to tidy the area. He collected the junk mail and ancient newspaper circulars and stuffed them into a trashcan. Unable to ignore the boxer shorts dangling from the back of a stained armchair, he reached into the bag and produced chopsticks, which he used to lift the undergarment and deposit it into the garbage.

Turning his attention to the dead plants, Kwan was taken aback when Mr. Shirley stealthily crept up behind him and barked, "Freeze!"

Kwan nearly fell over.

"Stop right there! Navy Seal! I'm a trained assassin!"

Kwan slowly turned around, hands in the air. Shirley took one look at him, sniffed in the direction of the brown paper bag, and relaxed. "You the Chinese delivery guy?"

"Emperor's Kitchen," Kwan said crossly, speculating that the fat landlord had never served with an elite military unit. He pointed to the bag of food across the room. "There's your order. Twenty bucks."

"Ha!" Shirley made a move for the food. "I told you I wasn't paying if it got cold, and you let it sit here for more than...HEY!"

Kwan had been a student of Kung Fu since he was three years old and in the blink of an eye, had flipped backward off the wall, hand-sprung across the room, and had the bag in his hands before Shirley had moved two muscles.

"Hey!" Shirley repeated, lunging for the bag. "Give me that!"

Kwan passed the aromatic bag back and forth under the landlord's nose. "Hungry?" he taunted.

Shirley began to salivate. "I'm not paying twenty bucks."

"Plus two bucks delivery charge and the mandatory twenty-percent tip."

"What?!" Shirley's forehead turned a shade of vermilion not found in nature.

Kwan smiled pleasantly. "Okay," he said, heading for the door. "I didn't have time for lunch today, so this succulent Kung Pao chicken, simmered in spicy garlic sauce, will certainly hit the spot. And the broccoli and mushrooms? Whoa. Don't even get me started on the black bean sauce we serve with it. If there's nothing else..." He headed toward the exit.

Mouth watering, Shirley reached under his caftan and extracted a twenty-dollar bill and a damp five from a sweaty money belt. "This is robbery with violence."

"Thank you," Kwan said. By the time he had pocketed the cash, Shirley was already in the elevator, hungrily tearing into the bag.

"You forgot something." Kwan waved a clear plastic bag filled with fortune cookies. Shirley hopped out of the elevator, and with great cow eyes looked at the cookies, then at Kwan. Kwan walked over and handed Mr. Shirley the chopsticks, with which he had picked up the discarded underwear. "Gotta go authentic, right?"

Shirley pouted like a kid whose trip to Disneyland had been cancelled. "I want cookies."

Kwan held them out of reach. "Buck-fifty a piece."

The landlord grudgingly snatched the chopsticks and disappeared into the elevator.

With Shirley gone, Kwan had all the time he needed to correct what he could about the bad Feng Shui in Charlotte's lobby. He removed the dead plants and litter. He repositioned the chairs and table in the sitting area, and lastly, he used his shirttail to polish Charlotte Nightingale's mailbox. Satisfied, he headed for the elevator.

He reached into his pocket, pulled out a small black ceramic turtle the size of a fortune cookie, and pressed the button for the fourth floor.

風
水

CHAPTER NINE

Charlotte had a spring in her step that afternoon as she took her final walk down the driveway of Eebner Brothers Lincoln-Mercury City—and she would have been on the sidewalk, home free, had it not been for the service manager, flanked by two swarthy mechanics who tore through the crowd in her direction. Many customers, still exploring the values at Eebner's gigantic price rollback sale, stood between her and the sanctity of the public walkway.

Grabbing the first person in front of her by the shoulders, Charlotte spun him around and announced, "If you buy today, they're offering free oil changes and filters for life. There's the service manager and the guys who'll be looking after your car." She pointed to the angry men coming her way. The man handed his hotdog off to his wife and stepped in front of the service manager.

Charlotte pushed ahead and repeated the story to another customer, and that person and his mate turned toward the service manager as well. Word of the fabulous sales incentive swept through the new car lot with a fury, and within seconds, even the salespeople were excitedly telling prospective buyers of the tremendous offer.

The service manager and his crew were quickly incapacitated, and Charlotte turned onto the sidewalk, feeling that she had been perfectly fair in dealing with the travails of a difficult morning. It was even a little thrilling to think that she had finally left her mark on something. She would be remembered at Eebner City. *Oh, yes.*

En route to the bus stop Charlotte came across the homeless man from the night before. She rustled the papers covering him.

"Hello there," she said.

"Get lost," he replied from beneath the Sports Section. "This is public property."

Charlotte wanted to tell him she was no longer a person without a story. She wanted to tell him about the balloons and the cops and how she dealt with all the angry customers, but instead she reached into her purse, took out five twenty-dollar bills and tucked them into the man's hand.

She reached the bus stop just as the bus approached. She kindly let a lady with numerous shopping bags board ahead of her and then took the last available seat beside the woman. Charlotte offered to hold a couple of bags while the exhausted gal got situated. She stuffed two bags beneath the seat in front of her, and then looked covetously at the vacant space in front of Charlotte.

"Go ahead," Charlotte said, as she shuffled her feet to the side. The woman stuffed two more bags under the seat in front of Charlotte, and then took the bags from Charlotte's lap.

"Thanks a lot. I forgot my car was in the shop when I bought all this." She adjusted her purchases. "I guess I went a little nuts today."

"Didn't stab anyone in the neck, did you?" Charlotte joked.

"Wasn't that something?" the lady remarked solemnly. "Like a butcher, that woman."

"I actually know her," Charlotte whispered.

"The killer?"

Charlotte nodded gravely. "Worked with her for more than a year."

The two men sitting behind Charlotte leaned forward. "Did I just hear you say you know the nut job who hacked the woman to bits in Cerritos?"

Charlotte's seatmate turned around. "Yup, she's worked with her for five years. Saw her with the chainsaw!" Suddenly the whole bus was interested in Charlotte Nightingale.

"Is it true she dismembered the victim?" someone in the back of the bus wanted to know. Another passenger near the front asked, "Did she really eat the heart?"

Charlotte was taken aback by the attention, and the strange way the information had transmogrified into an episode of Criminal Minds.

"I don't know. She was a little weird," Charlotte said.

Suddenly the woman beside her jumped out of her seat. "I've missed my stop!" she wailed, reaching for the buzzer. The bus lurched to a standstill. The lady nearly toppled over, and a few passengers who had been leaning out of their seats for a better view of Charlotte fell forward.

Charlotte stood and helped the lady with her bags. The woman dashed for the door. "I wish I could hear more," she said as she made her way up the aisle.

The driver opened the door. "Pay attention. I want a full report," she ordered him, stepping onto the sidewalk.

The bus pulled away from the curb, and the woman waved at Charlotte. Charlotte smiled and waved back, then realized that the lady had forgotten the two bags stuffed under the seat in front of hers. She grabbed the bags, but it was too late. The bus had pulled into traffic.

A knobby-kneed, twelve-year-old girl in a plaid uniform skirt, stooped beneath the weight of a giant backpack, tapped Charlotte on the shoulder.

"Scoot over," she wheezed.

Charlotte slid to the window seat and studied the Nordstrom's logos on the shopping bags. "Excuse me," she called to the driver. "Where is the nearest Nordstrom's?"

"Behind us, at the Galleria."

The little girl dropped her book bag with a thud and sat down beside Charlotte. "Well? What else?"

Charlotte rifled through the woman's purchases. "She was having an affair with…" She suddenly realized that the person next to her was a child. "Never mind. It's not important."

"So, she was knockin' boots," the child reflected, rolling her eyes. "With who?"

"With whom." Charlotte was a stickler for grammar. "Her brother-in-law," she answered to the semi-interest of the entire bus group. It wasn't as juicy as cannibalism, but it was something. "He was general manager at Eebner Brothers Lincoln-Mercury City, and she was a new car sales associate." She found a charge card receipt in the bag. "They'd have her address at the store, wouldn't they?"

The kid shrugged. "Your friend is a ho," she said knowledgeably.

Charlotte suddenly flashed on the image of Joey and the stripper, causing her armpits to heat up. She stood up, flapped slightly to cool her underarms, and then squeezed past the child and over the giant backpack. By the time she got to the front of the bus tears were rolling down her cheeks. The driver smiled kindly, and handed Charlotte a tissue.

"I'm sorry about your friend the murderer," the bus driver said. "People can be such a disappointment."

Charlotte wiped her face. "That has been my experience."

A major sale was in progress when Charlotte arrived at Nordstrom's. She made her way to the first available cashier and waited in line. There were women in front of her with their arms sagging beneath the weight of sale purchases they couldn't afford not to make. When it was finally her turn, Charlotte set the bags down and began pulling items out in search of the receipt. She placed a matronly navy dress with a fussy lace collar on the counter.

"I hope they're paying you for that thing," a female shopper behind her commented.

Charlotte spun around. "Pardon?" A few women anxious to make their purchases could only groan and shift their weighty hauls to their other arms.

"Next," the clerk barked.

Charlotte handed over the receipt. "A woman left these bags on the bus and I saw on the receipt that she charged everything. I figured you'd have her address on file and you could...."

The big sale had taken its toll on the frazzled clerk. She exhaled loudly through her nose. "You've got to be kidding me."

The woman behind Charlotte moaned, "Oh, for God's sake. Go upstairs to customer service. Come on, my arms are getting tired." Charlotte stuffed her bus companion's garments into the shopping bag and quickly stepped aside.

The woman dumped her purchases in front of the cashier with a grunt. Unburdened, she turned to Charlotte. "That's an interesting outfit you're wearing. I wouldn't have thought to mix those patterns and colors, but somehow it works. Michael Kors?"

Charlotte looked down at her faded bellbottoms. "I don't think so."

"There is a pair of Miu Miu mules that would be just darling with that. They're toward the back, and they're a yummy military pink. You'll love them."

Charlotte considered this for a moment, appreciative of the alliteration. "Where are the Miu Miu mules?"

The woman nearly fell over. "Have you been living under a rock? Hello? The shoe department."

Charlotte looked at the women in line, with all their many purchases cradled in their arms like cherished redeemers in stained glass church windows, and she had to ask herself the same question. Where had she been that she had overlooked the eighth wonder of the world?

"Don't move," the woman said, scribbling her name on a charge slip. "I'll personally take you over there." She looked at the clerk. "Wanna get a move on, Toots?"

After hastily shoving the woman's purchases into shopping bags, the clerk was simply relieved to be out from under the onus of having to provide any further customer service—and had nothing to lose by smiling at both Charlotte and the helpful shopper.

"Great. Have a nice day. Buh-bye. Next."

"I'm Carmen," the woman said, handing Charlotte a shopping bag. "You're gonna die!" She broke into a trot, and then took off at lightning speed toward the Holy Grail—the shoe department. "You're just gonna die," she declared over her shoulder. When they were within striking distance of hallowed ground, Carmen stopped dead, and with great reverence, held forth on the meaning of one's virgin visit to shoe Oz. "There it is. You will go, and nothing will be the same."

She sprung forward and disappeared among the throngs of women, each of whom was holding one shoe in her hand, right foot bare and ready for action. Charlotte followed, but had no chance of keeping up with a veteran and was quite content to inch her way over to the sale racks to peruse the size sevens. She spotted the pink satin mule to which Carmen had referred, kicked off one of her own sloppy loafers, and slipped her foot into the elegant Italian. It was a pretty shoe with admirable architecture, but Charlotte's droopy knee socks bulged over the sides, distracting from the shoe's silhouette. She hobbled to the mirror, one foot in the sexy high heel, the other in her loafer, which was similar in design and appeal to a gunboat.

A salesperson dashed by and Charlotte managed to grab him by the sleeve. His shirt was wet and stained under the arms. His hair was wild, his skin pallid and slick, and he appeared to be foaming at the mouth.

"Excuse me." She wiggled her pink-shod foot. "Do you have the mate for this?"

"Miu-Miu?" He blew sweat off his lip.

She backed away. "I think so."

"Wait here." He took a deep breath and ran off in the direction of the storeroom, plowing through a cadre of women brawling over a discounted pair of Jimmy Choos.

Charlotte stepped closer to the mirror and realized in horror that she now had three shopping bags that were not hers. Just then Carmen arrived and shrieked in her ear, "Well, look at that! I told you that shoe was just made for you!"

Charlotte studied her reflection in the mirror and liked what she saw. "It is nice."

"And what a deal," Carmen enthused. "You rarely get that kind of bargain on Miu-Miu." The clerk returned with the mate, and Carmen took all the packages from Charlotte so she could try both shoes at once. "You've got to get them," she coached, as the salesman looked hopefully at Charlotte.

"You taking them?"

"How much of a bargain are they?" Charlotte wanted to know.

He looked at the sticker on the shoebox and whistled. "They were originally six hundred eighty-five dollars. They're down to two hundred and fifty bucks. You're stealing them."

Charlotte gulped and kicked the right shoe off so quickly that it flew past the clerk and hit another bargain hunter in the calf. Looking about to discover what had struck her, the lady spotted the pink projectile on the floor and dove for it, beating a mother and daughter team from Sherman Oaks to the punch.

"Get me the mate!" she howled, victoriously waving the shoe overhead.

The salesman dropped to his knees and had the left shoe off Charlotte's foot before she knew what hit her.

Carmen glared at Charlotte, shoved the two shopping bags belonging to the bus lady into her hands and sniffed, "You are an insult to women everywhere." With that, she disappeared among the racks and shoppers.

Charlotte felt no guilt about disappointing Carmen or the clerk, but the remark stung. She watched all the women happily trying on shoes, paying for their purchases, and obviously experiencing some kind of pleasure the likes of which she had never known. Charlotte looked at the rows of size sevens, a collection that promised to transform her from a person without a hope into a Nordstrom shoe department connoisseur. Charlotte was therefore compelled to sample as many right shoes as possible. After a solid hour's effort, she had it narrowed down to one, low-priced pair of sensible taupe Naturalizers. The salesman walked by and she requested the mate.

"You buying this time?" he asked skeptically. Charlotte lifted her chin and nodded.

"Excellent. Meet me at the cash register." He returned a moment later with the bland left shoe. "Cash or charge?"

Charlotte opened her handbag and removed the envelope with the Eebner money in it. "Cash."

"If you open a Nordstrom account, you get an extra ten percent off," he told her, pulling a little form out of a display on the counter. "Here. Fill this out." She stepped aside so other shoppers could pay for their life-giving shoes as she filled out the form.

The clerk glanced up. "You'll have to take that upstairs. Go to customer service. They'll issue you a temporary card and you can shop 'til you drop."

Charlotte had never done anything 'til she dropped, and it sounded like it might be fun. She had heard about retail therapy. *Maybe this is just what the doctor ordered,* she thought. She banished the image of Joey and the hooker from her mind, lifted her chin and marched toward Customer Service, where she filled out the requisite application. The woman behind the counter, a gal with a frosted pageboy, navy blazer and a string of pearls, took the completed form from Charlotte. She snorted and flicked her tongue across her lips, a nervous tic, and asked to see Charlotte's driver's license.

Charlotte handed over her identification. "Here you go, Sylvia," she said, reading the woman's nametag.

"This is going to take just a minute." Snort. Lick. "Perhaps you'd like to have a look around in Finer Dresses and come back in say, fifteen?"

Charlotte had only to walk a few feet to the department where lesser dresses were not sold to notice almost instinctively that the racks were farther apart in this sector, affording the customer a most pleasant environment in which to shop.

There were no neon green sale signs over these clothes; there were no pink dots or red tags. The dresses were grouped elegantly by color. The area lacked the spectacle found in the departments of subordinate apparel. Having only ever shopped in thrift stores, it was mostly lost on Charlotte, except that she liked the sedate atmosphere and the fact that she had the whole place to herself.

She went to the first rack, above which a sign advertised, "The LBD," and she was sure that buried deep within the piles of clothing on the floor of her closet she possessed no such thing. She took a dress off the rack and stared at it. It was a tiny confection of matte jersey that would seem too tiny to fit any standard-sized human, but Charlotte stalwartly carried it to the mirror for corroboration. She held the dress against her body, and it hung from its hanger like a tiny T-shirt.

A saleswoman seemed to materialize out of thin air. "Try it on," she coaxed. "Not many women have the shape for it, but I think it would be simply divine on you."

Charlotte stood frozen in front of the mirror and asked incredulously, "Is this a...size?"

"You look like a six, but this garment runs a bit large. It'll be fine." Guiding Charlotte to the fitting room, the clerk seemed to preternaturally float across the carpet like a supermodel on a catwalk, or a hovering spaceship. Charlotte went inside and quickly closed the louvered door behind her, questioning the woman's ability to ambulate without moving her legs.

"How's everything in there?" the saleslady inquired.

"Uh, nice, thanks. I just got here."

"How's the dress, dear?" she said with a bite.

Charlotte quickly changed her clothes. "I'm not so sure." She opened the door a fraction of an inch. Her hair hung straight down, her loafers jutted off her feet like skis and her knee socks bunched around her ankles.

"The dress looks incredible," the clerk gushed. "But you'll need the right shoes."

Charlotte looked into the three-way mirror and turned around to study the dress, and herself inside of it, from all angles. Nothing bulged out, but the material was definitely painted on. It hugged every curve and protrusion on her body from the top of her thigh, where its hem clung, to the cleave of her buttocks, to the definition of her breasts.

She stared at her reflection, unsure of the female staring back. To her, it seemed that the body and the dress, everything but the hair, shoes, and socks, must surely belong to some other woman who possessed great amounts of self-confidence—and a possible tendency toward going nearly nude in public.

The saleswoman rapped at the door and opened it without waiting for a reply. She handed Charlotte a shoebox, stood behind her and pulled her hair up.

"There. You have a swan-like neck. Absolutely stunning. Your boyfriend's going have a heart attack when he sees you in this."

"I don't have a boyfriend." Charlotte bit her lip. She opened the shoebox and took out the strappy black stilettos the woman recommended to go with the daring dress.

"Go ahead," the sales lady urged. "You'll have ten boyfriends before you can say Christian Louboutin."

Charlotte dropped the shoes on the floor and kicked off her loafers. She slid her knee-socked feet into the sexy shoes and teetered toward the mirror.

"Ah, look at that. That's an absolutely terrific look for you. I'd lose the socks, though." The saleslady was adamant.

"Really?" Charlotte had never been sure about clothes.

"Definitely. The socks have got to go."

"No, I mean do I really look terrific? Is that the word? Terrific?" The woman oohed and ahhed over Charlotte's figure and the dress and the shoes, all the while nodding profusely. "Do I look nice?" Charlotte pointedly asked.

The clerk checked out Charlotte's provocative rear view. "Define nice."

"Well, I have to go to this dinner tonight where my sister's going to announce her engagement to a doctor. My mom said I should look nice."

"Do you like your sister...much?"

Charlotte shrugged. "We're not really close. She's beautiful and happy."

"I understand perfectly." The woman's tone suggested that she had a sister of whom she wasn't terribly fond. "The dress is just the right thing for tonight." The woman turned to leave.

"Wait," Charlotte said. "What does LBD stand for? I looked high and low for the tag, but I couldn't find one."

The clerk stared at her; sure Charlotte must be pulling her leg.

"Well?" Charlotte said.

"Little. Black. Dress. Please tell me you knew that."

Charlotte looked at her reflection. "It sure is little."

Charlotte approached the customer service counter clutching the little black dress and a shoebox. She was certain that her credit card application would be rejected, but nonetheless set the dress on the counter. She smiled weakly at Sylvia, the one person who could see to it that she get an additional ten percent off her purchases—if by some miracle her credit were approved. Lo and behold, Sylvia was delighted to see her.

"There you are! I was hoping you'd be back." Charlotte took it as a form of encouragement. Sylvia pushed the dress and shoes aside and leaned forward. "I see from your application that you work at Eebner Brothers. Did you work with Phyllis Schlotzky, Charlotte?"

"Yes, I did, Sylvia."

"Call me Syll," she said, with a conspiratorial air. "Your credit app was borderline. I'm sure you know what I mean, but you seem nice." Snort. Lick. "I have some latitude during these sales events, and I want you to have a Nordstrom charge." She winked and gave Charlotte a piece of paper that would enable her to enjoy the shopping/dropping experience she had been assured would change her life. Charlotte reached for the brass ring, and then Syll yanked it away. "I want to know stuff that hasn't been in the news. Did you go to any of her orgies? Did you ever see her carve a pentagram into someone's flesh?"

Charlotte sighed. "No on the orgies. No on the flesh carving."

Snort. Lick. "Come on! You must know something about her that's too gross for the mainstream media."

Group sex and maiming aren't gross enough? Charlotte thought, and she couldn't have cared less. But experience told her other people felt differently, and everyone was interested in the inside dope on Phyllis Schlotzky. "She was having an affair," she offered, hoping that the little tidbit might be enough. Sylvia snorted and licked double-time. "With her sister's husband," Charlotte added wearily.

"Wear that dress tonight and you'll be having relations with anybody you want. Just kidding. What else?"

"I don't know. Let me think." Charlotte glanced up at several pencils protruding from the ceiling tiles and wondered how bored someone had to be to do that.

"Ahem." Sylvia rapped her knuckles on the counter.

"Sometimes she wore very tight clothes and inappropriate footwear." Charlotte touched the edge of the little black dress. "Kind of like this."

The customer service woman was stunned. "She wore Chanel to work?"

"She wore a lot of flashy stuff."

"Tell me more." Sylvia waved the temporary credit card.

"Her brother-in-law was the general manager." Charlotte was running out of ammo.

"Was?" It was titillating info. "Did she decapitate him, too?"

"No, well, not yet, anyway," Charlotte speculated. "The police came to question everybody today, and they took him away. I guess they figured since he was intimate with her, he might be able to speak to her frame of mind or something. Know what I told the cops?"

Snortlicksnortlicksnortlick. Syll rested her breasts on the counter. "What?"

Charlotte could feel the woman's soggy breath on her eyeballs. "I told them he was banging her." Charlotte shivered, surprised by her own brass.

Sylvia rolled her eyes. "Big whoop. Did the wife know?"

"I have no idea, but I did overhear something about Phyllis and Don, that's her brother-in-law, my former boss..." She caught herself. Sylvia's eyes narrowed. Charlotte held her breath.

"What? Do you think he'll be fired?" Sylvia asked.

Charlotte exhaled, relieved. "He was fired this morning. Anyway, I heard that they were planning on running away together."

Syll snorted, licked, and shook her head all at the same time.

Charlotte sighed, exasperated, "She was a real pain. And high-strung." She thought about Phyllis peeling out of the lot hell-bent for the beauty supply store, leaving Charlotte behind. *Thank God*, thought Charlotte.

"It must have been something when you found out she murdered that poor woman in Cerritos, huh?"

"To be honest, I wasn't all that surprised," Charlotte said "A lot goes on at a place like that. Let me tell you."

"Her own sister's husband." Sylvia's tone turned grave. "I'm sure there's more to that story than meets the eye." A tiny ball of spittle had formed at the corner of her mouth.

Charlotte took a small step back and wiped her mouth in an exaggerated way. "Yeah, well, I think that's probably the whole thing."

"Pity." She handed Charlotte the piece of paper containing the digits that activated her Nordstrom buying power. "Enjoy," she said dryly, disappointed that Charlotte didn't have better Intel.

"Oh, geez, I almost forgot," Charlotte said as she handed over the two shopping bags belonging to the lady on the bus. "A woman forgot these on the bus. I thought you could find her from the credit card receipt."

"I'll get right on it," Sylvia said, preparing to launch a pencil into the ceiling tiles.

Charlotte returned to the clerk in Finer Dresses and proudly presented the scrap of paper with the magic numbers, the high-heeled shoes, and the little black dress.

"You're taking the shoes?"

"I'm thinking about it." Charlotte wasn't about to pay Miu Miu moola, and although she looked for a price tag on both the dress and shoebox, she couldn't find one. "What are the damages?" she asked in a tone she thought made her sound like an old hand at retail therapy.

The woman waved the scanner in the general direction of the shoebox, pingpingping, and then slipped it into the dress—pingpingping. "Thirty-five fifty on the nose. How 'bout that? It's a real bargain, my dear. You'll never get into Chanel and Christian Louboutins at this price again. Trust me. You are literally saving thousands."

Charlotte had never spent more than seven dollars on an outfit in her life.

"Thirty-five fifty. Geez, that is a bargain," she used what she imagined was a sophisticated tone. *I owe myself something nice for once,* she told herself. "I'll take it."

Charlotte handed the woman the significant piece of paper. So thrilled was she with her purchases, and so ignorant to the ways of shopping, that it never occurred to Charlotte to compare decimal points on the receipt with decimal points she had ascribed to the transaction in her head when she signed the charge slip and handed it back.

"I think you are going to be very pleased with your new things," the gal said, patting Charlotte's hand. "Have fun tonight, honey."

A reality television show played quietly in the background as Mr. Shirley dozed on the sofa, Kung Pao sauce dripping from his chin and fingers. On the TV, a shriveled Chinese man with a snow-white goatee stood in the center of an overgrown garden and shook his head. The nervous homeowners, a middle-aged couple living in rural Minnesota, fidgeted as the old man gravely surveyed their yard. He pointed at an abandoned koi pond choked with ivy and weeds. He pulled his lips back and hissed through his teeth. The homeowners nodded their acknowledgement. The thing was an eyesore.

One floor above Mr. Shirley's apartment, the plumbing in Charlotte's apartment sprang to life. What began as a low steady hum in the pipes was rapidly morphing into a rumble and shake. The walls of Charlotte's bathroom began to vibrate. Water slapped the sides of the toilet bowl. The sink tap sputtered, seemed to clear itself, and then spewed a torrent of water into the basin where Charlotte had dropped her hand towel that morning. The showerhead sputtered for an instant, then burst forth with tremendous pressure, immediately soaking the bath towel Charlotte had dropped into the tub. The towel drifted toward the drain and lodged itself at the end, blocking all possible water outlets.

Charlotte arrived at her apartment building as a team of firefighters packed up their trucks. "What happened?" she asked a hale woman wearing a yellow jacket and a big red hat.

"Water main burst." The female firefighter slid a leather sheath over the blade of a shiny ax. "You live here?"

Charlotte nodded as several firefighters exited her building. "Was there a lot of damage?"

"Not too bad," the woman said, smoothing a Frida Kahlo unibrow. "Caused a little damage to the landlord's place, though. He's going to have to replace the ceiling in his bathroom."

Charlotte knew that her own apartment was directly over Mr. Shirley's and feared the worst. "Do you know what caused it?" There was a discernible trace of guilt in her voice borne of the fact that most things that ran amok were attributed to her.

The woman ran her tongue across her upper lip. "Sure do," she said.

Charlotte clutched her shopping bag and braced herself, convinced that she would somehow be revealed as the culprit, but not really certain of the reason.

"The landlord's a little unbalanced. He claims that it's the fault of some woman who lives above him. The plumbing is so bad in this building that we had to turn off the water main just to get the situation under control. The pipes are ancient. It's nobody's fault, except for maybe the landlord's. This should have been addressed a long time ago." She removed her hat and attempted to fluff the hair matted to her forehead. "He's been cited for a ton of code violations."

She smiled warmly and extended her hand. "Hi, I'm Kelly. What's your name?"

"Charlotte." She grinned at the thought of Mr. Shirley being in trouble with the authorities.

"I like your outfit," Kelly commented, appraising Charlotte's mismatched pink combo from top to bottom.

The compliment cheered Charlotte. "You're the second woman to tell me that today, thanks."

"You're just trying to make me jealous," Kelly said slyly.

Charlotte blinked, unsure.

"You're a doll," Kelly clarified.

When Joey, masquerading as Frank, called her a "doll," Charlotte felt tingly and special and just a little bit silly. When Kelly the female firefighter called her the same exact thing, Charlotte felt her forehead heat up uncomfortably. "I have to go now," she said, blushing.

As Charlotte turned toward the building, Kelly grabbed her by the shoulder. "We found this in the hallway on the fourth floor. Right outside 4-D. Have any idea who lives there?" She held out the ceramic turtle Kwan had taken from his pocket.

Charlotte grinned stupidly. "Yes, I know who lives there."

"Do you know if this belongs to her or…?"

"Sorry, I don't."

Kelly pressed the little charm into Charlotte's palm. "Why don't you hang onto it? It's pretty. Like you."

Charlotte muttered a lame thank you, pocketed the turtle, and dashed into the building. She stabbed the elevator's call button, and as she waited for the doors to open, Mr. Shirley burst into the lobby behind her.

"Yoooooooooo!"

He wore a psychedelic caftan that billowed around him as he hurtled toward her, reminding Charlotte of a Rose Bowl float she had once seen veer off course during a parade. The driver had suffered a heart attack, and the floral tribute to milkmaids careened out of control until finally running up the curb and smashing into a falafel cart.

"You!" he bleated. "I knew you would do something like this!"

"The firefighter said…"

"Said what? That some dipshitz stuffed the drains full of towels and left her water running all day?" He was hysterical. "You are a plague!" He shoved her against the elevator door. "You are sooooo out of here!"

"But it's not my fault!" she protested, wriggling out of his grasp. "There was no water when I left!"

"If you're not gone by tomorrow morning, I'll personally throw your crap on the street!"

"You can't do that to me! I've been without decent plumbing for months. I've begged you to fix the pipes!"

"My cactuses are all dead. Root rot. And now my ceiling is hanging down into my bathroom like… like …" He searched for the word. "Balls. There, I said it. This is what it has come to. Balls. You're history, Nightingale!"

The simile was all too vivid, and Charlotte suddenly realized that she was not in a mood to put up with the abuse.

"Send me the paperwork," she said curtly. "I'm tired, and I have a party to go to." The elevator whooshed open and Charlotte stepped inside. "And you can shove your stupid cacti up your…" Whoosh. The doors closed.

She reached for the fourth floor button, but on second thought, pressed the third floor button instead. She could use the exercise of running up one flight of stairs, she reasoned, and perhaps the fourth floor would be less unlucky if she were to sneak up on it instead of announcing her arrival with the elevator's ding.

When the doors opened on three, Charlotte stepped out, then quickly popped back in, and pressed the number for her floor. "This is ridiculous," she chuckled. "Bad luck, my foot."

However, when the doors opened on four, she was greeted by chunks of drywall and wet wood leaning against the walls. The shabby hall carpet had been rolled up and shoved to one side. There also appeared to be a pile of crunched up fortune cookies in front of her apartment door. *Pigs*, she thought, envisioning people who littered.

Charlotte stepped over the debris and unlocked her door, fearing what might await her on the other side of the threshold. Then, steeling herself, she entered. Surprisingly, the place looked okay. She dropped her keys onto the credenza and carried her shopping bag into the living room, breathing a premature sigh of relief as she blithely headed toward the bedroom.

When she reached the bathroom, she stopped dead in her tracks—flabbergasted. The entire floor was missing. She looked directly into Mr. Shirley's bathroom through the gaping hole where the cheap linoleum had given way.

"Oh, my God!" she gasped.

Mr. Shirley appeared at the bottom of the hole. "If they red tag me I will kill you! Do you know what this is going to cost me?!"

"How'm I supposed to use the bathroom?"

"What?!" He was knee deep in water with a crocheted Cinderella toilet paper cover bobbing at his knees. He snatched it and shook it at Charlotte. "I crocheted her myself," he blubbered. "She's ruined." He threw the soggy yarn ball into the swirling water and picked up a plunger, which he raised ominously over his head. "You're a scourge, a pestilence! I should come up there and…"

"When are they going to fix all of this?" She cut him off.

Incensed, he lobbed the plunger at her. The projectile missed its intended target, but managed to hit a piece of the flooring that dangled precariously over his head. The saturated plank was knocked loose and subsequently knocked the toupee off his head.

More than the weight of the lumber, the sheer trauma of the situation seemed to have been the catalyst for him to fall face first into the floodwater. He pushed his massive body up and stared in horror as his hairpiece floated away. He was speechless, and from where Charlotte stood looking down onto the peculiar scene below, it appeared as though the little pink Cinderella was paddling toward a hairy atoll.

She had seen enough. She walked into the bedroom, sat down on the bed, pushed her loafers off and wiggled a big toe through a hole in her sock.

"You are a herpes," she mimicked Shirley's hostile tone. "Cinderella swam off with my hair." In spite of the fact that she wondered whether other people had days like this, Charlotte brightened and concluded that if no one had days quite this bad, at least Mr. Shirley must come close. She winked at her big toe.

"Bride of Satan!" Mr. Shirley roared from below. As she pulled off her socks, she could hear him sloshing around and cursing her for the ruination of his life.

"Demon spawn!"

She crossed the room and hurled the balled-up socks at Mr. Shirley's head as he swished a mop through the floodwater. He muttered another affront, gave up, and slammed his bathroom door behind him. Charlotte peeked down into his bathroom, where a geyser began to sprout from his toilet and the water level was rising rapidly.

Charlotte surveyed her bathroom to learn what might be preventing her sink, tub, and toilet from falling off the thin strip of linoleum that remained in her bathroom. She was curious as to whether the narrow piece of flooring that held the fixtures aloft was also strong enough to support her. She had new shoes and a dress that would require the use of some sort of cosmetic enhancement—and only the yawning chasm that led straight into Perdition was separating her from her make-up.

She gingerly inched her right foot onto the slender plank that ran the length of the bathtub, and it held. With a damn-the-torpedoes aplomb that was reminiscent of the five-gallon jug hair-rinsing method, she swung herself around the doorjamb and made a four-point landing in the tub. A few crumbs of plaster and mortar dropped like little paratroopers around Cinderella in the water below.

Emboldened, Charlotte carefully reached over the sink for the shoebox of cosmetics on the back of the toilet; and she would have had it, too, if it weren't that the sink suddenly gave way and hurled itself atop Mr. Shirley's sink, which in turn crashed onto his toilet. She hung over the edge of the bathtub holding onto a towel bar as Mr. Shirley flung open his bathroom door. He shrieked when the first wave crashed over him, sweeping Cinderella out the door, then again when he saw Charlotte balancing over the hole.

"It's not my fault," she said immediately.

He furtively scanned his surroundings, searching for something new to throw. Snatching a can of "Flowers of the Meadow" Glade air freshener drifting toward the door, the obese landlord hoisted himself atop his shattered sink, atop his demolished toilet, and began jabbing at Charlotte with the spray can.

"You must be stopped!" he screeched, simultaneously realizing the peril in which he had placed himself by perching desperately as he had atop the rubble. It logically gave way, and the water displacement his enormous body produced ensured that the rest of his apartment was flooded forthwith. He was a beaten man.

"Are you okay?" Charlotte called down.

He turned his head to the side and burbled through a mouthful of water, "I'd like to be alone for a minute."

Clutching the box of make-up, she swung out of the tub and into the hallway. Charlotte entered the bedroom and, as she began to undress, spotted the flyer from her Freshman Cavalcade. Charlotte thought for a moment, scanned the spines of all the books piled high atop the dresser, and located the correct volume. A dried flower marked the page where Charlotte's class picture appeared. She studied the photo—a girl with a glimmer of promise in her eyes—and her thoughts drifted to the day the picture was taken.

The handsome, young photographer had flirted with her; though she knew he used this technique to gain a smile for his camera, she felt pretty and alive and realized that this would be a day she would remember always. She tucked the flier into the book and closed it. Looking in the mirror between piles of junk, Charlotte Nightingale thought she caught a glimpse of that same hopeful young girl.

As she disrobed, the little turtle fell out of a pocket. She set it on the dresser beside her yearbook and made a mental note to track down its owner. Charlotte bit her lip and turned to the shopping bag on the bed, swallowing hard as she took the first step toward wearing Chanel and looking nice for her mother—as was promised by the knowledgeable saleswoman.

風
水

CHAPTER TEN

A converted warehouse just east of Little Tokyo seemed like an odd place for an audition, but Joey chalked it up to the fact that the movie was probably going to be shot nearby and the producers were working on a budget. Although the parking lot was overrun by crack-heads and a pack of mangy street dogs, Joey admired the filmmakers' quest for authenticity.

According to Jimmy Jordan, the project's executive producer, the lead actor had suddenly dropped out due to creative differences with the studio. Joey heard about it from a guy at a bar, and without an agent or manager or even having read the script, he boldly called Blue Ball Productions and demanded an audition believing that, if he turned it on, he could land the role of a lifetime. Jimmy Jordan told him to get his ass downtown pronto.

Wearing jeans, a plain white buttoned-down shirt and sneakers, Joey had toned down the Rat Pack look in favor of something more…actorly. He pulled a baseball cap out of his back pocket and groaned as he plopped it backward on his head. He rang the bell–a huge red knob positioned next to a thick, solid-steel door.

"Yeah?" A voice crackled through the intercom.

"Uh, Joey Lozzi." He spoke into the big red knob. "I'm here for the audition?"

The door buzzed and Joey pushed it open. It was dark inside, made more so by the fact that Joey had been standing outside in the blinding light and his eyes hadn't adjusted. He stood motionless. Suddenly, a grid of overhead lights flared on, illuminating the room with an intensity usually reserved for operating rooms and nuclear reactors. His hand flew to his eyes, protecting his retinas.

"For god's sake," a man chuckled. "Don't tell me you're shy."

Joey slowly uncovered his eyes. In the center of the room, directly beneath the lights, a naked girl with gigantic breasts pointing due north was on her back, knees hanging open, reading Daily Variety. She glanced in his direction.

"Hey," she said blandly, turning a page.

"Shit," Joey said quietly.

Jimmy Jordan emerged from a dark corner. "Let's see what you got."

"I didn't know this was a porno."

"Adult entertainment," Jimmy clarified. "It makes the permit thing easier. Let's see your junk."

"I, er, uh, well…"

"Pal, they're hiring at McDonalds. Come on. I ain't got all day."

"Which one?" Joey inquired.

"What a putz," the naked girl commented, ensconced in the magazine.

"I heard you worked before." Jimmy appraised Joey from head to toe, lingering at the area south of the waistline. Joey shuffled his feet, took off his hat and put it back on, and finally stuffed his hands into his pockets.

The female porn star irritably flipped a page, throwing Joey the hairy eyeball. "I ain't a fluff girl."

"How much does it pay?" Joey asked.

Jimmy frowned. "You got a big shlong, you get big money. If you can do the deed."

"Do it well," the girl added, putting down the reading material. "And I don't do ass. Mine or yours."

"I thought this was a movie role." Joey's shoulders drooped. "A real movie."

"You got the meat or not?" Jimmy had lost patience.

Joey grinned. "Yeah, an anaconda."

"Fire in the hole!" Jimmy clapped and headed for a director's chair at the foot of the bed.

"Shit, Jimmy," the girl bellyached. "My nails aren't dry yet."

Joey handed Jimmy a sheet of paper. "Could you just sign this that I auditioned? For unemployment." The overhead grid went dark with a clang.

"I'm still down here," Jimmy shouted. "Turn the freaking lights back on!"

"Sure, but I can sit here in the dark, right?" The girl flung Variety at Jimmy's head. As the lights flared back on, she flopped back on the pillows and blew on her nails.

Jimmy tucked Joey's paperwork under his leg. "Okay, kid. Saddle up."

Joey shook his head. "No."

"I don't hire anyone without an audition. Period."

Joey took a deep breath and then sighed. "Look, I don't want the job. I just want you to sign that piece of paper."

"You into male-on-male?"

Joey squared his shoulders and stood taller. "I'm a serious actor."

The porn star laughed out loud. "Which restaurant do you work at?"

Jimmy's leg shook, and he bit his nails, ripping a piece of skin from his cuticle and then spitting it onto the floor. "I'm gonna level with you. I am behind the eight ball here. Thor Magnum had to go back into rehab and he left us high and dry without a dick. I'll pay you double. Come on. Crystal gives the best head in the business."

Joey glanced over and noticed a festering cold sore above Crystal's lip. "She seems nice. I really thought this was a..."

"Serious film," Jimmy sniffed. "I got it."

He handed Joey the paper and got up. "You didn't audition." The grid of overhead lights went dark with a clang.

"Goddammit! I'm still down here!" Jimmy yelled.

Joey swatted at the wild dogs with his baseball cap as he made his way across the parking lot to the street. It was true. He had worked in "the industry" before. And true, a person with certain attributes could make a lot of money, but it had left Joey feeling... depressed. He feared that he'd lose all interest in pornography if he were working in it. A guy could become anesthetized, he reckoned. But that wasn't why he turned down Jimmy Jordan and Crystal. Charlotte would never understand. She's a good broad. He straightened his back. She deserves a stand-up guy.

Heading to the bus stop, Joey checked his messages. His cousin Frank had phoned to ask whether Joey might consider helping him out at his waiter job in Las Vegas. Frank needed to take a leave of absence and was reluctant to turn the job over to just anyone. The pay was good. The tips were great. And best of all, according to cousin Frank, it was temporary, so Joey could get back to livin' large in L.A. ASAP. Best of all, thought Joey, it was a job. And a job was exactly what he needed most.

風
水

CHAPTER ELEVEN

I t had just begun to pour when Charlotte stepped out of her apartment building to wait for the taxi she had called more than an hour earlier. She stood shivering beneath a tattered awning, wiping away raindrops as they splattered her face. A white Toyota swerved to the curb and slammed on the brakes. Kwan leapt out, holding a brown paper bag over his head as he ran to the building. Charlotte opened the door for him.

"Rotten night to be out, Kwan," she said sympathetically.

Oblivious to the rain, he stood in the doorway looking at her in the sexy new outfit. "Charlotte Nightingale. You look very…nice." The black Chanel dress was a second skin, and the heels made Charlotte's legs look five feet long. The tiny bit of make-up she wore gave her face a high-voltage charge.

She squeegeed some water off her dress with the back of her hand. "I do?"

His head bobbed emphatically. He took a deep breath and swallowed hard. "How are things?"

"Don't ask."

"Really?" He seemed quite surprised. "Are you sure?"

"Yes, really." She wondered what was wrong with him.

"Things looked bad before." Squinting, he sought clarity in the troposphere. "Nope. Things must have improved by now," he said adamantly.

"Yesterday I had a job, a car, a boyfriend, and a bathroom. Today, I do not. Does that sound better to you?"

He mulled it over. "Yes." *And you look devastating*, he thought.

"Yes?" Her head snapped back slightly. "On which planet is any of this an improvement?"

"I have something for you." He reached into his pocket, subsequently dropping a fortune cookie, a jumble of dollar bills, and some coins onto the sidewalk.

As Charlotte bent down to retrieve the items, Kwan dug into his other pocket, pulled out a small red crystal heart, and surreptitiously deposited it into Charlotte's purse.

She handed him his money, but held onto the fortune cookie. "Did you leave some of these by my door today?"

"Good fortune is what we make of it. If a person is open to it, which is the result of arranging things in one's life in such a way as to…"

"What are you talking about?" she asked, but the cab arrived before Kwan could answer. "I've gotta run." Charlotte stepped into the rain.

"You could help a little," he called after her. "There's only so much I can do!"

Charlotte lunged for the cab in an effort to get out of the pouring rain and away from Kwan, who seemed more than a little kooky. Standing in the downpour, she banged on the cab's passenger window until the driver realized his fare was locked out. He reached behind to open the door from the inside.

"Sorry," he mumbled, with no trace of apology.

Kwan waved goodbye as the cab pulled away. Charlotte wondered how a guy like that got along in the world, and whether he delivered Chinese food to other people who hadn't ordered anything.

When the taxi pulled into the driveway of the Nightingale's tract home half an hour later, Charlotte realized it hadn't rained at all in her parent's neighborhood. The pavement was dry as toast, as was the shiny, silver Rolls Royce parked in front of the house. The sky to the west gave every indication that there had been a splendid sunset.

She handed the driver a fifty-dollar bill and ran her hands through her wet hair as she waited for change. She tipped fifteen percent, not overly generous considering he kept her waiting in the rain for nearly an hour, and not stingy, considering she was unemployed. She thanked him for the ride, he grunted, and she got out and walked to the house.

Finger poised over the doorbell that she had just rung; she heard the unmistakable bang of one car hitting another. Her father opened the front door as the taxi shifted into drive with a loud clunk, subsequently ripping the rear fender off the Rolls. The cabby hit the gas and burned rubber down the street.

"That's Dr. Belmont's car, for the love of God!" her father exploded. "What have you done?" He looked at Charlotte as though she had personally wrenched the good doctor's bumper from the back of his car. "Well, I'm not telling him. You're a big girl." He walked into the house and left Charlotte standing on the stoop.

She took a deep breath and walked inside, directly into the living room where Charlene, Dr. Belmont, and Mrs. Nightingale sat on the sofa together. Charlotte's mother had a wide piece of white tape covering the bridge of her nose. There were strips of gauze and bandages beneath her eyes, around her ears and under her chin, which pulled her skin taut as she stood up and frowned at Charlotte.

"What happened to you?" Charlotte's mother used an extra-syrupy Southern accent reserved for guests and special occasions.

Charlotte touched her soggy hair. "I got caught in the rain."

"Nonsense," Mother declared. "There was a beautiful sunset. Can I see you in the kitchen, Charlotte?"

Dr. Belmont sprung from his place on the sofa. "How thoughtless of me." His voice was deep and confident. "I'm Dirk Belmont, and you must be Charlene's beautiful sister, Charlotte." He was tall, dark and handsome, and he looked directly into her eyes as he shook her hand with a firm yet warm touch. "It's so good to finally meet you."

She didn't know what to say to the beautiful man so it came as a relief when her father grabbed her by the shoulders and shoved her in the direction of the kitchen. "Your mother needs you."

Charlotte's mother paced nervously around the kitchen. "I thought I told you to wear something nice." She scowled at Charlotte, which caused her bandages to pinch, and which seemed to make her even grumpier.

Charlotte tugged the hem of the skimpy dress. "The saleslady told me I looked nice."

"Was she blind? There's an apron in the top drawer over there." She pointed to the place. "Put it on."

"Mom, what happened to your face?"

Her mother smiled with some discomfort. "Isn't it wonderful? Charlene's doctor gave me the family discount on some reconstructive surgery."

"Reconstructive surgery?"

"You remember when I had that terrible accident at the club."

"What terrible accident?" Charlotte had no recollection of any such thing.

"Well, of course you do. Last summer when I was playing tennis with Helen Webermacht."

"You got hit in the face with a tennis ball," Charlotte recalled.

"I might not have known it at the time, but my septum got deviated and Dr. Belmont has been kind enough to undeviate me and rebuild my nose to its original state. End of discussion. Now put that apron on and cover up. You look like a prostitute."

Charlotte fumbled with the apron strings as Charlene walked in. "Hey, Charlene, I hope you guys will be very happy. I'm so pleased for you." She leaned in to give her sister a kiss on the cheek, but Charlene sidestepped her.

"Ever hear the word congratulations?" Charlene inquired with a decidedly bitchy delivery.

Charlotte took the high road. "I read in an etiquette book that you're never supposed to congratulate the woman. Saying congrats to the woman is like saying 'Yahoo! You finally hooked a live one!'"

Charlene exhaled loudly and looked up at the ceiling.

"So, you congratulate the man and tell the woman you hope they'll be very happy," Charlotte finished.

Mrs. Nightingale stared blankly at Charlotte for a moment, put her hand gently on Charlene's shoulder, and concluded, "I think Charlene has done very well."

Charlene waved her left hand in Charlotte's face, flaunting a golf -ball-sized diamond flanked by baguettes the size of actual bread.

"Isn't it gorgeous," she gushed. "He's loaded!"

Charlotte admired the ring. "Congratulations. And awfully nice of the doc to do Mom's facelift."

Mrs. Nightingale was not amused. "That'll be enough, Charlotte."

"Isn't he just wonderful?" Charlene squealed. "He said when the time came, which obviously won't be 'til I'm old as the hills…" she looked at her mother. "Sorry, Mom. Anyway, he said he'd do my face, boobs, lady parts, anything at all I want. I'll be beautiful forever!" She looked down at her crotch. "They have special hair dye now, too, you know, in addition to trimming it into shapes and doing a nip/tuck here and there."

Charlotte shrugged, self-consciously crossing her legs.

Mr. Nightingale completed the family picture, announcing it was time for Charlotte to tell the doctor about his bumper. Charlene staggered back, toppling a fake fruit arrangement on the kitchen table.

"What about his bumper?" She kicked a wax banana across the floor. "What have you done?"

"I didn't do anything," Charlotte protested. "The cab hit the car when it backed out of the driveway."

"Oh, God, no!" Charlene squalled, clouds of fury gathering in her eyes. "Not the Rolls!"

Dr. Belmont had either become bored or lonely as he waited by himself in the living room. He casually strolled into the kitchen, producing a silence that fell over the Nightingales like a dead trout.

"Did I interrupt something?"

Mr. Nightingale pinched Charlotte on the back of her upper arm. "Well…?" He shoved her forward. "Don't you have something to say to the doctor?"

Charlotte wished that Charlene would just pummel her into a coma with the giant diamonds, but it was unlikely that the younger sibling would risk any damage to the valuable gems. Charlotte looked at Dr. Belmont. He smiled affably, with perfectly straight white teeth.

"Call me Dirk, please." He had dimples and a manly cleft in his chin, which accentuated a strong square jaw line, setting off a set of broad shoulders that complemented his small waist and flat stomach.

"My taxi hit your car and ripped your bumper off. It's lying in the street," she confessed, prying her eyes off his body.

"Your taxi?" His cheeks began to color.

"The taxi that brought me here." Her peripheral vision hinted that the Nightingales had just stealthily backed away from her, most probably so that none of them would be injured if it came to blows between her and the doctor.

Dirk cocked his head as if he had water in his ear. "You weren't driving the taxi then?"

"Why would I be driving the taxi?"

"Charlene told me you drove a cab or bus or something, and I just naturally assumed when you said that your cab hit my car you meant your cab."

Charlotte squinted at Charlene. "I drive a bus?"

"Well, I knew it had something to do with transportation!" Charlene snapped. "I can't remember every little detail about everything!"

Charlotte's father stepped forward and put his arm around Charlene. "Now listen, Charlotte. This is your sister's night. Let's not have any sniping. Doctor, er, Dirk," he said awkwardly, "I'm sure Charlotte can organize the repairs. She works for a car dealership."

Furrowing his brows, Dirk wasn't convinced. "With an author-ized Rolls Royce service department?"

Mr. Nightingale turned to Charlotte and spoke through clenched teeth. "Well?"

"You know we sell Lincolns and Mercuries, don't you, Dad?" He responded by noncommittally sticking out his lower lip.

"That won't do at all," Dirk informed them. "I'd never dream of letting those monkeys touch my Roller."

"Well, whatever the damages are," Mr. Nightingale said with great assurance, "I'm sure Charlotte will be glad to reimburse you."

Charlotte's jaw dropped. "But it wasn't my fault!" Her father again pinched Charlotte on the back of her arm, where bruises are most likely to form.

"No, of course not," Dirk said kindly in Charlotte's direction. "I have insurance. Let's not have this ruin our evening, shall we?"

Charlotte's mother announced that dinner was ready and for everyone to please take a seat in the dining room. "Dirk," she said with a gleam in her eye, "Where are your people from?"

"My people?"

"Your parents." She pointed to the chair she wished for him to take.

"We're all from California, Mrs. Nightingale. I was born and raised in Beverly Hills."

"Beverly Hills," she repeated wistfully. "We hope to move there one day ourselves." She believed it was imminent once her favorite daughter married the physician and Mr. and Mrs. Nightingale took up residence in the spacious in-law suite she had been designing in her head for days.

"And you?" he asked, unaware of her plans for his future. "That's a lovely accent you have."

"I'm from the South, Doctor," she drawled, pouring it on thick. "Born and raised."

"You moved to Nebraska when you were a year old," Charlotte interjected.

Mrs. Nightingale shot Charlotte a withering glance. "Once a Southerner, always a Southerner." She tweaked Charlotte's upper arm, where the skin was turning a sickly yellow. "Where ladies dress appropriately and they wear stockin's to dinner."

Dirk held a chair for his bride-to-be, and then sat down to a large drink of wine. He performed like a true gentleman, and Mr.

Nightingale thusly raced around to the other end of the table to do similarly for his bandaged bride. Unaccustomed to such acts of chivalry, Mrs. Nightingale's hand flew to her face in a coquettish gesture and her cheesy wedding ring caught on a piece of gauze, tearing her flesh when she took her hand away. She let out a muffled cry of pain, took her seat, and laid her napkin genteelly across her lap.

Charlotte remained standing, thinking there was a good likelihood that her father would seat her on his way around the table, but Mr. Nightingale went the other way and kissed his engaged daughter on the top of her head before taking his place. Charlotte sighed and slid out her own chair.

"Oh, no!" Dirk sprinted around the table. "Please." He took the back of her chair. "Allow me." She sat down uncertainly. "Aren't you going to remove your apron?" he asked.

Charlotte looked to her mother for some sort of cue and wasn't sure whether the contortion on the elder Nightingale's face was due to Charlotte's skimpy dress or the epidermis she had just torn from her cheek.

"That's a really terrific dress," Dirk went on to say. "Chanel, isn't it?"

Charlene burst out laughing as Dirk took his place beside her.

"What's so funny?" he asked.

"I seriously doubt it's Chanel, Dirk," Charlene snickered. "If anybody in this family's going to wear Chanel, it'll be me. Anyhow, Charlotte doesn't give a rat's petootie about clothes, which is really just as well since she has absolutely no fashion sense whatsoever."

"Charlene," he scolded gently.

"No, it's okay," Charlotte said offhandedly. "She's absolutely right, but this is Chanel. What's for dinner, Mom?"

All were taken aback as Charlene vaulted from her seat, raced around the table, untied Charlotte's apron, and yanked it over her head.

"What are you doing?" Charlotte asked, swatting her sister.

Charlene pushed Charlotte forward and inspected the tag inside her dress. She looked at her mother and bit her lip.

"It's Chanel, all right," the younger Nightingale confirmed.

Dirk was pleased to have been correct. "I know women's clothes, but who wouldn't, with all of Charlene's fashion magazines lying around. It doesn't take a genius." A look of hurt flitted across Charlene's pretty face. "Oh, no offense, honey," he apologized.

"None taken," she replied, mentally choosing something expensive from Tiffany's in exchange for Dirk getting out of the doghouse for his thoughtless remark.

"Roast beef," Mrs. Nightingale irritably announced, removing a silver dome from a platter containing the evening's fare. "Pass your plates, please."

As Mrs. Nightingale served dinner, Charlene stared at Charlotte with such a burning intensity that she looked down the front of her dress fully expecting to find a blob of gravy or something equally offensive clinging to her bosom, but the dress was clean.

"Things must be going awfully well at Auto Land," Charlene mocked.

"Eebner Brother's, Charlene. You've been there," Charlotte told her.

Dirk sat forward. "Eebner Brother's Lincoln-Mercury City?"

"Yes," Charlene answered for Charlotte, lightly resting her hand on Dr. Belmont's upper thigh.

"Isn't that where that woman worked, the one who stabbed the lady in Cerritos?" he inquired.

Charlotte nodded slowly.

Dirk pushed Charlene's hand away. "Do you know her?" he asked Charlotte, fascinated.

"I'm sure she doesn't know any such people," Mrs. Nightingale said emphatically, hoping to quell the murder-speak at the dinner table.

"I was supposed to go with her to the beauty supply store, but I had to work through lunch." For the second time in one day, Charlotte shuddered to think that she might have been witness to the gruesome slaying.

As if reading her thoughts, Dirk shook his head empathetically. "I bet that's one time you're glad you had to work though lunch."

Charlotte couldn't have agreed more. "It was ugly enough. The police came and questioned everybody."

Dirk reached across the table and benevolently patted Charlotte's hand. "What did you tell them?"

"Just what little I knew. That she was having an affair with our general manager, and the owners illegally dispose of toxic waste."

"Do you think that had any bearing on the murder?" he asked, as Charlene reached for the butter, knocking his hand from Charlotte's.

"No, I think she was just a mental case who happened to be screwing her sister's husband," Charlotte theorized. "Even the cops said you'd have to be insane to stab someone to death with tweezers."

Mrs. Nightingale nearly jumped out of her skin. "Well, that's enough!"

"Did you do something to irritate her?" Charlotte's father wanted to know.

"Excuse me?" Charlotte looked numbly at him.

"Did you do something to set her off?" He spoke slowly, loudly, as if he were talking to someone French.

"Well, I accidentally scratched the side of the Navigator she signed out. She seemed a little tweaked by that." Charlotte began to wonder whether she might have been the cause of Phyllis Schlotzky's murderous rampage.

"You work at a gull darn car dealership," her father chided. "How in the hell do you scratch the side of somebody's car? How could you be so…stupid?"

"I had a stapler caught on the hem of my skirt, and when I went to tell Phyllis that I couldn't go to lunch with her, it banged against the side of the car. It was an accident."

"You had a stapler caught on the hem of your skirt?" Charlene closed her eyes and shook her head from side to side. "Why?"

"The hem was falling down," Charlotte responded, as if this were the most natural explanation in the world. "I was going to staple it up."

Charlene slapped Dirk on the arm. "What'd I tell you? Chanel, my ass. That dress is a knock-off."

"What's the big deal about Chanel anyway!" Charlotte cried in exasperation.

"What's the big deal about Chanel?" Charlene repeated it as though Charlotte had belittled the discovery of life on Neptune.

"Well?" Charlotte asked.

"I told you this was your sister's night," Mr. Nightingale chastised. "For crying out loud, Charlotte, stop antagonizing her!"

"I'm not antagonizing her." The hair on Charlotte's neck began to bristle. "I just don't see what the big deal is."

Throwing etiquette out the window, Charlene sat forward, elbows on the table. "Okay, Charlotte. Where did you get the dress?"

"Nordstrom's. And the shoes. I got everything at Nordstrom's."

Charlene lifted the tablecloth and looked underneath. "Loubies? Are you kidding me?" She sniffed out expensive shoes like a swine hunting truffles.

Charlotte bit her lip. "Loubies?"

Charlene rolled her eyes. "Christian Louboutin."

"You can tell just by looking?" Charlotte was genuinely amazed.

"Let's change the subject, please," Mr. Nightingale implored.

"Dad!" Charlene bleated. "She usually dresses like a homeless librarian and now she's got about eight grand on her back. And feet. Don't you think that's a little strange?" They turned expectantly to Charlotte.

"Don't be ridiculous. There was a sale. It didn't even come close to that!" Charlotte was astonished it was possible, even if one did have the resources, to spend that kind of money on clothes. "Librarians make decent money, by the way. No reason a working librarian would be homeless," she clarified.

"They weren't giving the stuff away, were they?" Charlene was a dog with a bone.

"Of course not." Throwing her shoulders back, Charlotte turned to her mother. "I have a Nordstrom charge card."

Charlene was bound and determined to gather all the facts. Fashion was, after all, her life. "I would like to know, if I may be so bold, just how much you paid for the dress and shoes."

"Thirty-five fifty," Charlotte said definitively, hoping to put an end to the inquisition.

"Sounds like a bargain to me," Dad noted. "Now can we change the subject?"

"Thirty-five hundred dollars, Dad!" Charlene spat a fine mist across the table, then she sat back in her seat. "Wow, that is a bargain."

A piece of roast beef dripping in gravy fell off Mr. Nightingale's fork and plopped into his lap. He looked at Charlotte. "Well?"

"Well, what? That's ridiculous."

"Charlotte, I know about these things," Charlene stated, and Dirk nodded his accord. "Did you even look at the receipt?"

Charlotte thought for a moment—her face went white.

"Oh, dear God, Charlotte." Mrs. Nightingale wrung her hands. "What have you done now?"

Charlotte began to weep. It started as a tiny twitter in her throat, which blossomed into full-blown anguish. She put her head in her hands and in an uncharacteristic display of emotion, regardless of the many days she had survived that were nearly as bad as this, she sobbed.

"This is real nice for your sister." Mr. Nightingale shook his head in disgust. "Real nice."

Dirk burned a hole through Mr. Nightingale with his gaze. "What's wrong with you?"

The question and tone caught Mr. Nightingale so off guard that he dropped an entire fork full of mashed potatoes onto his lap to accompany the roast beef nesting in his crotch.

"Did I say something to offend you?" Charlotte's father asked politely.

Staring open-mouthed at the handsome doctor, Charlotte dabbed at her eyes. No one had ever come to her defense for any reason in the past.

"Just about everything you've said tonight has been offensive to Charlotte," Dirk said.

Charlotte gasped, her father's jaw dropped, and Mrs. Nightingale's entire face twisted in fury, then physical pain, giving every indication that she held Charlotte to blame for the whole debacle. By the time Charlotte glanced across the table at her sister, Charlene was out of her chair and headed for the door.

"Charlene, wait!" Charlotte cried.

Charlene dramatically turned around and wiped away an imaginary tear.

"I'll go. Dad's right. This is your night, and I've ruined everything," Charlotte said, certain they'd insist that she stay.

Charlene returned to the table and sniffled daintily into her napkin. Mother and Father had resumed cutting their meat. Charlotte sighed, went quietly to the door, and walked out.

"Didn't you take a cab here?" Dirk called after her, but she had already closed the front door behind her. He bolted out of his seat in a flash, charged across the living room, and was outside before anyone said a word.

"Let me give you a ride!" he said, running to catch up with Charlotte.

The remaining Nightingales were speechless as they rose in unison and headed for the picture window in the living room where all three pressed their noses to the glass, watching the scene unfold without a clue as to how something this bizarre might have happened. Like witnessing a horrible accident over which one has no control, their eyes followed the doctor as he opened the door of the Rolls Royce for Charlotte, and she got in. He closed the door behind her, picked the wrecked bumper off the pavement, tossed it into the trunk, slid behind the wheel, and drove away.

"Please tell me the apple falls far from the Nightingale family tree," he chuckled.

The Nightingale house disappeared behind them as he swung the car around the corner. Charlotte put her head back and closed her eyes. She never meant for any of this to happen, but the universe had a way of working against her and she often had the uneasy feeling that she had been incarcerated in some sort of bad luck penal colony.

"It's my fault," she conceded. "I shouldn't have come."

"Why on earth not?" He didn't seem to think the answer was at all obvious. "Is your family always like that?"

"No." She opened her eyes. "They were pretty nice tonight."

Stopping for a red light, he turned to her. "You have an interesting nose, you know."

"You're a plastic surgeon, right? I bet you see a face like mine and can think of ten ways to fix it."

"I wouldn't change a thing."

Eyes becoming damp as though he had just seen a public service announcement about puppy mills, Dirk intensely scrutinized Charlotte. "Your face has great character," he asserted.

"Character," she repeated. "That's a very diplomatic way of putting it, Doctor."

"Call me Dirk. So, where are we going?"

Charlotte was lost in his shiny eyes and the question took her aback. Her head swam with possibilities. Was he suggesting they go out dancing, or perhaps back to his place for a nightcap? This was her sister's husband-to-be and she wouldn't be much better than a common tweezer murderess if she did anything at this point but go home, change her clothes, and put the day to bed—alone. She understood herself to be the unworldliest woman to ever don a Chanel dress and found herself unable to speak.

"Excuse me." He cleared his throat. "Where do you live? I'm taking you home, right?"

In the second burst of unbridled emotion to surface in less than an hour, Charlotte began to laugh. She laughed at the dress and the shoes. She laughed at her stupidity in thinking someone like Dr. Dirk Belmont might want to take her dancing. She laughed hardest of all at herself for being in a Rolls Royce with a plastic surgeon from Beverly Hills who meant to marry her beautiful sister some lovely day in June. She threw her head back and laughed until tears rolled down her face.

At first Dirk thought she might be a little unbalanced, for her reaction to a question of such a simple nature did seem peculiar, to say the least. Then there was the weirdness at dinner about her clothes. Surely her parents and sister knew something about her that was not immediately perceptible to a newcomer. Maybe he should be worried. After all, she did consort with murderers and car salespeople, and her family, sister Charlene included, were all a little nuts.

These were the questions that perplexed him, but her laughter changed all that. With one eye on the road and the other on Charlotte, he realized how very pretty she was when she tossed her head back and exposed the milky white skin of her graceful neck. He wondered how she could look so unlike her remarkably beautiful sister and yet more heart stopping than any woman he had ever seen.

As she squirmed under his impassioned gaze, they rear-ended a police car. All went silent in the Rolls Royce as an officer got out of his squad car, not looking terribly pleased. From the run of bad luck that comprised her life, Charlotte suddenly found clarity in God's plan for her and it made her laugh even more. She was the definitive test case for the if-it-can-go-wrong-it-will experiment to which she had heard so many people refer, but until now had doubted its actual existence. She found this truly hilarious.

Memorizing every detail of her perfectly imperfect face contorted in a fit of glorious laughter, Dirk powered the window down without taking his eyes off Charlotte. The policeman snapped his fingers next to Dirk's ear.

"Stop your engine, sir," he ordered. "License and registration, please."

Dirk leaned over and took the car's papers from the glove box. He handed them to the officer and fished in his pockets for his wallet, and then he began to laugh.

"My wallet's in my jacket!" He slapped the steering wheel. "I left my jacket at your parent's house when we ran out. Ha! What are the chances?"

"About one in one," Charlotte said bleakly, hoping the officer wouldn't cart them both off.

Perhaps Dirk was a lucky man, or perhaps because he was a medical doctor (in any case, his story checked out with the policeman), Dr. Belmont and Charlotte were sent on their way without further incident. By the time the smashed-up Rolls pulled up in front of Charlotte's building, the moon and stars shone brightly. Dirk jumped out of the car and ran around to open the door for her. Moonlight danced over her cheekbones and flashed in her eyes as he extended his hand to help her out of the car.

"Thanks so much." She stood and smoothed her dress. "I hate to say it, but this was really fun. I'm glad Charlene found someone like you. She's got all the luck."

She kissed him on the cheek and walked away, not considering whether walking away was the right thing to do. She unlocked the door to the building and let herself in. While waiting for the elevator doors to open, it did not occur to Charlotte to turn her head to see whether Dirk remained in front of her building staring longingly her way—because in her heart, she knew that nothing good would ever come of looking for such things.

When the elevator opened, Charlotte immediately recognized the pungent lingering aroma of Emperor's cashew chicken. She pressed the unlucky number four, and when she stepped out on her floor, she smacked into Kwan and his ubiquitous brown paper bag, squashing the food between them.

"I know," she grumbled, "the number four is unlucky." A thick, sticky sauce leaked from the bottom of the mashed bag and subsequently down the front of Charlotte's dress.

"You can say that again." He handed her a napkin. "I've been waiting fifteen minutes."

"For what?"

"You ordered Emperor's cashew chicken for two."

"I did not. You saw me go out earlier. When would I have ordered food?"

He looked at the receipt stapled to the top of the bag. "Four-D," he said grimly. "Four is death."

"But I'm telling you it wasn't me. I did not order this food. I didn't order it last time. I was told that you don't even have Emperor's cashew chicken on the menu anymore!" She had reached her absolute limit; shoving him aside, she stomped across the hall, let herself into the apartment and slammed the door shut.

He knocked.

"Go away!"

"You look hungry," he shouted from the hall. "Your Emperor's cashew chicken for two is getting cold."

"But I'm only one," she said, slumping against the wall, tears welling up in her eyes.

"Then you'll have leftovers tomorrow," he countered. "It's like Emperor's cashew chicken for one, twice. Come on, I have stuff to do. Sixteen-fifty. Open the door."

"Sixteen-fifty! Last night it was fourteen-fifty!"

"You said yourself it wasn't on the menu last night," he argued.

Charlotte flung open the door and took a step toward him. "But you charged me fourteen-fifty just last night," she said firmly, wiping away a tear.

"We now do special orders, which are sixteen-fifty." He reached into the soggy bag and produced a greasy menu, which he attempted to hand her and which she pushed back distastefully. "If you want Emperor's cashew chicken, you have to ask for number seven…"

She cut him off. "Whatever." She seemed to shrink. "Whatever." Charlotte flipped her handbag upside down in search of the envelope of Eebner cash, but it was nowhere to be found. Out of the Kleenex, coupons, tampon wrappers, and junk scattered across the tabletop, she plucked the crystal heart Kwan had dropped into her purse.

She looked at him. "What's this?"

"Crystals bring luck in a variety of areas," he said rapid-fire, then even more quickly changed the subject. "I think we could probably start an account for you. You know, you could pay once a month or something. I mean, if you're a little short tonight."

"My money's gone," she said ruefully, but not completely surprised. "It's typical… for me." Posture crumpling, she let out a long-suffering sigh like air escaping a leaky tire.

He put his hands on his hips and stared at her, wanting very much for the negative chi to evaporate. All she could think of was the argument that was about to begin anew, concerning the food that she had neither ordered, nor as luck would have it, could afford.

"I will give you credit." The way he said it implied two meanings, but the word credit caught Charlotte's attention.

She squinched. "No! No credit."

The telephone rang.

"Go ahead." He waved his hand. "I'll wait."

Moving toward the phone, Charlotte was careful to avoid the dead fern on the floor, which was not there. She glanced around, but the phone continued to ring—and Kwan continued to wait for her to pay him. More than anything she wanted him to leave and take the maddening Asian entrée with him. The missing foliage became the least of her worries.

"Hello?"

"Charlotte." The voice belonged to Mrs. Nightingale, and it was more of an accusation than a greeting.

"By any chance did I leave an envelope at your house, Mom?"

Kwan unfolded a stack of napkins, laid them out on the credenza, and set the soggy bag on them. He went into the living room where Charlotte was huddled with the phone, and began scrutinizing the room like the host of a home and garden TV makeover show.

Charlotte wondered what he was doing, but she was more concerned that her mother would become hysterical due to the hasty departure of Dr. Belmont from the dinner table.

"He'll be back, Mom. I think he really loves Charlene." She meant it to sound reassuring.

Charlotte's mother sipped a highball at the kitchen table with Charlotte's envelope full of money in front of her. Charlotte's father sat stone-faced on the opposite side. Charlene was lying on the floor with teabags on her eyes to reduce the ersatz puffiness caused by excessive fake crying.

"We're worried about you, Charlotte," Mrs. Nightingale said. "As it were."

"That's nice, but I'll find somebody some day. Don't worry."

Kwan picked up a cocktail table and moved it to the center of the room.

Charlotte's mother held her hand over the mouthpiece and looked at Charlotte's father. "She thinks we're worried that she isn't going to meet anybody," she whispered.

Mr. Nightingale TiVo'd Dr. Phil every weekday afternoon. "She's in denial," he diagnosed with authority.

"Dad says you're in denial, Charlotte."

Kwan began rearranging the furniture, placing pieces in an attractive seating area around the cocktail table.

"What?" Charlotte said distractedly into the phone.

"Are you on drugs right now?"

Charlotte sat down on the sofa and switched ears with the phone. "What did you just say?"

"We know everything, Charlotte. It's okay. We're here for you." She took a sip of her drink. "In a manner of speaking."

Kwan spotted a wilted philodendron peeking out from behind a stack of books. He grabbed it and set it on the floor at the corner of the added-on closet, softening the harsh angle. He ducked into the kitchen, filled a small glass with water, and returned to tend the thirsty plant.

"What in the name of God are you talking about?" Charlotte was utterly confused, and not liking the tone of this particular misunderstanding one bit.

"Charlotte," Mother cajoled. "The dress, the expensive shoes, the envelope of cash. We know you don't make diddley-squat at the car wash. Charlene's the one who figured this out. She's up on current events."

"Current events." Charlotte rolled her eyes. "Did Vogue come today? And it's a dealership! Not a car wash."

"You know your sister does a lot of reading," Mrs. Nightingale asserted. "Car wash, dealership. Same thing."

"She reads fashion magazines!"

"And other periodicals," her mother said haughtily. "After you left we all sat down and took a quiz in *Cosmo* and found that we have…" Grasping the magazine, she recited, "'Do You Have A Loved One With A Dark Secret?' We got twelve out of fifteen right, Charlotte. Anything over ten and the article says your loved one is concealing a dark secret. That's you."

"I'm a drug dealer?" Charlotte was stupefied. "That's my dark secret?"

Mrs. Nightingale read aloud, "You're moody, your appearance has suddenly changed, you're argumentative, and you're constantly behaving in an inappropriate manner. There you have it, and thanks to Charlene, we can nip this nastiness in the bud."

Charlotte mulled over the reasons for which she was believed to have a dark secret and a thought occurred to her. "You only named four of the reasons, Mother. What are the other eight?"

"Are you fulfilled in your career? Do you have a lasting and meaningful relationship with a single member of either sex? Do you have a pet? Do you have a good relationship with your parents? Siblings? Are you fun to be around?" She paused. "Shall I continue?"

"Those are reasons to stab yourself in the brain with a fork," Charlotte reasoned, putting her feet on the cocktail table that Kwan had placed in front of the sofa. "I don't see how any of that makes me look like a drug dealer."

Kwan found a shallow glass bowl on a bookshelf beside which was an unopened box of blue votive candles. He carried the bowl into the kitchen, washed and filled it half way with water and placed the candles inside the bowl, where they bobbed at the surface.

"Your sister says it fits the pattern. You keep company with murderers and whatnots, and you're suddenly pouring yourself into a million-dollar wardrobe and walking around with envelopes stuffed full of cash. I rest my case."

Kwan carried the bowl with the candles into the living room and placed it on a side table. "Does that window face north?" he asked.

Charlotte turned away and hunkered with the phone.

"This is absolutely the most idiotic thing you people have ever come up with," she said. Meanwhile, Kwan shoved Charlotte and her sofa a few feet away from the wall.

"What are you doing, Kwan?" she asked irritably, regaining her balance on the settee. He apologized by way of shrugging, and then continued on his mission.

"Ah ha! An Oriental!" Mother spouted, convinced this was all the evidence she needed to prove her point.

"Yes, Mother. He's got some really good Asian shit."

Mrs. Nightingale nodded knowingly at Mr. Nightingale. "A drug lord is there right now."

Kwan perused every surface in Charlotte's apartment, flinching here and there, shaking his head. He removed two obelisks from the windowsill and hid them behind a stack of books.

"Is that your call waiting?" Mrs. Nightingale asked as the phone began to beep.

"I don't have call waiting," Charlotte answered as her phone beeped again. "I can't afford it."

"It's not my phone," Mother said. "So it must be yours."

"Hold on," Charlotte sighed. "If I lose you, it's because I don't have call waiting and I've disconnected you." Charlotte jabbed various keys on her phone, each time saying hello again to her mother. Becoming cross and wanting to put an end to the conversation, she stabbed one last button determined to finish the nonsense with her family.

"Yes, Kwan is an Asian drug kingpin. In addition to bringing me bags of drugs so that I can continue to be moody, have no pets, and dress inappropriately, he also delivers Chinese food that I didn't order. Welcome to my little slice of heaven!"

"Charlotte?" Dirk Belmont's voice was uncertain.

"Dirk?" Charlotte was equally uncertain as to how she had conjured the man, given the fact that she did not have call waiting.

"We need to talk."

"Hold on." She tried to remember which button she had pushed to summon Dirk's voice in the hopes that the same button would enable her to say goodbye to her mother.

"Mother?" Nothing. She punched another button. "Mother?"

"So, you do have call waiting," Mrs. Nightingale said curtly.

"I have to go. Dirk Belmont is on the other line."

Mrs. Nightingale seemed pleased to hear that the good doctor was involved. "Tell him to call us if he thinks we should perform an intervention."

"You perform an appendectomy. You host an intervention."

"Just wear something decent," Mrs. Nightingale counseled, relieved that someone other than herself might possibly resolve this unpleasant family problem.

"Mother? Hello?"

"It's me, Dirk."

Kwan took a compass from his pocket, got his bearings, and finished by hanging a strip of old Chinese coins strung together with red thread from a sconce on a northern wall.

He stood before Charlotte.

"Hold on a minute," she said covering the mouthpiece, looking up at Kwan. "What?"

"I've finished."

"Finished with what?" She was unsure of what he had been doing, but suddenly her apartment looked a lot better.

"The Emperor's cashew chicken is on me." He crossed the room, made a final adjustment to the Mandarin ducks on the credenza, and walked out.

A nanosecond later, Joey blew in.

"There's my gal." Tipping his hat rakishly over one eye, he sniffed. "Chinese? What a dame! I'm starving."

Charlotte imagined she must have done something truly awful in a past life. Holding her hand over the mouthpiece of the phone, she told Joey to get cleaned up in the hopes of getting him out of the room so she could finish the conversation with Dirk.

He clucked as though spurring a horse. "I'll be right back, Baby, and you can tell me where it hurts."

Charlotte slowly removed her hand from the mouthpiece, and then suddenly remembered the gaping abyss in her bathroom.

"Joey, wait!" she warned. "Frank! Don't go into the bathroom!"

He peeked around the corner. "You rang?"

"Wait in the bedroom," she mouthed.

"Ring-a-ding-ding! Bring the ice bucket and the gasoline, wouldya, Baby?" He winked and threw in a sexy lip curl.

Charlotte stared in horror at the phone and wondered what the doctor must think. "Hello?" she said tentatively.

"Sounds kind of busy over there. Is this a bad time?"

She tried desperately to think of any time that hadn't been bad and came up with nothing. "It's as good as any other."

"Can I come over?"

"When?"

"Now."

"What for?" She switched ears when no answer was forthcoming. She tapped the phone with her hand. "Hello? Hello?"

"I don't know how to explain it. I just need to talk with you."

She heard Joey crooning in the bedroom and knew it was only a matter of time before he'd come looking for his crystal tumbler and the bottle of Jack Daniel's she had been instructed to keep at the ready.

"I could meet you somewhere," she offered, desperate to get off the phone before Joey warbled his way back into the living room.

"Really?" Dirk sounded hopeful.

Joey sauntered in wearing nothing more than his fedora and a wicked grin.

"I'm leaving now," she said quickly. "Where?"

"The bar at Musso and Frank, ten minutes," he answered.

Charlotte hung up the phone.

"What was that all about?" Joey's eyes roamed all over her body, cashew chicken sauce notwithstanding. Although he looked relatively ridiculous wearing nothing but the hat, Charlotte felt a spark, which she fought to douse with all her might.

"I need you to leave," she told him firmly.

"Baby, we're not going to let a few Samolians get in the way of a beautiful thing, are we?"

"Do you actually have my money?"

"Look, Baby…"

"Don't 'look Baby' me." Her blood was beginning to boil. "Get dressed and get out."

"You're lookin' like a million Samolians yourself." He ran a finger under the strap of her dress, sending electrical impulses from her shoulder all the way to her toes.

"That stuff's not going to work anymore, Joey," she said, expressly because she thought calling him Joey would sting—nonetheless, he remained unfazed and surprised her further.

"Oh, all right, I've got your dough. I was hoping you'd let me hang on to it for a little while. I need to buy a tuxedo."

"Please tell me you got a job as a maître d'," she sighed.

"Baby, do you really see me waiting tables?"

She looked at his hat, then his face, then his naked torso, then below.

"Not at the moment, no."

He laughed, the corners of his eyes crinkling in a way that always made her melt. He was a gorgeous specimen and, she recalled with a sudden ache, a real louse.

"When did you have another girl here?"

He was most assuredly busted, but a big part of him wanted to believe that the age-old masculine ploy of denying everything at all times might still work with Charlotte. He thought about how to phrase his opening statement, and then he looked into her eyes.

She was no longer angry. There wasn't a shred of spite or vitriol in her expression, yet the look she leveled upon him bored into his soul, and automatically erased all the pat lines he had practiced and stored up for occasions such as this. He suddenly felt two feet tall.

"It was a long time ago, Charlotte. Remember when we first met at that party?"

"You borrowed ten bucks from me."

"Right, right." He was pleased that so far their memories were in sync. "Anyway, I came by the next day to pay you back, but you weren't here. Your landlord was in your apartment looking at the plumbing, and he let us in."

"Mr. Shirley was here? And what do you mean us?"

"Well, I kind of had a thing going with this strip, uh, young lady, and we were just stopping here on our way to a club. Point is, your landlord left and we waited for you, but you never came."

"That makes one of us."

"Come on," he implored. "I didn't even really know you then."

"And you never thought it would be a good idea to tell me, just for the heck of it, that you brought some woman in here and had sex on my bed while I was away? And who the heck uses a Polaroid camera in this day and age? Don't you have a cell phone, Joey? Couldn't you just be a normal guy and take a damn selfie like everybody else?" The idea royally ticked her off; then another thought occurred to her and her anger meter shot to livid.

"Who took the picture?"

"I never touched the sister."

"Get out."

"I've gotta go out of town for a few days, Baby. I was hoping you'd send me off with a good luck kiss."

"There are two kinds of luck in my world, Joey…" she began, but the telephone interrupted. She was late to meet the doctor. Perhaps he was calling to say that he couldn't wait any longer, or maybe he had changed his mind entirely, come to his senses, and he was right this moment calling from the Nightingale's home where he was wooing back Charlene.

The last thing Charlotte expected was a collect call from Phyllis Schlotzky.

風
水

CHAPTER TWELVE

"All right," Charlotte said to the operator as Joey disappeared into the bedroom. "I guess I'll accept the charges. Phyllis, is that you?"

"Charlotte, everything's just gone to shit." Phyllis sounded remarkably upbeat considering.

"That's a bit of an understatement."

"Don's gone back to his wife."

"Your sister."

"We were never close," Phyllis said defensively. "She always got everything she wanted and she loved to lord it over me. But that's not the point."

Charlotte thought about her own sister and future brother-in-law and a shiver ran down her spine. "What is it then, Phyllis? I was just on my way out."

"You have all the luck," Phyllis said wistfully. "What I wouldn't give to start over and have life by the tail the way you do. I suppose you're going somewhere trendy with a hot young stud. Who's the lucky bastard?" She was obviously interested in making small talk, which was odd since she rarely made the time to speak civilly to Charlotte in the year they had worked together.

"Just a friend," Charlotte said.

Joey walked into the room fully dressed. He winked, but it was a gloomy wink, sluggish and without pizzazz. He kissed her cheek on his way to the door.

"Gotta run, Baby."

"Don't forget your glass, Frank. Joey. Whomever."

"You keep it, or throw it away. I don't want it anymore."

Phyllis squawked into the phone, "How many guys you got over there, anyhow?"

"One guy, and he's just leaving. I really have to get going, Phyllis. There's somebody expecting me and I'm late."

"I remember when I used to have four, sometimes five dates in one night," Phyllis reminisced. "Man-o-man, have you got the life, Charlotte."

Charlotte sat down and considered Phyllis's remarks. Maybe she was right. Phyllis, who had never so much as given her the time of day, was a famous murderess and suddenly Charlotte's new friend. A handsome doctor thought she was beautiful, and although she theorized that she would never be more than a friend to her sister's suitor, it was enough that he considered it an option. And even though Joey did leave without repaying her the money he borrowed, he had been more or less a gentleman.

More importantly, Charlotte realized, she wanted to color in the lines of her own life and didn't need him to do it for her anymore. She ran a finger around the rim of his chipped glass. She just knew that if it had any liquid in it at all and someone asked, she would have to say that it was half full. This brand new sense of optimism fit her as perfectly as the tight Chanel dress and made her feel twice as terrific.

"Phyllis, I really have to get going," she said brightly.

"Are you wearing something nice? You do have the most peculiar taste in clothes."

"You'd be proud, Phyllis." Charlotte tugged the hem of her super-snug outfit. "My dress is painted on, and I accidentally ruined my sister's engagement party by running off with the groom-to-be. It's been a very weird day."

"Sounds like fun." Phyllis' voice was full of longing, then her tone turned grave. "How are things at the lot?"

Charlotte was stunned that this woman, this woman who had murdered a defenseless shopkeeper with a pair of tweezers, was concerned for the operations of the business at which she was formerly employed and having an illicit affair. "Wow, Phyllis, I'm surprised you give a crap about what's going on at Eebner with everything else you have to worry about right now."

"Don't be ridiculous," Phyllis said like her old self. "I give a rat's ass what those pricks do or don't do."

"Okay then, if there's nothing else..." Charlotte impatiently eyed the time.

"If someone had cheated you out of commissions and treated you like shit, wouldn't you do something to get back what belongs to you?"

Charlotte thought about the envelope of money and shifted uncomfortably. "I suppose I would."

"Would you?" Phyllis asked skeptically. "Really?"

"You don't know the half of it, but I have to go."

"Okay, Charlotte, here's the story. I took what was mine and a little something extra, but I want you to know I didn't do it because of greed or anything like that. I took the money because I don't believe they should be dumping battery acid and motor oil into the ocean. You know that's where the drains wash out, don't you? Right into the Pacific Ocean. It's murder on the marine life."

"Yeah, I just found out today that they've been paying people off to let them get away with it."

"Well, that's the thing," Phyllis explained. "They haven't been making the payoffs."

"But Abe and Ed said…"

"When I found out that they were dumping all that shit down the drain, I confronted them, but they told me to go fuck myself. That made me mad."

Charlotte nodded. It made her mad, too.

"Anyway, I went in one day and told the Eebners that the fellas from OSHA came by and said we had to clean up our act or the dealership would be fined. Well, there were no fellas from OSHA, but I figured it would scare the Eebners into doing the right thing, you know?"

Charlotte wasn't at all sure she knew what Phyllis was talking about, but she sensed it would add up to something bizarre. Phyllis was just that kind of person.

"The Eebners asked me how much the fines were gonna be. I had no idea, so I made up a figure and I made it high enough that they'd wanna dispose of the stuff legally. At least that's what I thought would happen."

"How much did you tell them?" Charlotte asked.

"Two-hundred and fifty thousand dollars. So they took me into the office, opened up the safe, handed me fifty grand, and told me to offer it to the OSHA people to overlook the situation. That was last year. So far those idiots have given me a quarter of a million dollars to pay off inspectors who never even came by."

Phyllis took a deep breath. "Don and I were going to take that money and start over somewhere else, then I was going to call OSHA and tell them about the battery acid and oil, but, well, shit, I got arrested, that stinking bastard went back to his wife, and he'll get his mitts on that money over my dead body!"

"Geez, Phyllis," Charlotte said, genuinely amazed. "That's some story."

"I want you to have the money, Charlotte. I'm never getting out of here after what I've done." Charlotte didn't know what to think. "Well, don't you want to know where it is?"

"Why'd you do it, Phyllis?"

"The fish, the mollusks, the sea lions..."

"Why'd you kill that woman at the beauty supply store?"

"Oh, that." Phyllis sounded as though she was sick to death of the subject. "That's all been blown out of proportion." Charlotte didn't see how that was possible. Murder seemed like a big deal no matter what.

"There wasn't one single product in that entire store that was cruelty-free. I tried to talk some sense into the woman about animal testing, and she said if God hadn't put the animals here for us to do with as we please, why did he put them here at all? He, so god-damned sure it's a man."

"Oh, boy," Charlotte whispered.

"I told the fruitcake what I thought of her, and she told me to fuck off. I believe we've established that I don't like being told to fuck off." She was silent for a moment. "I admit I may have overreacted just a bit."

"Yeah, stabbing someone with tweezers."

"Nail file," Phyllis sniffed indignantly. "The news in L.A. is for shit."

"Well, Phyllis, it's been great speaking with you, but..." Charlotte tried to get off the phone, but was cut off.

"You take that money and have some fun with it," Phyllis ordered. "Don'll leave you alone or I'll blow the whistle with his wife. Make your life count for something, Charlotte. And don't let anybody push you around. As of tonight, you have a pocket full of 'fuck you' money."

"I couldn't."

"Oh, get off it, Charlotte. That money's no good to anybody else. You can call OSHA yourself and fix the damned waste problem. Don's just lucky I don't call his wife for the hell of it. He doesn't deserve one nickel of that money, and the Eebners ought to be locked up for what they've done. Those pricks have been robbing our customers blind for years. I've got a young public defender with buns of steel, and I have no use for money where I'm going. It's yours, Charlotte. Take it and have some damned fun on me."

Charlotte weighed the possibilities.

"It's in the trunk of your car," Phyllis added nonchalantly.

"My car?" Charlotte was flabbergasted. "Why would it be in my car?"

"I needed a place to stash it. I couldn't very well leave it in a company car. Don and I were supposed to leave last night and I knew you'd be working late on the balloons, so I figured I could just run back there before we left and grab the cash. Your car was hidden behind the service department and it seemed like a logical place at the time. Anyway, it all works out just fine."

"Not exactly! I was fired this morning and nearly run off the lot. I left my car there!"

"Then I suggest you go back and get it," Phyllis calmly advised.

"You don't understand! I took the money they owed me out of the cash drawer. If they see me anywhere near the lot, they'll kill me or have me arrested for sure!"

"Charlotte, I have to get off the phone. My time's up."

Click. The phone went dead.

Charlotte looked down at her stained dress and then at the clock. She raced into the bedroom, grabbed a sweater that more or less concealed the cashew chicken sauce, and dashed out the door.

風
水

Twenty minutes later, when she arrived at Musso and Frank, a crusty old waiter was placing chairs upside down on the tables. Dirk Belmont sat alone at the bar, dejectedly sipping a drink. He rushed to greet Charlotte when she walked in.

"I didn't think you were coming," he said, pulling her toward the bar. "Can I get you a drink?" There was no bartender in sight. "The owners are friends of mine. I hope you don't mind. It's quiet and we can stay as long as we like."

Flitting his fingertips over a thin butter-soft wallet lying on the bar, he added, "You'll never guess what I found under the seat in my car. It was there the whole time! What can I get you?"

"Jack Daniel's. Two ice cubes, please." She hopped up on a barstool and tried to look sophisticated. "I'm glad you found your wallet."

"Call me lucky," he said, hurrying around the back of the bar to fetch her drink. "I suppose you're wondering why I needed to speak with you."

"Not really."

"Am I that transparent?" He looked down in an "aw shucks, my name is Jethro" kind of way. "Is it that obvious?"

"You and my folks got off on the wrong foot," she said sweetly. "Tomorrow morning you'll wake up, call Charlene, and everything will be just fine." She took a sip of her drink and coughed, unaccustomed to hard liquor, and wondered how Joey managed to choke it down with such gusto.

"That's not what I want. You've changed all that. I'm in love with you."

Charlotte fell off her seat.

"I know it must seem sudden," he said. "I can't really explain it myself, but I feel it in my bones, Charlotte. And it would be a terrible thing to let this slip through our fingers."

Charlotte regained her balance on the barstool. Dirk grinned. "Are you all right?" She knocked back the rest of her drink and pushed the empty glass away. He immediately refilled it.

"I don't understand," she lamented. "You're supposed to be in love with my sister. You're supposed to marry her." She downed the second glass of whiskey and he refilled it again.

"You," he said looking deeply into her eyes. "Call me crazy. I want you."

Charlotte gulped the third glass. "This is…unnatural. I'll have another, please." She rubbed her temples. He poured another, and then leaned across the bar on his elbows, mooning. "Well, this is just bizarre! How could the same person be in love with my beautiful, perky, perfect sister and then turn around and love someone like me? It doesn't make sense."

"You're being awfully hard on yourself."

"You don't understand. Charlene and I are nothing alike. We are mutually exclusive." She was beginning to feel the effects of the liquor. "There are people who love people like my sister and then there is a whole different breed of person who might be attracted to me. It doesn't make sense," she slurred and then gulped down the drink in front of her. "It's ab-thurd."

"After tonight, Charlotte," he said, reaching for her hand, "nothing makes sense. All I know is that I have to have you." He mercifully poured her another tall one.

"You haven't spoken about this to Charlene, have you?" She hoped desperately that he had not.

"She didn't take it well."

Charlotte snatched the glass of whiskey and swallowed it in one gulp. She slid off her seat and grabbed the bar to steady herself. "I have to go."

"We can't deny this, Charlotte!"

She staggered toward the door. "I need air."

He ran around the bar, took her by the arm, and walked her outside. "I don't feel well," she said, inhaling deeply.

"I'll take you home, honey. My car's just around the corner."

She pulled away from him and leaned against a parking meter. "Don't call me honey. I'll wait here. Off you go."

He dashed down the street and around the corner. The second he was out of sight, she took off in the opposite direction, and she would have made it to the bus stop in time to catch the last bus to Glendale had it not been for the sky-high Louboutins.

As the right heel caught in a sidewalk crack, crumpled beneath her and snapped off, Charlotte stood frozen in time—then buckled and slumped to the pavement. Dirk's Rolls Royce glided to the curb just as the bus stopped at the corner a few feet in front of Charlotte. There was no one waiting for the bus, except for Charlotte, and she couldn't get up fast enough. She stared helplessly from the sidewalk as it pulled away.

"Are you hurt?" Dirk asked, helping her off the ground.

Charlotte dusted herself off and watched the bus disappear into the night. "That was my bus," she said somewhat incoherently. "I have to go to Glendale."

"Now?"

"I have to get my car." She closed an eye in order to focus.

"Charlotte." He took her gently but firmly by the shoulders. "You're in no shape to drive."

"I have to get something out of the trunk!"

"I'll take you. Calm down."

When the Rolls pulled up in front of Eebner City, Dirk had to shake Charlotte to wake her.

"Charlotte," he sang, but there was no response. "Charlotte!"

"Huh?" Groggy and seeing double, Charlotte nearly fell out as she opened the passenger door. Before Dirk could come around to help her, she attempted to scale the gates to the lot. He took her gently by the hips and pulled her back.

"Don't you have a key?" She pushed him away and tried again to climb the fence and again he gently pulled her down.

"Where's the car?" He hoisted himself up and threw a leg over the top of the chain link. "I'll get whatever you need."

She looked up at him and everything began to spin. She grabbed the fence and hung on for dear life. "Behind the service department," she said, swaying. "The keys are in the ignition. It's in the trunk," she mumbled, collapsing to the ground. "The trunk…"

He dropped onto the driveway behind the gate. "What's in the trunk?"

Charlotte had passed out.

Dirk glanced around, spotted a squat cinderblock building with big roll-up doors, and darted toward it under the glare of sodium vapor lights. He went around the back, and as Charlotte had hoped earlier that day, the weeds had indeed grown so prolifically that her car was nearly obscured.

Dirk crept slowly into the thicket, avoiding the barrels and drums of sludge and waste that littered his path. He saw a glint of metal buried deep in the brambles and fought his way through until he found Charlotte's Jetta. He yanked the door open against the hearty plants and grabbed the keys. After tramping down the shrubbery at the rear of the car, he opened the trunk. The helium canisters looked like World War Two shells, which generally would have seemed weird except that it was dark, something was crawling up his leg, and Charlotte was waiting for him back at the car, more or less.

"It's in the trunk," he told himself.

He slapped the back of his leg, squashing whatever it was creeping up his pant leg, and began to unload the tanks. Even in the darkness he was able to make out an animal print. In the back of the trunk, wedged behind the helium canisters and the spare tire, sat Phyllis's faux fur leopard print overnight case. Trimmed in fake, black, patent leather with a handle and lock of tarnished brass plate, it looked like something a runaway teenager from the wrong side of the tracks might carry while hitchhiking her way out of Kentucky. All Dirk saw was an overnight bag, and it gave him a thrill.

He shook it, weighed it, and finally opened it. A lurid pink see-through nightie embellished with hot pink boa erupted from the luggage like a gag snake popping out of a can of peanuts. Fingering the slippery fabric, the doctor did a little jig.

"Oh, yeah!"

Without delving deeper into the bag, he stuffed the lingerie back in, snapped the case shut, tossed the helium canisters back into the trunk, and bolted to his Rolls Royce, all the while envisioning Charlotte in the negligee.

There she was, slightly drooling and fast asleep.

Harold and his younger brother Walter stood on the sidewalk in front of Emperor's Kitchen attempting to block Kwan, preventing him from reaching his car.

"I don't want to go," Kwan said determinedly. "I don't like to gamble, and I've got stuff to do around here."

"We cleared it with your old man," Walter countered. Kwan zigged left, then zagged right.

"Dragon style," Harold noted. Walter digested the info, then ambled toward Kwan with high, loping steps.

"Mmm, Walter's going with the crane. Interesting. What's so important you can't hang with your homies for a couple of days, Kwan?" Walter swept his arms from side to side, continuing forward in high, inelegant strides.

Kwan held out his middle and index fingers, curling his thumb, ring, and little finger into his palm, beckoning his opponent. Walter struck out with his fist, which Kwan plucked out of the air and squeezed until Walter dropped to his knees.

"I've started a project and…"

Harold viewed him warily. "What kind of project? Nice praying mantis, by the way."

"Thanks," said Kwan, helping Walter off the sidewalk. "A little Feng Shui thing I've been…"

"I knew it," Harold said shaking his head. "It's that chick, isn't it? The one with shar chi coming out her…"

"No. It has nothing to do with her. It's something for one of my dad's friends."

"Walter, go ask Dragon Breath in there who Kwan's working for." Walter had dropped to all fours and was creeping toward Kwan. "Oh, for God's sake. The dog? Fight like a man, Wally."

Kwan bent his right arm up at a ninety-degree angle to his elbow, making his wrist parallel with his lower arm. He advanced toward Walter with four fingers pointing out and his thumb curled underneath, giving his appendage the appearance of a pissed-off cobra. "Maybe we can help with your little project," Harold said sarcastically.

"Yeah, right. You don't know the first thing about Feng Shui," Kwan replied with a lightning strike to a pressure point in Walter's neck. Walter flopped onto his back like a beached sea lion.

"Snake fist, very nice." Harold extended his hand to Walter and helped him to his feet. "This is messed up, Kwan. You don't want to get into that shit. Trust me. The chick is whack."

Walter spun around and windmill-kicked Kwan square in the solar plexus. Kwan didn't flinch.

"Iron shirt? Whoa," said Harold, impressed. "You've been doing some serious ab work, bro." Walter sat down to rub his injured foot. "You're coming with us, Kwan. End of story. We'll be back by Monday morning. The biatch and her bad luck will be here when you get back."

"It's not that. I feel…responsible. I have to stay and…" Walter had sprung into a monkey position.

Kwan widened his stance and looked directly into Walter's eyes. "Don't even." He turned to Harold. "And don't call her a biatch. You are Chinese. Not cool. Not a rapper. You sound ridiculous."

Harold stood back and looked hard at Kwan. "What have you done?"

"I didn't do anything. I'm a little out of practice and I thought here's this girl with…"

Walter got a gleam in his eye. "Did you bang her?" Kwan did a back flip and kicked Walter in the head. Stunned, Walter hit the pavement with a thud.

"Nice one," Harold remarked. "Didn't see that coming."

Walter staggered to his feet. "Come on, man. It's just a couple of days, and it won't be a party without you." Walter's eyes glazed over from the head kick, giving him the further appearance of a dimwit. Harold put his arm around Walter's shoulder. "This is what I'm left with, dude," he said to Kwan. "Come on."

Kwan sighed. "Two days. That's it."

Harold slapped Walter on the back and smiled. "Kwan, you drive. I just got my ride detailed."

Walter nodded thickly, unsure of what happened.

風
水

CHAPTER THIRTEEN

By the time Charlotte opened her eyes, the sun was peeking over the horizon and the desert was coming to life. She swallowed hard and tried to shake the cobwebs out of her head.

"Where are we?" she asked, desperately trying to remember if she should have known the answer.

"We'll be there in a couple of hours." Dirk lifted her hand from its place across her chest and kissed it like a prince in a fairy tale.

She quickly withdrew her hand and pinched herself on the cheek. "We'll be where in a couple of hours?" She squinted at the desolate beauty of the Mojave and wished she had a pair of sunglasses.

"Las Vegas."

"Pardon?"

"I wasn't sure you felt the same way I did until you sent me for your overnight bag. Correct me if I'm wrong, but I assumed that meant you wanted to spend the night with me. I don't know what came over me, but you were sound asleep and I felt like driving."

"Las Vegas," she repeated, shocked.

"Why not? Let's live a little. You have your things already packed, and I can pick up a shirt and whatever else we need when we get there."

"My things?"

"In your overnight bag, you naughty girl," he teased.

"My overnight bag?"

"From the trunk of your car, silly. You're not much of a drinker, are you?"

She closed her eyes and tried very hard to remember what had happened the night before. A lot had happened, and she was accustomed to so little that she couldn't fathom a single detail. Yet all the events of the past twenty-four hours circled around in her head like turkey vultures over fresh road kill. She touched her temple and groaned.

"I took the liberty of picking up a few supplies in the event you felt a little fuzzy when you woke up." He reached into the back seat and grabbed a Louis Vuitton Rolls Royce Edition ice chest. "Go ahead. You'll find everything you need."

She opened the chrome and leather cooler and found a chilled bottle of Cristal champagne, a small carton of freshly squeezed, organic orange juice, a bottle of Extra Strength Excedrin, and an ice-cold pair of Gucci sunglasses. She immediately shook four pain relievers into her hand, tore open the orange juice, and knocked back the pills. She wiped her mouth, closed the cooler, and put on the frosty dark glasses.

"The overnight bag? From the trunk of my car?"

"Yes, of course. Now do you remember?" There was a twinkle in his eye.

"Did you look in the bag?" She stared straight ahead, stealing a sideward glance to gauge his reaction.

His eyebrows went up and down, up and down. "I saw the negligee, if that's what you're driving at."

"What negligee?" He reached over and optimistically squeezed her leg. Charlotte suddenly imagined the sort of sleepwear that belonged to Phyllis and cringed. "Did you see anything else… interesting?"

"Honey, I'm a gentleman. I saw the nightie and that was all I needed to know."

She fought to keep down the Excedrin and the orange juice and the Jack Daniel's from the night before. "I can't go to Las Vegas. We can't go."

"Give me one good reason why not?" Charlotte didn't have a hope of getting a word in edgewise, as he had apparently thought the whole thing through. "It's the weekend, we're probably on everybody's shit list, and I say we go have some fun and get to know each other."

He turned to her with a dreamy expression. "I love you."

"I need to use a bathroom," she responded, not at all the response he anticipated. He swung the huge car off the road at the next exit and pulled into a truck stop. "Where's my bag?"

"I'll get it for you. It's in the trunk."

Please, let there be a pair of sneakers in the bag, Charlotte thought, noting she wore one hyper expensive and very tall shoe while the other lay broken and pathetic on the floor of the car. Kicking off the good shoe, she was out of the car before it had come to a complete stop. She snatched the small suitcase the instant Dirk popped the trunk and made a beeline for the ladies room. She bolted herself in a stall and opened the case. Bits of hot pink boa floated out, making her sneeze, and the tacky, see-through negligee made her queasy, but there beneath the god-awful thing were piles and piles of cash.

Dirk had just finished topping off his tank when Charlotte raced out of the truck stop café and jumped into the car. "I have to go home," she said urgently. "Now."

He stuck out his lower lip like a disappointed child. "I thought we were going to…"

"This isn't right. You belong to Charlene. Geez, my parents are going to kill me."

Charlotte held a mental vision of an awkward family scene, at whose center she would be defending the standard position that this was not her fault. She closed her eyes in an effort to blot the unholy picture from her mind and could only wonder if, indeed, she might have done something that would lay the blame at her feet. Was it the sexy shoes? Then she remembered that with one of the heels snapped off, the shoes weren't so alluring anymore—at least not the right one.

As Charlotte pondered whether the Nordstrom people would understand that the merchandise was defective (and she couldn't possibly be expected to pay for it), she glanced at the tacky bag planted firmly between her bare feet and pictured the wads of bills inside.

She dreamed of a life where money wouldn't be a constant worry, but the dream was contaminated by a gnawing fear that she would someday be arrested. As she considered all the angles—the reasons for which and the reasons against which she could or should keep the money—the doctor took her lack of protestation as a sign that they would be enjoying Las Vegas.

He got behind the wheel and continued to drive through the desert.

風
水

CHAPTER FOURTEEN

Joey checked into his new digs at the Glittering Gulch Trailer Court and Mobile Home Estates, his temporary home in Las Vegas. Joey's cousin Frank (it was, in fact, his cousin's given name) had taken a leave of absence from his position as a waiter during the nightly show at the Flamingo to pursue the loftier goal of blackjack dealer and was attending card dealer's school for a couple of months. Frank had a lucrative post during the big show and couldn't afford to let anyone other than family take over during his bout with higher education, lest he prove all thumbs and truly need the waiter's job.

Armed only with Charlotte's rent money and a genuine desire to make something of himself, Joey availed himself to his cousin, found a place to hang his snap-brim hat and had only to buy a tuxedo before fulfilling his destiny. If he were to win Charlotte back, he would have to be able to repay her the rent, at the very least, and demonstrate that he was not a bum. Taking over for his cousin was a step in the right direction and certainly a cut above working in porn.

A wiry, old gal wearing a micro-mini toga and shiny gold high-heeled sandals with leather straps that wrapped around her calves and up her baggy thighs crunched across the gravel parking lot with Joey in tow. She unlocked the door of a tiny trailer and handed him the key.

"I'm gonna be late for work," she said, hacking up part of a lung. "You'll find everything you need inside the canned ham here." She lit a cigarette and shimmied her bony butt across the parking lot.

"Where can I buy a tux?"

"Come with me." Her high heels sank into the stones. "I'll drop you on my way to work." They got into an ancient El Dorado and she hit the gas with a lead foot, spraying pebbles all the way out of the parking lot.

"Do you work at Caesar's Palace?"

She blew smoke out of the corner of her mouth in his direction. "Yeah, right," she cackled. "You can find me at Ernie's Kabob House on the Woodbury Beltway."

"Is that a Greek place, I mean, with the toga and all?"

"We're kabob goddesses. Like there was ever a goddess for meat on a stick. A god maybe, but a goddess? No way. Said on your application you'll be working at the Flamingo. What they got you wearin'?"

"A tuxedo, remember?"

"Could be getting hitched. You never know. The Flamingo," she wheezed. "Classy place." She glanced at his crotch. "I know how you can make a little somethin' on the side, if you're interested."

Joey squirmed uncomfortably. Why does everyone assume I'm a sex machine? He wondered. "I think I'll just stick to my job, thanks."

"Suit yourself." She tossed her cigarette butt out of the car. "They pay pretty good money for stitching them feathers on. It ain't a dream job, but it's piece work, and a guy like you'd probably be pretty good with needle and thread."

"What are you talking about?" Joey twisted in his seat to face her.

"Makin' up the headdresses for the showgirls. You're queer, ain't ya?" She expectorated something brown into a tissue and lit another cigarette.

"Gay? You think I'm gay?"

She inhaled deeply and held the smoke in her lungs for a moment. "I'm a poor judge." She emitted a big blue cloud. "Especially when it comes to men. You always wanted to be a waiter?"

"I wanted to be a professional singer, but that didn't pan out. And I am not gay, by the way, but I have many friends who are."

"I wanted to be a Mars-Venus practitioner, but my Jimmy thought it was stupid."

"I don't understand."

"That's exactly what I said." She slapped him on the thigh, her hand lingering long enough to be awkward. "It would have been worth the three grand to get the license. I'd already paid fifteen hundred for the course."

"I don't know what a Mars-Venus practitioner is." He pointed to the road, indicating she should pay attention and drive with both hands.

Pouting, she placed her hands on the steering wheel at ten and two o'clock, the cigarette dangling from her lips. "Now you're starting to sound like Jimmy. You've heard of Men are from Mars, Women are from Venus, I assume?" He nodded, although he wasn't up on modern psychology.

"Well, they offer a course where you can learn," she spoke as if reciting a brochure, "the fundamentals of the healing methods and communication skills necessary for inter-relationship development, understanding, and growth." She shook her head. "I found it to be very useful and informative, but old Jimmy said getting the license would just be throwing good money after bad."

"Has your husband passed on?"

"What? No. We're divorced."

Joey laughed out loud, which seemed to hurt her feelings. "I hope to use all that I have learned from the Mars-Venus course on my next and hopefully more receptive husband," she said in defense of the Mars-Venus method.

She swung the El Dorado off the main street and drove down a narrow alley, coming to a stop outside a single-story brick building with a red fire door. "Knock three times and tell 'em Hilda sent you. If that fails, tell 'em you're a cop." She slapped him on the leg and hooted with laughter, causing her to cough up her other lung.

Joey got out of the car and Hilda peeled rubber, taking the corner on two wheels. He approached the red door and knocked three times. It opened a crack.

"Whaddya want?"

"Hilda sent me." The door whooshed open and Joey was pulled through by the lapels. The heavy metal door clanged shut behind him. His eyes had to adjust to the low light and it took a moment before he realized he was standing in a huge warehouse chock full of tuxedos. Boxes of them lay open on the floor, with more piled high along the walls. There were racks and racks in every conceivable color, shape, size, and shimmering fabric. A stout man in a powder blue tux with a ruffled red shirt led Joey to the center of the room.

He sized Joey up. "Forty regular, I expect. What are you in the market for?"

Joey took in the wild assortment of eveningwear. "Black!" he blurted, touching the cuff of a double-breasted pink lamé number with rhinestone buttons.

"We got that," the man said, reaching for a classic tuxedo.

Joey removed his thrift shop jacket and put on the formal one. "Do you have a mirror?"

"It fits like a glove. Take my word for it."

"Can I try the pants?" Joey asked, unzipping his trousers.

"Hear about the guy with five dicks?" The man's belly rose and fell in short bursts. "Pants fit him like a glove!" He removed a pair of black slacks from a hanger and handed them to Joey. Joey stepped into the slacks and looked down. The length seemed about right, but it was hard to tell without a mirror. He buttoned the jacket.

"Well? How do I look?"

"You look like a million damn bucks for just a hundred fifty, no tax."

"What about a shirt?"

The man's thick fingers flitted over the ruffles of his shirt. "You want something nice?"

"Simple," Joey articulated, glancing at a rack of vividly colored, satin dress shirts. "Something simple."

"Suit yourself," conceded the "tailor" as he reached into a cardboard box. He grabbed a white shirt in a cellophane packet and shoved it at Joey. "We'll call it two hundred even. You getting married?"

Joey pulled up his pants and produced the money for the tuxedo. "Nope. Got a job as a waiter at the Flamingo."

"You got a girl? 'Cause my daughter's due back any minute, and she's…"

"I have a girlfriend, thanks. Name's Charlotte."

The man stepped forward and looked into Joey's eyes. "You sure about that?"

No, I'm not sure, Joey thought, but he was going to work hard, keep his nose clean, and show Charlotte that he could be a good man—and a functioning member of society. The huge, metal door swung open, and a stunning young woman walked in wearing a flesh-colored leotard. It took Joey a moment to realize that she wasn't naked.

"There she is now," the man said, kissing his daughter on the cheek. "This is Giselle. Giselle, this is…?

She smiled at Joey with straight white teeth, revealing perfect dimples on either side of her full mouth.

"Uh, Joey, hi."

"You still sure about that thing we were just discussing? She's with Cirque du Soleil," the father shared as an obvious selling point.

Giselle was a looker by anyone's standards, and apparently quite flexible, yet all Joey saw was someone who was not Charlotte—and that was not enticing to him any longer.

"Thanks for everything. I gotta run." Joey headed for the exit.

"Good luck," the man called after him.

K wan sat behind the wheel of his Toyota trying to blot out the thundering hip-hop booming from the speakers as well as the voices of Harold and Walter, who were shouting to be heard over the music. His head was pounding and his eyes hurt from the bright sunshine. He reached under his seat and felt around for the sunglasses he had loaned to Harold, that Harold claimed to have returned, but that Kwan knew were lost. He switched off the radio and glared at Harold, daring him to turn it back on.

"Okay, okay... chill, Dog." Harold pulled his hand away from the controls.

"We're running with the big dogs now," Walter chirped, bouncing up and down in the back seat like a four year old. Suddenly he frowned. "Ouch!"

Reaching under his backside, Walter pulled out a spool of red satin ribbon that had lodged between his butt and the seat back. Kwan steered with one hand and attempted to snatch the ribbon with the other, but Harold plucked the spool from Walter before Kwan could nab it.

"What up, my little red friend," Harold said, twirling the ribbon around his finger. "Christmas shopping early this year, Dog?"

Kwan ignored him.

"Buy me some cool shit for Chinese New Year?" Harold wound the ribbon around his head à la Rambo. "Well?"

"Well, what? It's probably been there for years."

Walter picked up a receipt from the floor of the car. He leaned forward and waved it in front of Kwan's face, causing the auto to veer across two lanes. "Says on the receipt you bought the ribbon yesterday," he reported.

"Oh, that. My dad needed it for…"

"You think we're buying that shit?" Harold vigorously shook his head. "We know what red ribbon is used for, man."

"I don't," Walter said. "What's it used for?"

Kwan turned the radio on, but this time Harold switched it off. "Uh, uh. It's Feng Shui time, Wally. Sit back and learn from the master." He punched Kwan in the arm. "You gonna tell him, or should I?" Kwan hunkered in his seat and stared silently ahead.

"Okay. Our boy Kwan here is going to use this ribbon to attract love. Now we must ask ourselves just who he plans to use it on." He smirked at Kwan. "Word."

"I have to pay attention to the road."

"It's a straight freakin' line from L.A. to Vegas, bro."

Walter sat forward. "Who is she, Kwan? Come on… I tell you guys all my shit."

Harold turned to face Walter. "You haven't had any shit since the earth cooled, Wally. But Kwan…that's another story. He's been hittin' on this chick who has the worst luck in the entire universe."

"I have not been hitting on anybody," Kwan snapped. "I need to concentrate here. Our exit is coming up." A sign at the side of the road told them the exit for Las Vegas was fifty miles away.

"The girl lives in Hollywood. Apartment 4-D. The death number, of course. She drives a hoopty ride circa the Iron Age, has stringy hair, and a shar chi target painted on her ass." Harold looked at Kwan. "Sound about right to you, man?"

Kwan focused on the road. Walter pulled the ribbon off Harold's head, waved it around, and sang, "Kwan's got a girlfriend. Kwan's got a girlfriend."

"God, take me now," Kwan muttered under his breath. "I'm surrounded by twits."

Harold took the receipt from Walter and a sly smile spread across his face as he studied it. "Dragon Breath needed a pair of Mandarin ducks, too. He gettin' freaky with Mrs. Dragon Breath?"

"Don't call her that, or him."

Touching his chest in a sarcastic mea culpa, Harold apologized, "Sorry. What up with the ducks, Kwan? For real?"

"They're for a friend." Kwan hoped this would put an end to things.

"What's the deal with ducks?" Walter asked, showing Kwan the error of hoping for such things.

Harold slapped the dashboard. "It's the most basic, ancient, no-fail mating call there is. Get yourself a couple of those babies and WHAMMO! You're peeling off your silk boxers like a newlywed."

"Where did you put them, Kwan?" Walter tied the red ribbon to Kwan's ponytail.

"The love sector, be my guess," Harold teased.

Kwan sat erect and took a deep breath. "Charlotte Nightingale is a project. Nothing more. Nothing less. Her life, it appears, is fraught with misfortune. I endeavor to correct that in any small way I can. I expect nothing in return. I am not looking for anything in return. I am here to help." He exhaled a long, full breath and relaxed his grip on the steering wheel. Walter sat back in his seat, satisfied with the explanation. Harold, on the other hand, hit the roof.

"I have two words for you. That's a load of crap!" Counting on his fingers, he added, "five words."

Walter seemed confused. "I've seen him do Feng Shui for lots of people."

"Mandarin ducks, Wally. That's not 'I hope you get that big promotion' Feng Shui or, 'I hope Uncle Louie's goiter goes down' kind of shit. Freakin' Mandarin ducks, Dog."

"I feel sorry for her," Kwan insisted. "That's all."

Harold sat back and crossed his arms over his chest. "A Feng Shui mercy fuck? Na, na, na. A man has one thing and one thing only on his mind when he does the ducks, man. You are in deep."

"Do you guys really believe in that stuff?" Walter asked innocently.

"Four thousand years in the making, Bro. Generation after generation. You gotta believe in it. Any minute now Kwan's 'project' is gonna drop what she's doing and fall religiously in love with Kwan. Right, Kwan?"

Kwan rolled his neck from side to side, trying to work out a terrible knot forming at the base of his skull. "I gave her a black turtle for solid support in her endeavors, but that seemed to fail. I placed a red, uh, just a crystal in her handbag for general improvement."

"This is some serious shit," Harold said solemnly. Kwan was just pleased that he hadn't been pressed about the fact that the crystal was red. No way was he going to mention that it was in the shape of a heart.

"Go on," Harold nudged.

"I reduced the shar chi entering her home by making a few simple adjustments to her habitat. She told me she lost her job, her car, and her boyfriend all in one day. The ducks were merely my attempt at..."

"Yeah? What?"

"I just want her to be happy," Kwan said softly.

"You stickin' to that story, Bro? Fine. I hope she finds a dude that'll rock her world. I hope your Feng Shui works."

When Joey arrived at the Flamingo showroom for his appointment with Mr. Fred Utech, his new boss, he fully expected to find a man. Instead, Fred Utech appeared to be no more than twelve years old, although he later mentioned to Joey that he would be returning to Harvard in the fall to complete his MBA.

Joey walked into the big theater and spotted a small person sitting at the bar, reading what appeared to be a newspaper. As Joey drew closer he saw it was a racing form. Fred wore large jewelry and too much cologne, although the jewelry was somewhat exaggerated by Fred's diminutive stature. Giant cufflinks spelled out his initials in pavé diamonds- F.U.

Joey extended his hand and his eyes immediately began to water from the strong bouquet of Dark Temptation Axe body spray in which Fred had recently doused himself.

"I'm Joey Lozzi," he said to his new boss. "Achoo! Frank Lozzi's cousin."

Fred appeared confused. "I heard his cousin's name was also Frank." His voice cracked as though he hadn't finished puberty.

"Right, I go by Joey now." Prisms of light reflected off a colossal diamond horseshoe ring on Fred's tiny pinkie finger.

Fred slid off the barstool and dropped onto the floor, several feet shorter than Joey. "I like Frank. He's a hard worker." He tilted his head back in order to look up at Joey's face. "You a hard worker like your cousin?"

Wanting desperately to ask Fred how old he was, Joey nodded instead.

"You start work at eight o'clock. That's when the doors open. Show's at nine, you'll finish about midnight. Keep moving—you'll sell more booze and stay out of the customer's way during the show. Any questions?"

Joey was just dying to ask the guy's age, but he shook his head. "I got nothing."

"You sure?" Fred coaxed, as if reading Joey's thoughts. Joey again shook his head, biting his tongue.

"Fifteen!" Fred exclaimed.

Joey patted Fred's juvenile shoulder. "I was gonna guess more like 18."

"What are you talking about?"

"What are you talking about?" Joey asked.

Fred waved the racing form. "Bet the wad on number fifteen. First race. Starts in five minutes. Why, what did you think I was talking about?"

"Roulette?" It was all Joey could come up with.

Fred shook his undeveloped head. "Roulette's for pussies. Real men play the ponies."

Joey nodded and gave the little guy a thumbs up. "Got it."

"Okay, you own a tux, right? Rentals look cheesy and you'll go broke."

"Basic black, with a white shirt," Joey confirmed.

"Wear shoes and socks," Fred told him. Joey couldn't imagine a barefoot waiter in Las Vegas, much less one wearing a tuxedo. "You'll be getting a new boss in a couple of months when I go back to school. Harvard. Business."

"I'll be sure to hang onto the shoes and socks then."

A gaggle of showgirls swooped into the room wearing massive feathered headdresses. Fred clapped his hands like a seal with a new red ball. "Okay, beat it, kid. I wanna watch rehearsal."

The showgirls filled the stage as the orchestra took their seats and began tuning their instruments. Joey thanked his new boss and walked away. On his way out he stopped a seventy-five-year-old busboy.

"Who's the headliner?" he asked the old timer.

"What are you, a wise ass?"

"I'm new in town," Joey explained.

"I thought the whole world knew about Donny and Marie. A woman and her partner open for them. Singers."

"Is it cool if I hang around and check out the rehearsal?"

"What do I look like, a Mormon? I give a shit." He walked away. Joey took a seat in a white leather booth and pushed aside a half-empty cocktail that had created a puddle on the table.

"I believe that's mine," said a silky-voiced, large-busted woman in a sequined evening gown, whose make-up might have been applied with a trowel. Her bouffant smelled flammable from three feet away. She picked up the drink and licked her super-glossy lips.

"I haven't seen you around here before," she said seductively. "Mind if I sit down?" She was already sitting. Her long French-tipped nails tapped against the side of the glass and Joey thought that she would be quite pretty if she lost the big hair and garish make-up. She was, however, the kind of woman most men in Las Vegas would consider a dish.

"You an entertainer?" She scanned every inch of his body.

"I wanted to be a singer once." He looked away for a moment. "And you?"

"I open for the Osmonds. Me and my partner, Mike. What do you do?" She dipped a finger into her drink. "My name's Carla." She sucked her finger dry.

"I'm Joey Lozzi. I'm a waiter," he added humbly.

"I know a Frank Lozzi who's a waiter right here at the Flamingo. Isn't that a coincidence?"

"He's my cousin. I'm filling in for him for a couple of months while he goes to dealer's school."

Fingers flitting across her throat and down her plunging décolletage, she asked, "What kind of stuff did you sing?"

"I'll give you a hint. They used to call me 'Old Blue Eyes,'" he told her, noticing that when she swept the hair off her neck it sprang right back to its original shape.

She squinted and pursed her lips. "I see the resemblance. You got any kind of voice?"

Joey wasn't sure about anything anymore. Here was a bona fide Vegas bombshell practically undressing him with her eyes, who knew exactly what kind of drink said 'tell me where it hurts ya, Baby' to a guy like him, and he could barely tear his eyes off her hair.

"I'm running a little low on confidence at the moment," he said softly.

She pushed the glass away and shook her head. "Talent's nothin' without it, kid." She jumped up. "Damn, I'm late for my Brazilian, or is it a Playboy. I can never keep them straight."

Joey was pretty sure the Playboy was a complete denuding of the female form below the waist, but it seemed somehow unwise to tell her he was aware of the distinction. Even more unusual to his way of thinking, he didn't care one bit what Carla looked like—fully shorn or not. Something about her just made him want to sing.

"I've never waited tables before," he said as she turned to go. "Got any advice?"

Running her tongue over her teeth, she took a good long look at him. "Clench your tush whenever you're standing still. You'll get a lot of tips from the gals that way."

He smiled. "Got it, thanks."

She was halfway to the exit when she stopped and turned around. "And Kid," she added. "Be yourself. You're gonna do great."

風
水

CHAPTER FIFTEEN

As the Rolls sped into Las Vegas, Charlotte opened her eyes, then quickly closed them again. Each time the situation ballooned beyond her capacity to comprehend, like a narcoleptic, Charlotte would lapse into a somnambulist state, hoping that when she awoke it would all have been a hallucination. Observing the Las Vegas city limits sign and the handsome doctor mooning over her from behind the luxury automobile's wheel, Charlotte was shocked back into reality. The brief but taxing process made her want to go right back to sleep, but she fought the impulse to close her eyes.

"Where exactly are we going?" she asked.

He shrugged his shoulders. "I've never been to Las Vegas. You?"

Giving herself permission, under the circumstances, to be slightly cantankerous, she replied with an edge, "No, I never had the desire."

"Well, I guess we'll just drive into town and see what's available," he said pleasantly. "Separate rooms?"

She could tell from the way he said it that he was hoping she would answer in the negative. "Definitely separate rooms," she confirmed, teaching him a lesson about hoping for such things. "There." She pointed to a flashing purple sign at the side of the road. "That looks okay."

The valets in front of the Flamingo were quite impressed with the doctor's posh vehicle, and word was soon out that a high roller and his lady had checked in. The young man who opened the car door for Charlotte wrestled for control of the overnight case, but she had suddenly become a fierce competitor and successfully carried it into the lobby herself, barefoot, all the while clutching the leopard print bag tightly to her chest.

"Any luggage, sir?" another valet asked Dirk.

"Nope. We'll buy whatever we need," he said in an effort to impress both the valet and Charlotte, but she had already hurried inside.

Charlotte approached the registration desk and said to the gentleman behind the counter, "One room. One night."

"All right, miss." He entered the information into his computer. "And which credit card will you be using?"

"I'd like to pay with cash." She unconsciously tapped the overnight bag.

"We need to have a credit card number on file until you check out," he informed her. "Then you can pay with quarters for all we care."

"But I don't have a credit card. Oh, wait a minute." She dug into her purse. "Do you take Nordstrom's?"

He glanced up at the ceiling. "I'll have to get the manager."

Dirk stepped. "I'll take care of the rooms."

Charlotte shook her head. "Oh, no, you don't. I can pay my own way."

The clerk looked at Dirk, then Charlotte. He stuck his jaw out. "Why don't you let him put your room on his card until check-out, and then you can pay for it yourself with cash?"

"Would that be okay?" she asked Dirk, but he was already handing over a black American Express card. Upon seeing it, the clerk's fingers flew over the computer keypad, his disposition improving markedly.

"Any good shows in town?" Dirk asked. An officious man wearing a manager's nametag came up and whispered something in the clerk's ear. The clerk looked peeved as he walked away to help a less affluent customer at the other end of the counter.

"Dr. Belmont!" the manager gushed. "We are so pleased you have joined us." Dirk had no clue as to where or why anyone in Las Vegas had heard about him, but it did present a perfect opportunity for him to toot his horn in front of Charlotte. It did not occur to him, however, that the manager had uttered the identical compliment to each and every guest who cruised up in a Silver Cloud and who had the initials MD after their names on their shiny black Centurian cards.

"Why, thank you," Dirk said, rapping the granite countertop with his knuckles. "As plastic surgeons go, I've been blessed with a fantastic practice."

"Your rooms are comped, Dr. Belmont. We are delighted to have you and the young lady here with us at the Flamingo."

"I thought you'd never been to Las Vegas." Charlotte eyed Dirk suspiciously. "Two rooms," she added emphatically.

"Naturally," the manager oozed. "Doctor, would you care to secure a line of credit with us using your Centurian card?"

Dirk frowned. It sounded risky.

Sensing the doctor's hesitation, the manager continued, "That way the young lady is free to patronize any of our fine shops without the burden of carrying around a pesky handbag, and you will be free to enjoy our many diversions by simply signing your name on a charge slip at any of our gaming tables or restaurants."

The way he explained it made perfect sense. "That sounds fine," Dirk conceded. "How much do you recommend?"

"Well, Doctor, I might suggest you start with ten thousand." Charlotte whistled through her teeth, which Dirk took as proof that she was impressed. "Ten thousand?" Dirk spoke in a voice slightly louder than usual. "Surely that's not enough money for shopping and gambling."

"Very well, sir. How about twenty-thousand?"

Charlotte gasped.

"Make it fifty and we're done," Dirk said like a big shot.

The manager clapped his hands and gave Dirk two keys. He ding-ding-dinged a silver bell on the counter to summon the bellman. "Carl, take Dr. Belmont and the young lady to the Pent-house Suite." A man in a shocking pink Sergeant Pepper jacket and a Shriner beanie escorted them to the elevators.

"I'd like to buy you something wonderful," Dirk said, eyeing the stain on Charlotte's dress.

She glanced at her reflection in the elevator's smoked mirrors. Her dress was stained, wrinkled, and slept-in, and she found it odd that no one had given her heat about appearing in the lobby sans shoes, but on the other hand, she had never been to Las Vegas before. Perhaps this was how things were done here. While glancing down at her bare feet, Charlotte could not recall ever seeing such vivid carpeting in her life.

"You don't have to do that," she told him, mesmerized by the floor covering's avian motif.

"But I want to buy you a present. A gift."

Carl smirked.

"I can buy my own clothes," Charlotte insisted, hoping to wipe the smirk off the bellman's face.

Dirk turned to Carl, slightly embarrassed. "What's to do around here?"

"Gambling? Hello?"

"Any good shows?" There was a note of irritation in Dirk's delivery.

"Donny and Marie Osmond, but it's impossible to get tickets." Carl checked out Charlotte's body in the snug black dress and nodded appreciatively. "You'll want to take the lady somewhere nice. Talk to the concierge. She'll be able to do something."

The elevator doors opened on the top floor, and Carl directed them to their suite, where he unlocked the door and waited for them to enter. When he was certain that Charlotte was watching, Dirk reached into his pocket, extracted a fifty-dollar bill, and handed it to Carl. He was slightly put off when Charlotte turned away at the last second and missed the bestowal of the big tip.

"Please ask for me if you need anything at all," Carl requested as he retreated obsequiously into the hallway with the generous gratuity.

The door closed, leaving Dirk and Charlotte alone in an opulent sitting room. The furniture was gilded, as were a bunch of lilies in a Lalique vase.

"This is very nice," Dirk said, anxiously anticipating Charlotte's enthusiastic response.

"It's a little over the top, isn't it?"

"Charlene would just lo…" He caught himself. "I'm sorry. I wasn't thinking."

Charlotte sat down on a silk settee and hugged her travel case to her knees. She felt uncertain, uncomfortable and overwhelmed. "Now what?"

"Why don't we get cleaned up, you can go shopping, I'll play a quick round of golf, and then we'll go see a show? You take that room." He pointed to a thick eight-paneled mahogany pocket door. "I'll take the other one."

Sighing, she got up and crossed the room. She slid open the door and flinched. The bedroom was even swankier than the sitting room. The bed, large enough for an NFL play-off game, had a canopy of gold brocade that exactly matched the heavy draperies swagged over the windows, which offered a view of a miniature New York City skyline, a wee Eiffel Tower, a mega roller coaster and a giant creepy neon clown head that would make it difficult for her to sleep at night. She sucked in her breath and stood at the threshold, staggered by the extravagance of the stadium-sized boudoir.

The telephone rang and she could hear Dirk answer it.

"Luckiest guy in the world speaking," he said buoyantly.

Charlotte ducked into her room and quickly closed the door.

"Hello, Carl," Dirk said loudly. "There is something you can do for me."

Charlotte checked to see whether her door was lockable, and then locked it. She crossed the room, which took a good minute or two, and she sat down on the bed. She tucked the overnight bag under the damask dust ruffle and fell back onto the plush bedspread. The eiderdown duvet beneath it was ten inches thick, enveloping her like warm Velveeta cheese.

Running her hand over the smooth fabric, she could feel the occasional quill poking up. How many ducks? She wondered, and then unexpectedly flashed on the Mandarin duck carvings in her foyer, envisioning their new place on the credenza. Who had moved them? She figured it was Joey, probably scavenging for loose change, and then an image of Kwan popped into her head. He was smiling.

Kwan navigated the Strip with some difficulty. Each time he'd signal that he was turning into a particular hotel, Harold would insist that the place didn't measure up Feng Shui-wise.

"Yo!" he'd caution vociferously. "Those obelisks are daggers of death! Where is your head at, man?"

Walter would pretty much mouth whatever Harold yelled, making a mental note to inquire as to the meanings at a later date when Harold's blood pressure returned to normal—and Kwan wasn't swerving from lane to lane like a maniac.

"Not here!" Harold screamed as Kwan cut in front of oncoming traffic in order to turn into New York, New York. "Check out those angles! Why not just cut my heart out, Dog?! I'll lose my ass at Keno!" Kwan swerved back into traffic, cutting off a family of eight in a Saturn Relay with Utah plates.

"I thought you were the go-to Feng Shui guy, Kwan," Walter said, quickly re-buckling his seat belt.

Kwan pulled into the Flamingo Hotel and Casino against Harold's better judgment, exhibited by wild gesticulating and gagging sounds. "Screw it. I am driving no farther. Feng Shui isn't some magic you can channel for gambling. It's not a pair of fuzzy dice. This place is as lucky as the next."

Walter thought this over as they pulled up to the valet. "Life's a gamble," he commented wisely.

"Right on, Wally," Harold said. "But you can hedge your bets. Right, Kwan?"

Kwan was out of the car and had handed the keys to the attendant before Harold even finished asking. He marched into the lobby, plopped into a chair, and opened a book on Feng Shui. Harold and Walter followed him in.

"Check us in," Kwan told them. "I have a headache."

Harold and Walter spoke to a woman at the reception desk, and a moment later, the manager was summoned. Harold banged his fist on the counter. "You cannot seriously tell me that the only room you have available is number 444. This place is huge!" He leaned over the counter in an attempt to reach the computer keypad.

The manager slapped his hand. "Sir!"

Kwan glanced up briefly, and then returned to the Feng Shui text. He was convinced that he had overlooked some key detail in the arrangement of Charlotte's furniture, or possibly her knick-knacks. It just wasn't possible that her luck had actually diminished since he began the Feng Shui campaign. He had studied Feng Shui for years…it was in his blood. His grandfather was a Feng Shui master—old school—from Yangtze Province, where people traveled great lengths to seek his advice and counsel.

Great-grandfather had also been a practitioner rumored to have once performed his craft in the Forbidden City for none other than the Emperor himself. The monarchy's overthrow by Chairman Mao and the Communists was not considered the fault of Kwan's ancestor or his Feng Shui know-how, but, rather, of a eunuch's cluttered quarters. This was Kwan family lore, and they stuck to their story. Clutter was bad. No doubt about it.

Kwan turned the page and studied an illustration of a man and woman locked in a passionate embrace, a pair of Mandarin ducks prominent in the foreground like Olympic judges poised along the rails at a figure skating competition. The birds looked attentive and alert, ready to award a high score for superior mating.

He thought about the wooden duck carvings he had moved in Charlotte's apartment, how smooth they had felt, how sensual. He thought of Charlotte standing in the rain, mascara running down her face, her soaked dress clinging to her thighs and breasts as if it had been painted on. Suddenly, his cheeks were burning. He flipped the page at once.

"They offered to comp us a suite at the Bellagio," Harold pointed out for the manager's benefit. "But we prefer it here. Now what are you gonna do for us?" Harold smacked a thick stack of hundred dollar bills on the counter. "Now tell me you don't have any other rooms."

The manager typed on the computer. "Ah, we have a suite available."

"Which you are going to give us for the same price as room 444," Harold stated.

"Sir, I'm afraid I cannot do that."

Harold patted the big pile of Benjamins. "We're here to gamble."

Walter thumbed through the money, incredulous. "How much is this?"

"All my pay and tips from the past six months. I save a lot of money living with my mom and dad."

The manager smirked as he handed over a key card. "Top floor. Suite 1515. Enjoy your stay."

Walter blinked. "How much is that gonna cost?"

"It's comped, sir. Is there anything else?"

Walter jumped up and down, signaling that the transaction was complete. "Woo hoo! We are the big dogs! Lock up your daughters!"

Harold walked over and snatched the book from Kwan's hands. "It's all good, man. You'll work a little of your magic in the room, and shazam. We're going home winners."

Kwan smiled weakly, not altogether sure of himself or his skills.

D irk opened the door and Carl walked in, arms overflowing with tuber roses and gardenias. Per Dirk's orders, he chased here and there depositing the blossoms in vases, saving the fattest, most succulent for Charlotte's bedroom. The bellman knocked discreetly at her door and then pushed on the handle, but it was locked.

"Madam, it's Carl."

Dirk rocked back on his heels, hands in his pockets, chin extended smugly.

Charlotte slid the door open and peeked out. "Yes? Mmm, those smell amazing. Come in."

Carl distributed the bouquets around the bedroom. When his back was turned, Charlotte reached under the bed, slipped her hand into her suitcase and grabbed a hundred-dollar bill. After Carl had filled the vases with water, she tucked the money into his breast pocket.

"I'm not wealthy," she told him. "But I can take care of myself. I also know what it is to work for a living. Do something nice for yourself," she suggested.

"This is excellent, Miss," he said, figuring it had to be at least a fifty, or why would she go on like this. "If there's any way I can be of service to you, please don't hesitate to ask for me. Again, my name is Carl." He scraped and bowed, backing out of the room. The instant his feet hit the hallway outside the suite, he checked to see how much she had given him. "Thank you, beautiful!" he said to no one.

"I've got to say, the service here is extraordinary," Dirk said to Charlotte. "It pays to tip well. For example, I passed the guy a fifty just to make sure you and I were well taken care of."

Retreating into her room, Charlotte muttered, "Thank you," then slid her door shut. There was no end to his attempts at impressing her. She wished he would relax, not try so hard. She wished he were someone else, and once again, for some inexplicable reason, she pictured Kwan.

Shaking the thought loose as if it were a Styrofoam peanut stuck to a sweater, she considered calling Charlene, but the impulse quickly gave way to the knowledge that accusations were sure to fly and she had no excuse whatsoever for being shacked up with Charlene's betrothed in a penthouse suite at the Flamingo hotel, surrounded by fragrant and exotic flowers.

She pulled off the Chanel dress and wondered why anyone in their right mind, given all the facts, would spend such a considerable amount of money on a garment that didn't travel well or repel stains. She picked up the phone.

"Is there a women's clothing shop in the hotel?" Yes, there was—Pandora's Closet—and she was connected forthwith.

The senior saleswoman finished taking Charlotte's information, hung up the telephone, and snapped her fingers. On the other side of the boutique, a junior shop girl with painted-on eyebrows and dangly fingernail charms fussed over a display of jeweled thongs.

"Candy," the senior salesperson said. "The lady in the penthouse suite would like a few things sent up." Candy snapped her gum, like, whatever.

Dirk had finished brushing his teeth when the phone rang. He spit into the sink and picked up the wall phone beside the toilet. "Delivery from Pandora's Closet," Candy said unenthusiastically. Smack, pop went her gum.

Dirk mistook the sound for static on the line. "If you can hear me, come right up," he instructed. A moment later, there was a knock at the door and Candy stepped in, arms laden with parcels. Dirk took the boxes and set them on a table. Candy pulled the top packages off the pile and handed them to Dirk.

"These are yours," she said with a drop of warmth, thinking it would sure be nice to hook a rich guy. She looked around the room, imagining a life of privilege and comfort.

"Do you need me to sign for anything?" he asked.

"I forgot the slip. I'm pretty sure everything's well within your line of credit." He took a step toward her, and she could smell the hotel toothpaste on his breath. She swallowed her gum and ran her tongue over her teeth; thankful she had worn a nice bra. She squared her shoulders and stuck her chest out.

"How much is all this stuff?" he asked quietly.

"What?" Confused, she thought that perhaps he was going to ask for a quickie, or at least see if she wanted to make out.

Dirk nodded toward Charlotte's bedroom, from which the sound of a running shower emanated. "I'm crazy about that girl, okay? It doesn't mean I can't ask how much this is going to cost me."

"No clue," she replied flatly. "My boss said to bring it up. I don't really know what the deal is."

Charlotte emerged from a heavenly shower, prune-like. She cracked open the bedroom door and stuck her head out. "Dirk, have my jeans and stuff arrived yet?"

"That's fine," he said loudly. "Whatever it is, just put it on my bill." He promptly scooped up the parcels, rushed to Charlotte's door, and gallantly turned his head as he passed them to her. To his disappointment, she took the boxes and slid the door closed.

Candy came up behind him and cleared her throat, both as a hint that it was time for the tip and because a wad of Juicy Fruit had lodged somewhere in her esophagus. Dirk retreated into his bedroom and returned a moment later with two dollar bills.

"Thanks, mister," she said sarcastically, but he was unaccustomed to people being rude. He was, after all, a doctor.

"Doctor," he pleasantly corrected.

"Doctor." She held the small tip like it was used Kleenex.

Charlotte opened the first box, tossing the cover aside, expecting to find what she had ordered. Instead, a mink coat cascaded out. Next, she found a delicate hand-beaded evening gown, then a silk teddy and bikini bottoms, then a cashmere sweater and a lace-up leather miniskirt. She opened the remainder of the boxes and found several pairs of glitzy satin mules, rhinestone pumps, one pair of alligator cowboy boots, finally the jeans, and lastly, a tailored white buttoned-down shirt. She picked up the alligator boots, then the phone.

"Pandora's Closet, please," she said, slipping a foot into a boot. It was a handsome boot, she decided. "Hello, this is Charlotte Nightingale. You just sent some things to our suite."

The veteran clerk was hopeful that Charlotte might have decided to keep all of the items. "Yes, have any of the things met with your approval?"

Charlotte eyed the improvident garments spread out on the bed. "Yup," she said as the saleslady mentally added up her commission. "I like the jeans and the white shirt."

The woman's face fell.

"Also," Charlotte went on, "I thought I asked for a pair of sandals or sneakers, and all I can find are high heels and cowboy boots."

"Aren't they gorgeous?"

Charlotte wiggled her foot. "Hmm, all right. I'll keep the boots, jeans and shirt, but everything else is going back." She put on her new things and walked into the sitting room, where Dirk posed in front of a full-length mirror admiring the cut of his new Armani suit.

"Charlotte," he said, turning to her, disappointment spreading across his face like a rash. "Please let me buy you something nice."

She liked the clothes she was wearing, and the word "nice" as it pertained to attire made her a little queasy. To her way of thinking, it was one such "nice" terrific dress that had gotten her into this whole mess in the first place.

"They've made a mistake. They sent all kinds of stuff I didn't order."

"Don't you like any of it?" She shrugged noncommittally. "Hey, it's only money, right? And I've got plenty of that."

Charlotte had led an austere life to this point, and although she now had in her possession a quarter of a million dollars, she did not view this recent development as a catalyst to throwing her money away on foolishness. If she kept the money she would repay her student loans then enroll in graduate school, or maybe start her own business. Suddenly the sky was the limit in terms of her options.

"I'm not a spendthrift. I don't waste money on clothes."

"What's that supposed to mean?" He fiddled with an expensive silk pocket square.

"I just meant that some people think nothing of wasting all their money on superficial things."

"What?" He adjusted the silk tie that matched the pocket square. "I needed a new suit anyway." He slipped the cover off another parcel and pulled out a pair of lime green seersucker golf slacks and a pale pink Lacoste golf shirt.

She tucked her shirttail into her jeans. "That's not what I meant."

"You mean like Charlene?" He sounded a little confrontational. "I like that she wants to look good. There's nothing wrong with that."

"Not if you're a vapid, self-absorbed dimwit," she replied, verbalizing her feelings toward her vapid, self-absorbed, dimwitted sister.

"If it weren't for those dimwits, I wouldn't have a Rolls Royce and a fifty-thousand-dollar line of credit with this hotel. I have made a handsome living helping people with sagging buttocks, flat chests, and floppy labia. There is nothing wrong with people who want to look their best."

"At the risk of upsetting you, I think there are more important things than appearances," she insisted, cringing from the mental image of certain reconstructive procedures. "I mean, I realize that's how you make your living, but there has to be a limit to the lengths people will go to look good on the outside." She blanched. Inside— yick." She tried to banish the image in her head. "Whatever."

"What do you spend all your money on then?"

"Books. And my student loans."

"Charlotte," he said, bordering on condescension, "you have a great deal of potential, but…"

"Potential?"

He exhaled, exasperated by Charlotte's inability to see things his way. "I'm just saying that you're lucky. You don't really need plastic surgery to look terrific. With a decent wardrobe, a good haircut, and the right make-up, you could be every bit as beautiful as…" He caught himself before the words escaped his mouth, but they flew unspoken into the cosmos nonetheless.

"I knew it. Someone like you isn't capable of being attracted to someone like me. The real me. You can't get Charlene's perky looks and magazine-perfect clothes and me all wrapped up in the same person. I like who I am. I'm comfortable in my skin."

It wasn't as though Charlotte had ever suffered from low self-esteem—it was more that she had never considered it much of an option. "Even if I had hundreds of thousands of dollars, I wouldn't change a thing," she said confidently. "I'm starving. I'm going to have something to eat."

She went into the hall and pressed the elevator's call button with Dirk hot on her heels. Things were not progressing as he had hoped. He took her hand.

"I'm sorry. Let's start over. I don't want you to change. I really do think you are the most beautiful woman in the world. If you paid just a tiny amount of attention to your hair and make-up, you would be simply perfect. I was even thinking that you might enjoy the spa while I got in a quick round of golf."

She pulled her hand out of his and got into the elevator the instant the doors opened.

"A few highlights, maybe a touch of self-tanner..." His voice trailed off as Charlotte stabbed the button and the elevator doors slid shut between them. Dirk went glumly back to their suite, only to discover that he had locked himself out.

Charlotte looked hard at her reflection and felt a twinge of guilt. Why she had been so hard on Dirk? Sure, he went a tad overboard trying to impress her, but he had defended her and come to her rescue when her own family had belittled and made her feel small, and that had to count for something. Perhaps no harm would come from a simple haircut and maybe a tiny bit of mascara.

She reached into the pocket of her jeans and pulled out a wad of cash. When the elevator reached the lobby, she went to the concierge desk, where a woman in a neon pink jacket with a wavy peplum was busy shuffling papers.

"Excuse me, is there a beauty parlor here?" Charlotte asked uncertainly, wondering whether people still called it a beauty parlor or in the years since she'd been cutting her own hair they had changed the name to something more shicky micky.

Beaming, the concierge leapt out of her seat, revealing the massive spread that came with a sitting job. "I'll take you there myself, Mrs. Belmont! I understand that husband of yours is quite a miracle worker. Think he might have time to look at my butt?"

Charlotte figured she had either misunderstood or was truly the least worldly person ever to visit the vice capital of the world. She could only gape at the woman. The concierge understood that a plastic surgeon's wife must be constantly bombarded with requests of this nature and determined her tack should be less direct.

"Please forgive me," she said contritely. "I'm sure your husband is here to relax. Perhaps once he's had a chance to..."

"He's not my husband," Charlotte cut her off. "If you want him to look at your rear end, feel free to ask him yourself." She intended to sound sophisticated, but the remark came off as catty.

The woman didn't care much for Charlotte's tone and roughly pulled her through the lobby. Charlotte bumped into an elderly couple making their way through the hustle and bustle, and as she turned to apologize, she was nearly certain she caught a glimpse of Joey walking arm in arm with a bosomy woman in a sequined evening gown. Before she had the chance to get a better look, the concierge deposited her in front of Monsieur Henri's.

"Here we are, Miss," she said, emphasizing Charlotte's lack of marital status. "I might just ask that good-looking gentleman of yours to take a gander." She smacked her rump. "As long as you don't mind." She jiggled back to her post as Charlotte stood at the door to the salon, scanning the lobby for the man she thought looked an awful lot like Joey. It had been one heck of a twenty-four-hour day, and she told herself that her eyes were playing tricks.

At Monsieur Henri's check-in desk, a woman stuffed into a brown jumpsuit like a pork sausage, appraised Charlotte. "You've come to the right place. Henri will be right with you." She turned away and blared loudly enough for people in Reno to hear, "Miss-yur -on-reeeeeee, code blue!"

A tall man with hair plugs hurried over. "Er-mer-gerd!" Monsieur Henri gasped. "We're gonna fix you right up."

The view from the guys' suite was terrific, but the layout was all wrong, at least according to Harold. "Nope, this ain't going to work. They have to give us a different suite." He picked up the phone.

Kwan took the receiver from him and replaced it into its cradle. "I can fix it."

"Then get your ass to work, Dog," Harold said. Walter kicked off his Converse sneakers and opened a book on how to beat the house at Blackjack. Harold snapped the seal off the mini-bar and pulled out a beer. He dropped into a plush sofa and put his feet on the cocktail table. Kwan stood in the center of the room, eyes darting back and forth. He knocked Harold's feet off the table, slapped the book out of Walter's hands, and clapped.

"Chop, chop, boys. Move that sofa to the wall over there. Unplug that lamp and put it against the southern wall. See that silk plant? Put it in the entryway." Harold and Walter hopped to, quickly rearranging things to Kwan's specifications.

Kwan stood in the center the room while they hustled around him. In spite of the activity, all Kwan could see was Charlotte's apartment, Charlotte's knick-knacks, Charlotte's wet hair and the soap suds running down her legs, Charlotte's eyes following him as he moved the furniture, and the expression on her face when he told her she looked nice.

"Yo!" Harold barked in Kwan's face. "We've been done for like ten minutes. Now what?"

Kwan shook that last image of Charlotte from his mind. "Huh?"

"Let's go meet some girls," Walter suggested. "I saw some honeys in the lobby."

"Now, see," said Harold with a smirk, "that's what I'm talkin' about."

Kwan frowned. "You know they were prostitutes, right?"

"Oh, you're back," Harold replied. "I wondered where you went there."

"Kwan has a girlfriend, Kwan has a girlfriend," Walter sang.

"You guys go. I'm going to hang here for a while. Maybe take a nap."

Walter flinched in disbelief. "There is no napping in Vegas."

"Can't allow it, Bro. Sorry." Harold grabbed Kwan by the arm and pulled him toward the door. "Come on. Let's go."

Kwan pulled away. "I'll be down in a minute. Where are you going to be?"

Harold adopted a fatherly attitude, his tone suggesting that he would 'turn the car around' if need be. "I don't want to come back up here," he warned sternly.

"Ten minutes. For real." Kwan intended it to sound reassuring, but it came off a bit feebly.

Harold and Walter headed for the door. "Blackjack," Harold said over his shoulder. "And I'm not fooling around."

The instant they were gone, Kwan opened his overnight bag and took out a crystal fish, a portable plug-in fountain, some ancient Chinese coins, and a tiny pair of carved wooden ducks. Mandarin ducks.

Outside the suite, as they were exiting, Walter spun joyously in circles imagining his big winnings and the girls that were sure to follow a high-rolling winner such as himself. He spun right into

Dirk, who was locked out of his suite across the hallway, fiddling hopelessly with the door latch.

"Watch where you're going!" Dirk snapped.

"Sorry, Dude," Harold said, then eyeing Dirk's green plaid pants and pink striped shirt, added, "You in some kind of Rotary Club or something?"

Dirk looked down at the trousers and stiffly pointed out, "These are golf togs, son." He pushed past them en route to the elevator.

Harold grabbed Walter's sleeve. "We'll catch the next one, bro. That guy stinks of shar chi."

"You can tell from his pants?"

"I can tell from his smell. He's like, cursed."

Normally, Charlotte would have run in the opposite direction of a place such as Monsieur Henri's. The overwhelming smell of sweet perfume, ammonia-based hair dye, and noxious nail polish made her sick to her stomach. Not a single strand of hair, breast, fingernail, or leafy green plant looked remotely real.

As Henri towed her to the changing room, Charlotte looked at all the women who were being overdone to a ridiculous degree, and her thoughts immediately turned to Phyllis Schlotzky. *Geez, Phyllis would have loved this*, Charlotte thought with a pang of grief for the animal lover facing life in the clink.

Henri shoved her into the dressing room and stood in the door. "What are we doing today? The works, I imagine. Hair, make-up, nails," he spoke in a machinegun staccato. "Well?" He snapped his fingers. "Time is not on our side."

Dirk came down in the elevator and marched to the concierge desk. The woman looked up, quickly running her hands through her hair.

"Dr. Belmont!" she gushed, shifting her weight from one globular butt cheek to the other. "What can I do for you today?"

"A tee time in twenty minutes, please. And I'd like tickets to the Osmond show tonight. Oh, and I locked myself out of my suite."

"I'll let you in myself," she said, a full octave below her normal register. She consulted her computer. "Mind rounding out a four-some with three very nice gents here for the plumbing convention?" It wasn't whom he would have hoped to play a round with, but it was okay. The concierge clucked through her big white teeth. "Donny and Marie. That's going to be a tough one. Their shows sell out weeks in advance."

She glanced up and her body stiffened upon seeing Carla and Joey strolling through the lobby. When Carla glanced up, she spotted Dirk and she sashayed right over.

The concierge looked like she had sucked a lemon. "I'm with a client, Carla. Keep walking."

Dirk cleared his throat. "I'm only in town for one night. Isn't there anything you can do? I'm trying to impress a young lady, and it would mean the world to me."

"Yes," the concierge said brusquely. "We've met. I'm sorry, tickets for tonight's show are completely sold out."

Carla leaned over the desk, cleavage spilling over the top of her dress. "We both know if you really wanted to find a couple of tickets…"

"It's sold out," the concierge said emphatically.

"Oh, come on. He's trying to impress a gal."

Joey knew exactly how Dirk must feel as he put his arm around the Doctor's shoulder. "I'm sure I can fit you in at one of my tables. I know how it is."

"See, Honey?" Carla's eyes twinkled just a little wickedly. "It's not a problem." She turned her attention to Dirk with a look suggesting butter wouldn't melt in her mouth. "What's your name, Sugar? I'm Miss Carla; I'll personally put you on the guest list. And Joey here will take real good care of you and that special lady."

Joey gave a nod to Dirk's outfit. "You may want to wear a jacket."

Dirk scoffed. As if some punk waiter had to tell him how to dress to impress.

The concierge entwined her arm in his. "I'll see you to your suite now, Doctor. And I was wondering...is there anything you can do about my buttock region?"

Dirk observed her massive spread. "Have you considered going on a diet? And maybe exercising?"

She released his arm and picked up the pace. "It's hereditary. All the women in my family carry their weight behind them. I was wondering about liposuction."

Normally, Dirk had an acute bedside manner, at once making women feel that in his hands they would become the most alluring creatures to grace the earth. Contrary to this ability, however, Dirk simply shook his head. "That heredity stuff is a load of crap. Calories in, calories out. Eat right," he said, noting her rear end, "and get that thing in gear once in a while. Human fat looks just like chicken fat, if you can picture a forty-five pound bag of the stuff. There isn't enough liposuction in the world for that butt."

She stopped at the reception desk, cutting to the front of a very long line of people waiting to check in. She rapped her knuckles on the counter in front of the clerk. "This gentleman claims to have locked himself out of his suite. Have somebody deal with it."

She made a sound remarkably similar to a hiss. He wondered why he had been so rude, and then he chalked it up to his argument with Charlotte, having walked out on Charlene, and ultimately because he locked himself out of his room. He grabbed the concierge by her sleeve.

"My tee time? I'm good to go, then?"

"I'm sure you'll have a lovely time," she snapped, yanking her arm away.

The counter person frowned at Dirk. "Please go to the back of the line, sir. You can see there are people ahead of you." As Dirk stepped back, he bumped into Kwan.

"Excuse me," Kwan said politely, touching Dirk's arm. "My fault."

"Watch where you're going," he snapped, going to the end of the line.

Harold and Walter sat side by side at a twenty-five dollar minimum bet Blackjack table, jostling a drink between them. "I ordered the seven and seven, Bro," Harold groused, spilling half the drink. "It's not my fault if the waitress forgot your beer. Why don't you get up and get it?"

The dealer aggressively dealt the cards, slapping them on the felt tabletop. "Play cards, gentlemen. I'll have the cocktail waitress come back."

Harold had a stack of twelve chips in front of him, while Walter was down to just one. Walter grabbed his lone chip and got up. "I'm gonna get a Heineken."

Harold pushed his entire stack of chips into the green felt betting area before him. "Bring it," he told the dealer. The dealer had twenty-one. Harold went bust.

Kwan placed his hand on Harold's shoulder. "There you are," Harold said, turning around. "You're a little too late, though."

The dealer sneered. He didn't care much for Harold.

"Loan me a couple hundred, Dog."

"How much have you lost?"

"All of it. Come on, man. I'll pay you back. I gotta beat this guy, know what I'm saying?"

Kwan shook his head. "Throwing good money after bad."

"Are you playing or not, sir?" The dealer's tone was downright brusque.

Harold pulled Kwan close. "Got some Chinese coins on you, bro? Maybe a crystal fish or something?"

"They'll let you bet those things?" Kwan asked sarcastically. "Because I know you don't have any more money."

The dealer snapped, "Sir, if you're not placing a bet, please leave the table."

Harold rose in a huff. "Fine. What are we supposed to do now?"

"Vegas was your idea," Kwan said as they left the table. A woman smoking a cigarette and juggling two drinks in plastic cups sloshed into Harold. Without glancing up, she continued her journey, flicking ashes on the gaudy carpeting in the process.

"Well, I'm out of ideas. And money. Come on, man. Just a few bucks for the slots."

"I hate it here," Kwan stated unequivocally. "Everything about the place. I want to go home."

"No way. I can take some cash out of my credit card. We'll see a show or something. The buffet in these places is killer, Bro. Let's find Wally and do some damage, yo? Maybe hook up, know what I'm saying?"

Kwan knew exactly what Harold was saying. He was doomed, trapped in a land of bad carpeting with losers of every description, and everywhere he turned, shar chi seemed to be swirling around them. It was too loud, too colorful, too artificial. He did what he always did when he felt overwhelmed...closing his eyes, Kwan sought a beautiful flower garden in his head...

However, on this occasion, his happy place was elusive. He kept flashing on Charlotte's apartment and all the areas that still needed help. He pictured her cluttered bookcases and wondered what her bedroom looked like. *Was the dresser all wrong? Chairs heaped with clothes? Were the drawers organized, or jumbled and stuffed with mismatched socks? Was there a mirror in the room? Was her bed in the right place? What kind of bed was it? Were the sheets soft and...*

When he opened his eyes, Harold was staring at him. "You in there? I asked you three times if you wanted to go to a tittie bar, Dog."

"I'm going to my room."

"Man, Vegas never sleeps," Harold whined. "At least help me find Wally."

Pointing over his shoulder, in the opposite direction of his gaze, Kwan said, "He's over there." Harold turned around and, sure enough, there was Walter, standing behind a curvaceous redhead who was bent over a craps table throwing the die. Walter had his eye on her butt and not the game.

"If you knew he was there all along, why didn't we just..."

"I didn't...I'm going now," Kwan said, heading back to the suite.

While awaiting the elevator, without thinking, Kwan repositioned a tall cylindrical ashtray that had been placed too far from the wall, disrupting the flow of chi.

Dirk stood at the tee on the fourth hole and addressed his ball. He waggled, loosened his wrists, and squared his shoulders. He drew back his club in a powerful arc and let it rip. SPLASH! His ball curved gracefully into a water hazard to the right. His golfing companions, three middle-aged plumbers from Des Moines, laughed uproariously.

"Didn't think you could do that five times in a row!"

"On three holes yet!" another chimed in. "You have used up your mulligans for life, my friend."

Dirk was a scratch golfer. *Perhaps I got a bad batch of balls*, he thought, for it didn't occur to him that his game had just permanently gone to shit. He went to his bag, ignoring the plumbers, and pulled out a fresh carton of brand-new Titleists. He returned to the tee.

"You're counting all these strokes," one plumber informed Dirk as the others nodded. "You should just drop in the fairway. At least you'll be somewhat closer to the green."

Another man added, "On the hole we're actually playing."

Dirk pushed down his anger. It would have felt good to wrap his three wood around the guy's neck. He teed up the new ball, waggled, loosened, squared, and THWACK! SPLASH! This time he hooked the ball and it dropped into a water hazard two fairways to his left.

The doctor returned to the cart, stuffed his club into his bag, got behind the wheel, and peeled off before his partner could hop on. He bounced down the tee mound, careened over a wooden bridge crossing a little creek, and veered across two fairways to retrieve his ball. He parked on the lip of the pond, stripped off his shirt and dove in. A foursome playing that hole stopped their game to watch.

A few seconds later, Dirk bobbed to the surface clutching his golf ball. He wasn't sure it was his golf ball, but it was down there and, damn it, he was claiming it.

Golf shoes filled with silt and muck, pants heavy and ballooning up at the groin, he slogged out of the pond and onto the fairway. He snatched a five iron from his bag, dropped the ball on the grass, and began moving into his stance. At the same time as the onlookers pointed to Dirk with shocked expressions, Dirk felt something most unpleasant on his leg.

"Leeches!" someone shouted.

"Jesus, I never seen so many before," another commented. Dirk pulled up his pant leg and found a large bloodsucker attached to his shin. He tried to pry it loose.

"You can't pull 'em off!"

Dirk stared in horror at the slimy creature on his leg. "How do I get it off of me?"

"He's the least of your worries," one of the guys remarked.

The club marshal zoomed over in a bright orange golf cart. "We have a dress code, sir. I'm afraid I'm going to have to ask you to leave the course. Now." He waited for Dirk to make his move, but Dirk stood frozen on the fairway. "You'll want to get those off of you as quickly as possible, sir. We have a strict no-swimming policy for a reason."

At the same moment as he felt a tingling all over his body, Dirk glanced down and saw countless leeches on his arms and chest.

Kwan sat on the floor in the middle of his room, twirling a piece of red ribbon around his finger. He smacked himself on the forehead, stood up, and tucked the ribbon into his pocket. This is ridiculous, he thought. I can turn it around.

He pushed the dresser ten feet farther down the wall so that its mirror did not reflect the bed. On second thought, he pulled the dresser away from the wall entirely. He used a dime to unscrew the bolts at its back, then detached the mirror and stowed it in a closet. Closing his eyes, he invited the forces of chi to guide him.

When he had a clear mental picture of what needed to be done, Kwan took from his suitcase a compass, a crystal fish, a porcelain unicorn, a cloisonné peacock, three small wooden horses, a bunch of silk peonies, and a handful of crystal prisms.

風
水

CHAPTER SIXTEEN

It was nightfall before Henri had finished foofing and joozhing Charlotte, and Dirk had grown weary pacing the Persian carpet in the sitting room of the penthouse suite. His chest, back, legs, arms, buttocks, and one side of his face were traversed with bright red welts. He scratched himself as he walked back and forth, hoping the antihistamine he had purchased at the gift shop would soon take effect.

Finally, there was a knock at the door, and he rushed to open it. It had been a lousy day so far, but he was determined to have a good time with Charlotte. Perhaps a candle-lit dinner with a couple bottles of wine and a demonstration of remorse for the things he had said would place everything back on track.

He wasn't certain of what an apology required, but Dirk knew from the look on Charlotte's face as she left, that something was upsetting her. If it had been Charlene who was angry and moping, the remedy was simple, if expensive. Anything in a robin's egg blue box with the word Tiffany on it would suffice.

He had never met anyone quite like Charlotte, so he was going to have to play it by ear. He opened the door and staggered back. The last thing he planned to do was blurt out, "Marry me!"

It was either by some miraculous twist of fate or perhaps simply that Henri was having an off day, whatever the reason, but Charlotte had been made up to look radiant, elegant, and simply stunning. Whereas the other women in the salon had their hair teased and piled high atop their heads, Charlotte's was pulled into a silky chignon, and her make-up enhanced the features God had given her, and no more. As if Grace Kelly had been reincarnated, Charlotte stepped into the room with the regal air of cool silk.

"Marry me!" Dirk repeated, with no less enthusiasm the second time around. He tore at a nasty welt on his forehead.

"What happened to your face?" Charlotte asked. It was swollen, blotchy and bleeding where Dirk had scratched it. As he rubbed the abrasions on his neck, Charlotte noticed that his hands and forearms were also patterned with swollen ridges.

Dirk was usually good in a pinch. He could make up a convincing story to explain away almost anything on a moment's notice. It was something on which he prided himself. He wanted to invent a fantastic tale in which he rescued a child from the swollen creek on the tenth hole, or had bravely dived into the water hazard on seventeen to retrieve an elderly woman's wedding ring, which had flown off her hand as she hit a chip shot, but he drew a blank.

"Leeches," he said glumly.

"For real?"

Forgetting about his plan for making up with Charlotte, much less marrying her, he snapped back, "What kind of a stupid question is that? Of course, for real."

Charlene wouldn't have cared if the man were disappearing in front of her very eyes due to a flesh-eating virus—she'd plaster a smile on her face and suggest they go to an expensive restaurant, or shopping. Charlotte just stood there staring at him. "We are on the guest list for tonight's show," he croaked.

"I don't mean to be rude," she began, "but where did you come into contact with leeches? I mean, it's kind of weird. We are in a desert."

Ever since he had met her, things had been kind of kooky, but try as he might, the doctor couldn't logically lay any of the blame at her feet. She hadn't asked for a ride home from the Nightingales. She hadn't invited herself to meet him for a drink or suggested they go to Vegas or made him play golf; nonetheless, he couldn't shake the nagging feeling that somehow she was at the root of his recent misadventures.

"Golfing," he told her. "Did you hear my question?"

Tossing her head back in what she meant as a carefree, devil-may-care gesture, she assumed his proposal was some kind of cockeyed joke.

"Well...?" He was perfectly serious.

Charlotte could only think that leeches had sucked out some of his gray matter. "Marry you? We don't even know each other!"

Good point, he thought. This was one strange lady. How many women would turn down a marriage proposal from a plastic surgeon with a thriving practice in Beverly Hills? "Why don't you change while I take a shower, and we'll grab some dinner before the show? Then we'll get to know each other. And discuss our future."

"I like this outfit," she told him. She felt good in the fitted shirt, jeans, and cowboy boots. "The only other thing I have is the Chanel dress, and it's trashed. And there is no future for us."

He scratched his leg. "The girl from the shop came up to collect the clothing you were sending back, and I took the liberty of hanging on to a few things," he confessed. "The mink was a little over the top, but I sure liked that evening gown. Please don't be cross with me, but I told them you were keeping it. If you're not going to marry me it's the least you can do."

She emphatically shook her head.

"Please, Charlotte," he begged. "It's my treat."

"I told you I was capable of buying my own clothes, and I would never have occasion to wear something like that again. It's too extravagant."

"It isn't really," he argued, reaching under his golf shirt to claw at his ribcage. "At least try it on, would you?"

She sighed because she knew the kinds of things that happened when she succumbed to requests of this nature. "I can't. I know that dress costs a fortune, and it just isn't me."

"At least try it on. You can let me do this one thing for you." The itching was driving him insane and he wanted desperately to jump into the shower. "For God's sake, Charlotte. I have no problem buying you that dress. It's half the price of a rhinoplasty, and I can do twenty of those in a day."

"Why don't you buy it for Charlene?"

He stood back and looked at her. "She wouldn't do it justice," he replied honestly.

She was touched. It was a very nice thing for him to say, and her stomach was growling. "Okay, thank you. I can be ready in ten minutes." She went into her room and shut the door.

The celestial garment was laid out on the bed with its extravagant price tag prominently displayed. She looked at the dress and a pair of crystal beaded mules peeking out from under the bed skirt and she felt sick. The cost of the gown was dear in terms of money, but Charlotte was more concerned with the intangible price of wearing this particular piece of clothing. She unbuttoned her shirt, then picked up the hand-stitched dress and faced the mirror.

"Oh, brother," she said to her reflection.

She had never encountered a moral dilemma before, and suddenly her life was rife with them. She considered Charlene's feelings, and the two hundred fifty thousand dollars, and the way the doctor was attempting to buy her affections, and the nagging feeling that she had seen Joey in the lobby of the Flamingo Hotel. What did it all mean?

She couldn't fathom any explanation and tried to recall the starting point of this eruption of options, decisions, and choices—

when Dirk knocked at her door, interrupting any epiphany that might have been forthcoming. She dropped her jeans and stepped into the magnificent gown.

"I'm almost ready. One second."

"I haven't even showered yet," he grumbled, wondering how in the hell a woman could be dressed and ready to go in less than a minute. It took him longer than that to choose which socks to wear. He was particular about his appearance, which made the leech marks all the more annoying. "I just wanted to tell you that there are shoes that go with the dress."

A whole outfit, she thought. Until the day before, she had never owned one complete actual outfit. Now she had two of the most impractical and expensive ensembles imaginable in her possession.

"How long is it going to take you to get ready? I'm really hungry." She slipped a foot into one of the shoes embellished with Swarovski crystals. It fit perfectly. Don't even go there, she told herself.

"Give me ten minutes," Dirk replied, chagrined. He didn't like to rush through his ritual ablutions. He pulled off his shirt on his way to the shower, and it pissed him off that the stupid girl at the men's shop failed to send the socks he requested to go with his new navy blue suit. By the time he noticed the socks were missing, he raced down to the shop, but they had just sold the last pair to a very pleasant Asian man. Dirk then phoned every men's clothier in Las Vegas, and even a Wal-Mart and two J.C. Penney's, but came up empty-handed. He would have two choices—wear white athletic socks with his Prada loafers and Armani suit—or go without socks entirely. It's not the '80s, he told himself. White socks it is.

He flung aside the shower curtain, turned on the hot water and removed the rest of his clothes. He puffed up his well-developed chest and turned to the mirror. His jaw dropped. Bright red welts crisscrossed his entire body as though he had tangoed with a cantankerous porcupine. He immediately began to scratch.

Across the hallway in his suite, Kwan sat on the sofa tying his shoelaces. He liked his new blue socks and thought they nicely complemented his trousers and dress shoes. He had persuaded Harold and Walter to join him for a quiet dinner, after which they could do whatever they pleased. He decided to dress for dinner, and the navy blue socks from the men's shop in the hotel completed his elegantly casual look.

It wasn't like Kwan to give too much thought to his appearance, but things recently seemed just a little out of whack. He tied his other shoe, glanced up at the portable fountain in the corner, and realized that he hadn't turned it on. He wiped a speck from the toe of his shoe and got up.

Dirk stared in horror at his reflection until the mirror became shrouded in steam. He stepped into the shower and immediately felt better. He adjusted the temperature to cool, and the itching subsided at once. The hotel shampoo produced thick suds as he massaged his head. It came as a shock when the water temperature shot to freezing and even more so when the pressure dropped to barely a drip. He scooped foam away from his eyes and adjusted and readjusted the knob, but to no avail. There was simply no water.

風
水

CHAPTER SEVENTEEN

Joey crouched in front of a vinyl mirror over a tiny sink under the low ceiling of his mini-Airstream in an attempt to see himself in the new tuxedo. He took the ends of a black silk bow tie and tied a perfect bow. He combed his hair, brushed his teeth and made his way outdoors, where he could finally stand erect.

Rolling his head from side to side, he massaged the kinks out of his neck before hitting the main road to thumb a ride into town. As luck would have it, Carla was headed for work herself and pulled up alongside Joey in a sporty Cadillac convertible.

"You're a sight for sore eyes," he said, climbing in. Her face was fresh scrubbed, her hair was pulled into a loose ponytail, and she wore jeans with a plain white T-shirt. "Wow. You look great."

"Feel kinda naked without my hair and make-up," she answered, stepping on the gas. "But thanks. Are you nervous about your first night?"

"Should I be? What can go wrong?" It seemed fairly straightforward. Take orders, bring the drinks, pick up tips.

"Mostly it's okay, but sometimes you get a pain-in-the-ass customer and then look out. You gotta treat them with kid gloves. That comes directly from management."

"Fred Utech?"

She nodded. "He's a dolt. I dated him for a while, but it wasn't meant to be. He's really immature. I was a cocktail waitress back then. Glad that's over." She looked at him and shook her head. "I'm sorry. It's not so bad for a guy. You'll be okay."

"Well, I'm not going to be a waiter forever."

She laughed. "It's your first night, right?"

"I have to repay a debt and save a few bucks, and then I'm going to take some acting classes. I am going places."

"Good for you. It's important to keep your eye on the prize. Acting classes, huh? You wanna be a double threat?" She seemed genuinely impressed.

"Excuse me?" Joey said.

"Didn't you tell me you wanted to be a singer? With the acting, I figured…"

Joey sighed. "That career didn't really go anywhere. I need something steady."

"Acting. Perfect. You've really got it together," she said, admiring his chutzpah.

Joey suddenly felt as though he might be getting it together. He looked incredibly handsome in the new tux. That and a recent sense of responsibility made him feel grown up. He couldn't wait to see the look on Charlotte's face when he repaid her for all the money he had borrowed. He was certain she didn't know about half of it and would be delighted to have a thick stack of hundred dollar bills pressed into her palm. He would immediately tell her about the acting classes he joined and the many auditions he would be going on—legitimate auditions—the kind that didn't require the removal of one's pants.

Carla swung the Caddie into the employee parking lot at the Flamingo and, as they rounded the corner, Joey could have sworn he saw Charlotte exiting the hotel with a man. *Right*, he thought. *I've got Charlotte on the brain.* Carla parked the car and they walked to the rear entrance together.

"Good luck tonight, Kid," she said patting his arm.

"Break a leg," he responded, having decided to give up Rat Pack lingo in favor of show people talk. "Knock 'em dead."

Dirk and Charlotte had left the hotel and stepped onto the strip where Dirk puffed up his chest beside the vision that was Charlotte. Passersby and people in cars gawked. She had taken Dirk's arm to steady herself on the tricky heels of the beaded shoes and feared people were either staring at Dirk, with his welts and silly white socks, which would have been rude, or perhaps because something was amiss with her own appearance, but she was perfection. It didn't occur to Charlotte that they were irresistibly drawn to the beautiful young woman in a fabulous evening gown. Every few feet, she stopped to smooth the back of the clingy fabric to ensure that nothing that wasn't supposed to be sticking out, was.

A group of tourists with cameras swinging from their necks surrounded them on the sidewalk. "Can I have your autograph?" asked a heavy gal who thrust a small book and a pen into Charlotte's hands.

"Excuse me?" Charlotte looked around to see whether there was anyone else to whom the woman might be speaking.

"For my daughter," the woman answered, pointing to the place on the paper where she wanted the signature to appear. "Back in Milwaukee." She rattled her autograph book in Charlotte's face.

"But I'm not anybody," Charlotte protested.

"You're one of the showgirls. We've been to nearly every show in town." She stepped closer to Charlotte and said judgmentally, "I like the dancing, but I hate those skimpy outfits. Bits sticking out all over. Ooosh."

A colossal man with sweat dripping off his chins shook his head. "Christ, Tillie. What is wrong with you?"

"Sorry, hon," she apologized to Charlotte. "You look decent enough. I used to have a flat stomach, you know."

She screwed up her mouth and squinted at Dirk. "Who're you, the manager?" Her tone seemed accusatorial. She turned to Charlotte and smiled. "Write 'to Becky. Aim for the stars, love... whatever your name is, okay?"

"Sign the damned thing and let's get out of here," Dirk said crossly. Bewildered, Charlotte autographed the woman's book.

The woman looked at the signature. "Nightingale. I'm surprised you didn't become a nurse, but I suppose there's nothing as glamorous as being a showgirl, eh?"

"I don't know," Charlotte said uncertainly. "I always wanted to be a librarian, until just recently. I've actually been thinking about starting a small business with..."

Dirk cut her off, taking her by the arm and pushing past the tourists. His sores were beginning to itch again, and he hadn't been able to completely rinse the shampoo out of his hair. Housekeeping had sent up a maintenance man to fix the shower, but he was baffled and unable to get it to function. All of the other suites were booked up, and Dirk was not willing to downgrade to a lesser accommodation—so he had done his level best to rinse his hair in the sink with a small drinking glass. He literally itched from head to toe.

"Bunch of fools," he cracked.

Tillie turned around. "I heard that."

Dirk quickly pulled Charlotte down the street. "That was kind of weird," she said.

"Showgirl," he sniffed. "In a five-thousand-dollar dress. As if."

Charlotte pulled the hairpins out of her 'do.

"What are you doing? You looked great. How much did it cost to have your hair done?"

She shook her hair out and ran her fingers through it. "It was giving me a headache. And you didn't have to be so rude to those people. I paid for the hair-do myself, by the way."

風
水

CHAPTER EIGHTEEN

Charlotte faced Dirk across a Formica table in the booth of a diner where they were having a meal, such as it was. A mound of wilted lettuce heaped into a faux wooden salad bowl separated them. Dirk pushed gray meat around in coagulated gravy slurping over the sides of the chipped blue plate upon which it had been served. Charlotte used her napkin to wipe lipstick off her mouth and then rubbed the paper against her cheeks to rid them of blush. Each time she removed some artifact of the makeover Henri had given her, Dirk winced.

"You're not still mad about the tourists, are you?"

She shook her head and pushed the slimy lettuce to his side of the table.

"I don't feel like myself," she replied, never imagining that she would so dearly miss the person she had been just one day before. "I want to go home."

In his heart, Dirk knew the outcome—regardless of what he wanted, attempted, cajoled, or paid for. He thought about Charlene and how she would probably slather the damned salad in Thousand Island dressing and gobble it up just to please him. Before him sat a young lady to whom he was willing to offer the world, and all she had to do was put on a little make-up, a decent dress, and act like she was grateful. Charlotte didn't seem to care if he spent one thin dime or fifty thousand dollars on her, and just what kind of woman is that? It irked him to no end.

"You said you would stay one night," he refreshed her memory. "And we're on the list for the show."

"I can't wait," she said, with no enthusiasm whatsoever.

"I would have taken you to a better place for dinner, but every single decent restaurant in Las Vegas was booked solid. You heard the concierge yourself. You said you were hungry a million times. So here we are." He pushed the salad to Charlotte. "There is absolutely nothing wrong with that lettuce."

She shoved it back. "Dinner's on me. You eat it."

And just to prove his point, he did, and although he was certain it was done covertly, when Charlotte had turned away, she caught him spitting into a flimsy paper napkin.

Across town where the better restaurants were found, Kwan and party were seated at a low-slung table in an upscale Asian-fusion place started by a celebrity chef with his own TV show and a large line of cookware, utensils and hair care products distributed by Target. A gorgeous young Thai woman in a colorful sexy sarong snapped open a linen napkin, and in one smooth move placed it across Kwan's lap. She looked at Kwan and smiled.

"May I take your order?"

Harold and Walter traded glances. Kwan was on a roll, even if he wasn't aware of it.

Carla stood in front of a bank of make-up lights as a pretty showgirl zipped her into a nearly transparent gown. Carla bent over and adjusted the weight of her large breasts into the tiny cups of the dress, then stood erect, pleased with the way her décolletage bubbled over the plunging neckline. She sat at the dressing table and opened a large tackle box filled with cosmetics. Lip liner poised in hand, she leaned into the mirror and noticed her partner Mike standing behind her.

"Hey, Mike," she said chipperly. "Ready to knock 'em dead?"

Mike produced a small notebook from the pocket of his tuxedo jacket and then furtively searched in further pockets for something with which to write. He snatched the lip liner from Carla, scribbled out a note, and handed it to her.

"I don't think you've spelled laryngitis correctly," she laughed, crumpling the note. "Very funny."

He was not laughing, and from the way he was rubbing his throat and mopping the sweat off his brow with his shirtsleeve, it was plain to see that he was under the weather.

"You have got to be kidding," she moaned. "We bring down the house with that last number."

Mike plucked a tissue from a box on the dressing table and loudly blew his nose.

Charlotte and Dirk arrived at the Flamingo's showroom behind the noisy group of tourists from the Midwest. Tillie turned around and glared at Dirk, then quickly backed away. The welts on his face and neck gave him the appearance of a late-stage syphilitic. He stuck his tongue out at her.

Rolling her eyes, Charlotte stepped out of the line. "I'm going to find a restroom. I'll meet you inside."

Once Charlotte had walked away, Tillie stuck a finger in the direction of Dirk's face, careful not to get too close. "What did you do to her?" He was being accused of something, but for the life of him he didn't know exactly what it might be. "She looked like a real bombshell before," she said, and the Wisconsin contingent nodded their agreement. "The hair, the make-up…" her voice trailed off in disappointment.

There was no way for Dirk to fathom that his life had changed beyond the inexplicable occurrences of the past twenty-four hours. He couldn't know that his charmed life, once replete with cars, money, and unflagging good fortune had taken a turn for the worse in a bigger way than merely the strange goings-on since dinner at the Nightingale's. Had he been cognizant of these things, he most assuredly would have blamed Charlotte, for her luck in this regard leaned toward the rotten. However, as he was ignorant to the ways of the universe and its capricious way of turning the tables on people, he stood in line outside the showroom, figuring erroneously that this was as bad as it was ever going to get.

He missed Charlene and her simple ways and the only notion that brightened him was the thought that he would one day bring her to this glittering city and she would wear what he liked, eat her damned salad and be grateful for the opportunity to have done so.

"Well?" Tillie stood with her hands on her hips. "You're not exactly a prize. What is that, eczema on your face?"

"Back off, you heifer." Dirk said, failing to consider the number of tourists with Tillie, or their accumulated weight and muscle mass. Tillie's husband took umbrage, needless to say, but the remarkable thing was the heavy man's lightning-fast right hook, which thanks to Dirk's equally fast footwork, did not connect.

Dirk leapt back and threw his arms into the air. "My hands!" he cried.

Tillie stepped between Dirk and her husband. "Are you a musician?" she politely asked.

"Plastic surgeon." He kept his guard up lest the behemoth take another shot at him.

"Really?" she asked coyly. "Here in Las Vegas? Why, we're here another week. Maybe I should get my eyes done. What do you think, Harry?"

"I think you're nuts. The man just called you a cow."

"Do you do liposuction?" she asked Dirk, smoothing the Hawaiian shirt over her distended gut. The line lurched forward and the brassy entourage from the Midwest, each with an Osmond ticket in hand, proceeded into the showroom.

Dirk scanned the lobby for Charlotte, but she was nowhere to be found. He sighed and stepped up to the ticket taker. "Dr. Belmont. There are two of us."

"Tickets, please."

"We're on the guest list. Dr. Belmont. Two." He tried to get a look at the manifest in her hand, but she snatched the top-secret document away.

"We've suspended the guest list for tonight's show. I'm sorry." She took a pair of tickets from a young couple in line behind Dirk.

"That's impossible. The singer, Carolyn, put us on the guest list herself."

The woman exhaled loudly. "There is no such singer. And the concierge told me ten minutes ago that the show is oversold and we have to suspend the guest list. Please, step out of the way." Several more people came up, handed their tickets, and happily tramped inside.

By now, Dirk didn't actually care about the show, or Charlotte for that matter, but this was a function of principal and Dirk had had enough of being pushed around for one day. He stepped in front of the ticket taker, reached into his pocket, and produced a fifty-dollar bill.

"Will this reinstate the guest list?" He thrust the money into her hand.

"Security!" she shouted.

Startled, Dirk stumbled backward into a group of Shriners with tickets. Two muscular men wearing black T-shirts with the word SECURITY printed on them in big yellow block letters suddenly appeared on either side of Dirk and seized him roughly by the arms. He wondered how it was possible to be sitting at dinner with his fiancée and her family one minute, and then nearly be beaten in a fracas with a fat tourist from Wisconsin the next, and now this. As he attempted to shake the beefy men off his fine Italian suit, his jacket tore open and a button popped off and skittered across the floor.

Joey walked out of the showroom and over to the ticket taker. "Whoa, what's going on here?"

"Guy's having a fit 'cause we've suspended the guest list."

"He's a personal friend of Donny's," Joey lied. "He and his gal have seats at one of my tables. I was just coming to see whether they'd arrived, and this is what I find? Mr. Osmond will not be happy about this, Miss…?"

She quickly covered her nametag with the clipboard. "Smith?" she replied timidly. The security men unhanded Dirk and he shook himself off.

"Where's your lady friend?" Joey asked. "You'll want to take your seats." He winked at the ticket taker. "Isn't that right, Miss Smith?"

"Go right in," she said pleasantly, clutching the manifest to her chest.

"She's supposed to meet me inside." Dirk glared at the woman. "If that one will let her in."

"Your gal got a name, doc?" Joey asked.

"Charlotte."

The ticket woman noted the name. "Not a problem."

"Follow me." Joey led Dirk into the showroom. "I used to have a girl named Charlotte," he said sadly. "Do yourself a favor and treat her right. Some girls come along once in a lifetime, if you're lucky." He ushered Dirk to the premier seats at the front of the stage. Joey reached into his back pocket and produced a paperback book. In a hushed voice, he said, "Men are from Mars, Women are from Venus. Do yourself a favor and read it."

Dirk glanced at the paperback and pushed it away. "Thanks for the tip, pal," he snapped. "I'm a doctor. I know what I'm doing."

Joey shook his head. He knew better than anybody what it felt like to have a woman named Charlotte and then to lose her.

"What'll ya have, Doc?"

"White wine. My date's a big Jack Daniel's drinker. Couple of ice cubes. That'll do it."

"She sounds like a woman after my own heart," Joey said, his hand automatically patting the left side of his chest.

The last thing Dirk thought he needed was some meddling fool waiter offering him free advice about women. Still, the seats were fantastic, drinks were on the way, and Dirk held out the tiniest dram of hope that things could be rekindled between him and Charlotte, at least for the night.

He never would have grasped the notion that for him, hope was about to become a distant, unattainable grail, and destiny would take its place. Had he realized it, he might have looked back at his life to this point and been more thankful for the gifts he had been given and the luck he had enjoyed. He might also have considered reading *Men are from Mars, Women are from Venus.*

Charlotte arrived at the table wearing jeans and the white shirt. Her hair was pulled back into a ponytail and she had scrubbed every last molecule of make-up off her face. Rather than appearing underdressed, Charlotte looked fit in her new clothes, healthy and vigorous like a prize thoroughbred or a movie actress on vacation. She took her seat and a moment later, Joey brought their drinks.

"A white wine for the doc here, and a Jack Daniel's for the lady," he said placing a glass of whiskey in front of Charlotte. Their eyes met.

"Charlotte?"

"Frank?"

"Joey. I'm going by Joey now."

Dirk raised his eyebrows. "Charlotte?" He looked at Joey. "Your Charlotte?"

"Charlotte," Joey replied dumbstruck. Dirk watched the way the two of them had not taken their eyes off each other, and he dropped his head into his hands and scratched. The house lights flashed. "Geez, you look like a million bucks, kiddo. The drinks are on me."

The yin and yang of the universe pummeled Dirk over the head like a thousand ball-peen hammers. He was a plastic surgeon from Beverly Hills and this crazy girl was smitten by a waiter who ended up achieving what he couldn't, all in the simple and inexpensive gesture of buying a round of drinks. As if reading his mind and wanting to one-up him yet again, Joey leaned in and added, "All night. Whatever you want."

Charlotte took a sip of whiskey and was forced to move her chair closer to Dirk's as other guests took their seats around the table. The emcee appeared on the stage and introduced Carla.

Charlotte looked up at the brick house in the translucent dress and recognized her as the woman with whom she had seen Joey in the lobby. *That figures*, she told herself. *My rent money well spent.*

"Bet she paid under ten grand for the pair," Dirk snickered.

Charlotte could feel her scalp tighten. "Let's just get through this night and then we can both go back to being who we are," she said a skosh loudly. "You and Charlene can go back to picking on people and thinking you're better than everyone, and I can get on with my life and pretend none of this ever happened."

Normally, Dirk would have opted to leave well enough alone, but as his luck had recently packed a bag and taken a trip south he couldn't keep his mouth shut. "I'm just saying I would have done a better job, that's all."

As all good fortune seemed to be in transit, Charlotte hadn't noticed the room fall silent as Carla placed her lips near the microphone. Charlotte pushed back her chair with a loud screech and shouted, "I'm sure you'd have done a better job with her tits!" Blossoming in a deep crimson shade, she quietly slunk down in her seat.

Carrying a tray of drinks, Joey said proudly to no one in particular, "That's my girl." On principal, several women in the audience poked their husbands in the ribs. A hint of a smile flitted over Carla's glossy lips as she grabbed the microphone.

Duly castigated, but not yet silenced, Dirk sat forward. "I don't see why you have to get all pissed off at me. I'm doing you a favor."

Charlotte turned to face him. "Do yourself a favor. Call Charlene. You deserve each other."

The orchestra kicked in, making any further conversation nearly impossible. Dirk watched the seductive moves of the diva on the stage and considered his options, though for some inexplicable reason, his options weren't what they used to be. He could call Charlene and fix everything and be back in her perfectly manicured hands within a few hours, but Charlotte had somehow changed all that. No, it was decided; Charlene was no longer viable.

As for Charlotte, he wanted to be as far from her, the catalyst for his sudden insecurity, as he could humanly be; yet he was incapable of rising and leaving the room. So he remained in his seat, eyes glued to Carla as she finished a scorching tune to enthusiastic applause.

She moved closer to the edge of the stage and looked directly at Dirk. "This next number is dedicated to everyone who's having a rough time in a relationship," she purred. Launching into a soulful rendition of Stormy Weather, she took a big heaving breath, filling her large-capacity lungs to full capacity, which caused her breasts to strain against the flimsy fabric of her see-through gown. Had anyone told Dirk just one day prior that he would fall for a Vegas bombshell, he would have fallen over laughing, but on this particular night he never gave it a second thought. He simply fell for her, head over heels.

Carla finished a knockout interpretation of the song to a thunderous ovation. She took her bows and waved so long, but the audience, led by the Milwaukee contingent, would have no part in her leaving before the big number, her duet with Mike. Although the rest of the audience had clapped themselves out, the Midwestern bunch stood, stamped their feet, hooted, howled and smacked their hands together until everyone figured this was how it was done at the Flamingo and joined in.

"I am sorry to disappoint," Carla said to her ardent fans. "Mike Diamont, whom you all know as my fabulous partner, is out with laryngitis. The incomparable Donny and Marie Osmond will be out in a few moments. Thanks for coming, and good luck!"

As she walked across the stage, a few agitators booed. Dirk twisted around in his seat and shushed the offensive patrons, while Joey was less subtle and told a few of the potentially generous tippers where they might stuff their big tips. Charlotte was simply pleased that the night was creeping to a close, and if she and Dirk could make it through the rest of the show without further incident, then that was just fine by her. After all the years of conditioning, one would have thought that Charlotte Nightingale would have known nothing was going to happen the way she envisioned.

Carla returned to the microphone, shielding her eyes from the spotlights. She looked uncertainly into the spirited crowd. Joey delivered the drinks on his tray, and then waved the tray at Carla.

"Go for it, Babe!"

Squinting against the bright lights, she spotted him in the crowd. "Hey, Kid," she said into the mic. "Do you know *Witchcraft?*"

Everyone in the room turned to see with whom she was speaking. Joey shook his head and waved offhandedly, assuming Carla was joking.

"The Nelson Riddle arrangement?" she tempted.

In the time it took for Joey to ditch his tray and bolt onto the stage, one would have been hard pressed to blink. "Ladies and gentlemen, the Flamingo hotel is proud to present Mr. Joey Lozzi!" She crossed her fingers behind her back. "You ready for this?" she whispered to Joey.

"Not really," he said, taking a deep breath. He looked swell in his tuxedo, in the spotlight, beside a glamorous Las Vegas diva.

The orchestra hit the first tentative notes of the song, and from there on in it was magic, or as some might be inclined to believe, a sort of wonderful witchcraft. If Carla and Mike brought the house down with the number, Carla and Joey blew the roof off the joint. There was a chemistry between them that would make that performance of that song on that particular night...legendary.

Heads together at the microphone, Joey and Carla played off each other in a way suggesting they had been working as a duo for years. A stagehand dressed all in black darted out and handed Joey his own microphone. After that, no one could take their eyes off

Joey, prowling the stage like a pro, making every woman in the place swoon. And even though each one felt certain he was singing directly to her, his focus was exclusively on Charlotte.

"It's such an ancient pitch," he sang, "but one I wouldn't switch, 'cause there's no nicer witch than you."

Charlotte stared up at him with her mouth hanging open. He had crooned and sang and hummed and whistled to her on many occasions, but never had he sounded so sincere. Or utterly amazing. He hit each note with absolute confidence and gave the phrasing a unique imprint.

Swaying to the music, exhibiting some very smooth footwork, and singing like it was in his blood, Joey was no Frank Sinatra. In fact, the Chairman of the Board would have tipped his snap-brim fedora to Joey and said, "Kid, you own that goddamn song."

Even Carla was stunned. She stood at the mic holding her own, but ended up providing little more than back-up singing for Joey's incredible performance. The crowd went wild.

Charlotte leapt out of her seat and screamed along with all the other women.

"Wooooooooooooooo!"

Grown men openly wept.

Joey and Carla took their bows, and under the hypnotic spell of Carla's big lungs, and long before the raucous applause subsided, Dirk decided he would make her his own. He further knew he would help her realize her full beauty potential by redoing the breast implants, perhaps removing one or two wrinkles from around her eyes, and maybe even hoisting her tushy up a notch or two. Yes, he thought, she's perfect.

As people began filing out of the theater during intermission, Charlotte sat dumbfounded, desperately seeking to come to grips with the events of the past two days. Where she had once taken what life handed her without acrimony or question, she was now beginning to view things a bit differently.

Before, she would have simply shrugged her shoulders and figured that the cracked circumstances thrown her way were ordinary events in a life chock full of calamities. However, the catastrophes of the past day stood out against the daily mishaps of her life like a botched nose job and threw her for quite a loop.

Yes, Charlotte was accustomed to all the bad luck the universe could muster, and, yes, she coped with it all rather even-handedly, but all of a sudden she was in the midst of some type of excitement vortex, and, good luck or bad, could not remember the last time she felt so alive. It wasn't Joey's doing, although he was sure a big surprise, and certainly not through any good will of Dirk's that she sat up and smelled the coffee of self-confidence.

She turned to tell Dirk that it was time for her to leave, but he had vanished. She caught him making a mad dash for the stage door, and she thought Charlene was better off without him. As to whether Charlene would come to see it that way was another matter entirely; even the thought of the imminent encounter with her parents and sibling couldn't undermine her joyful awakening. *Let the chips fall where they may*, she told herself. *If they don't like it, they can lump it.*

For the very first time in her life, Charlotte Nightingale felt good about herself.

Dirk rapped on Carla's dressing room door and nearly fell over when she opened it stark naked. It was all he could do to utter his old standby, "Marry me."

Eyes bulging, he recognized that her ample assets were God-given and even he could not have done a better job at any price.

"How'd you like the show?" She held him in the palm of her hand.

"Marry me," he repeated, drinking in every inch of her voluptuous flesh.

"Yeah," she winked. "I will."

He didn't look up in the direction of her face and therefore didn't see the cunning ice blue eyes of a true performer. He stared at her body and decided that she was simply the most potentially ravishing creature he had ever seen.

"Dr. Dirk Belmont," he said, gallantly kissing her hand.

Carla was uninterested in appearances, and she didn't find the welts on Dirk's face the least bit disconcerting. The combination of the chivalrous gesture, the marriage proposal, and the lovely title that preceded his name were all that she needed to decide in that instant that she would be his.

"Charmed," she replied, licking her lips. "Doctor." She said it with great affection, and his life would never be the same.

Joey caught up with Charlotte as she made her way out of the showroom.

"Charlotte, what did you think?" He looked different, no longer a character out of a cheap paperback novel. Her heart raced, and she felt a lump in her throat. "Well? Are you proud of me?" he asked.

She nodded.

Charlotte had never doubted his talent; she just never thought it would see the light of day. Joey was a procrastinator, a dreamer, a lay-about who didn't seem to have a plan for getting from one day to the next. Then it occurred to her that those traits were exactly what she had wanted in a boyfriend. A comfortable old shoe.

Joey came with a price, of course, costing more than she could afford, but she could count on him to darken her doorway when she was lonely and then be gone by morning when she needed to face the world to earn the money to keep him around at night. He wasn't completely dependable then either, often disappearing for weeks at a time, but he came through in a pinch and she was grateful to him for saving her from herself.

"I'm going to pay you back every cent I ever borrowed," he vowed. "Then I'm going to..." She leaned forward and kissed him. It was the sweetest kiss they had ever shared—and it would be their last.

"I am proud of you." She smoothed his lapel. "You're going to be a huge star, Joey. I hope all your dreams come true. I really do."

He had had doors slammed in his face, been slapped hard across the cheek, and even once been pummeled with an umbrella, but in all his days had never been so gently or tenderly dumped by a woman. It made him feel good, and as Charlotte walked away, he was filled with gratitude. She had, in fact, saved him.

Charlotte hurried to the penthouse suite in an effort to be packed and on her way back to L.A. before Dirk returned with Carla. She knew he wouldn't be able to resist showing off the ostentatious accommodations for his new confection. She carefully laid out the slinky evening gown that would suit Carla perfectly and almost left behind the beaded slippers. With the heel severed from her Christian Louboutin shoe and in lieu of the fact that she intended to pay for the alligator boots and her new clothes, she tossed the pretty shoes into Phyllis Schlotzky's tacky overnight case and decided to accept this gift from Dirk—graciously.

風水

CHAPTER NINETEEN

Kwan picked up the dinner check and was informed by the lovely server that their entire meal had been comped. Word had gotten out that Kwan was an important restaurateur in Los Angeles, and the entire restaurant staff bowed and scraped in homage to him. Clearly, Harold and Walter had planted this seed with the manager, and as a professional courtesy, the caviar and champagne and five courses they enjoyed were all on the house.

Harold and Walter raced outside after dinner, anxious to get back to the casino as their luck seemed to be on an upswing, but Kwan hung back until they were out of sight and then left a tip large enough to have paid for the entire meal, including a twenty-percent tip. There was a yin and yang in the Universe, and it never seemed wise to try and outsmart it.

The three friends walked down the strip toward the Flamingo, dodging drunken tourists and the seedy-looking men who hawked escort services and nudie bars. Harold and Walter were animated and a bit tipsy themselves from all the "free" champagne they had consumed at dinner. They snatched every pornographic flyer thrust their way. Kwan quietly followed, mentally packing his bags, ready for immediate departure from Las Vegas.

When they returned to the hotel and he informed them he was leaving, Harold staggered toward an ATM in the lobby. Walter took off in the direction of a group of scantily dressed girls who were in town for a home healthcare convention.

Kwan went to the elevators and noticed that someone had moved the industrial ashtray back to its original position away from the wall. He stared at it until the elevator opened, then got in. As the doors slid shut, the opposing elevator opened and Charlotte stepped out with Phyllis's overnight bag clutched to her chest. She was shoved across the vestibule by a boisterous group of Filipino tourists anxious to see the sights, and rammed her shin on the ashtray. She looked down, rubbed her leg and pushed the ashtray into the exact same position as Kwan had done earlier in the day. That's better, she thought.

Kwan gathered up his crystals and books and unplugged the portable fountain. Emptying it into the sink, he felt his own good fortune swirling down the drain. My life is a joke, he told himself. I am an imposter. He finished packing, took one last look around the room, and spotted a fortune cookie peeking out from under his pillow.

Those idiots, he thought. *Always goofing around.* He walked out of the room, and then turned back. He grabbed the little plastic package and opened it. He smashed the cookie and pulled out the thin strip of paper inside. *Good fortune is what you make of it.* He dropped the cookie and the fortune into a wastebasket.

He took an envelope from a desk in the sitting area and placed enough money inside for Harold and Walter to take a bus back to Los Angeles. He didn't want to leave them high and dry without a way home. If they blew it all gambling and had no way to get back, that was their problem. He had done his best.

In the past, he would have hung around the room, patiently waiting for the weekend to end, reading or practicing Tai Chi. He told himself it was the assault of noise and light and bad carpeting that drove him to leave early. In fact, it was something else completely; he just couldn't put his finger on what it was. When he stepped out of the elevator at the lobby, he didn't notice that the ashtray had been repositioned, but his mood shifted ever so slightly. The drive will do me good, he thought.

Charlotte took a cab to the Greyhound station and purchased a one-way ticket to Los Angeles. Told the bus would be leaving in an hour, she decided to find a place to eat while she waited. A plumbing supply truck was stopped at the curb in front of the station, spewing noxious fumes into the air. She covered her mouth and coughed. When it pulled away, she had an incredible hankering for Emperor's cashew chicken. Across the street, a neon sign for the Lucky Eggroll Restaurant shone brightly.

Kwan drove down the strip on his way out of town and found it far more peaceful than the drive in. No one was talking at him, the radio was silent and he actually enjoyed watching the insanity surrounding him from the safety and comfort of his car. He rolled the window down, removed the rubber band from his ponytail and let the wind blow back his hair. He was glad to be going home, but home to what? Did he really want to spend the rest of his life working at the family restaurant, never measuring up to his father's expectations, never venturing out into the world to find out what he might be missing?

He didn't blame his father for being immovable. No doubt, times were hard back in the old country and a person had to be tough as steel to survive. Old Man Kwan was a success story in the truest sense and had managed to build a tidy little empire from one simple recipe. It was Emperor's cashew chicken that had put the Emperor's Kitchen on the map when it first opened. People lined up around the block to get a table. But the old man was stubborn, in addition to being tenacious, and he suddenly took his most famous dish off the menu just to prove it was him and not the damned food that made his restaurant a success.

Kwan shook his head and vowed never to shoot himself in the foot. His dad didn't need to know that the chef secretly prepared the dish every day from the same old recipe, or that they served it covertly to customers who asked for it by its top secret name, Number 7, hold the pork. It was Emperor's cashew chicken and it kept 'em coming in.

He made a mental note to remind Charlotte of this development. It would make ordering by phone a lot easier for her when Old Man Kwan took the call. He wondered where Charlotte was at that moment. Was she stuck in traffic, causing gridlock? Had anything at all he had done improved her lot in life? No, he decided, he could barely keep his own head above water these days.

He swung around the corner in front of the Greyhound station, just as Charlotte stepped into the Lucky Eggroll Restaurant, and decided he no longer believed in Feng Shui.

Charlotte stepped up to the counter and scanned the menu on the wall. They had Lucky Orange Beef, Lucky Kung Pao Pork, Lucky Egg Drop Soup, but nowhere could she find Lucky Cashew Chicken. A pimply blonde boy wearing a paper hat stood at the cash register waiting to take her order. He looked at her as though she were a great inconvenience.

"I don't have all day," he griped.

"Do you have cashew chicken?"

He glanced over his shoulder at a large illuminated menu on the wall. "Do you see it?" The photographs of the various dishes were faded, with a decidedly green cast. Not a single dish looked remotely edible.

"No, but maybe you call it something…"

He pulled the silly hat off. "It's my break." He walked away.

Donning the hat, another pockmarked teen took the kid's place. "Can I help you?"

"Uh, I was wondering if you have anything like cashew chicken. It's pretty simple, I think. It's chicken and…"

"Let me guess, cashews?" The kid chuckled. "Yeah, I can hook you up. Morrie!" he brayed. "Throw together some cashew chicken. Chop chop! Get a move on!"

An elderly, stooped man scurried into the kitchen. Charlotte felt badly that an ill-mannered teenager was ordering him around so rudely. She took a deep breath and decided to do something about it.

"May I speak with the manager, please?"

"I am the manager."

"Do you have to treat him like that? I mean, couldn't you ask nicely?"

The boy crossed his arms over his chest. "That's my grandpa. He's lucky I got him this job. Social security's for shit. Why don't you sit down and he'll bring your food when it's ready." He turned to the kitchen and clapped. "Move your ass, Gramps. We don't got all day."

Charlotte took a window seat and watched a white Toyota turn the corner as the light turned green. The driver's long, black hair blew in the breeze, and she wished that she were on her way home, not waiting for an octogenarian to jump through hoops to fix her meal.

The senior citizen brought a plate to her and smiled as he set it on the table.

"Don't mind him," he said, nodding to his grandson behind the counter. "What goes around comes around."

She tucked a hundred dollar bill into his apron pocket and patted his hand. "Thank you," she said. "This looks delicious."

She ate her meal, which wasn't bad, though it wasn't nearly as good as the Emperor's Kitchen version. The ingredients seemed roughly the same, but something was definitely missing.

Her thoughts turned to Kwan and how kind he had been to her, if a little wacky at times. He seemed a misguided soul. Then Charlotte laughed out loud. Of all the people to think someone else is misguided. But something had changed, and Charlotte wasn't nearly as lost as she once had been. She finished her food, rearranged the condiments in a more pleasing manner on the table, and went across the street to catch her bus.

風
水

CHAPTER TWENTY

Charlotte disembarked from the bus at the Greyhound station in Hollywood, caught a cab and finally arrived at her apartment building just before dawn. Mr. and Mrs. Nightingale and Charlene were sitting on the curb. Charlotte paid the taxi driver and stepped out of the car.

"Wow," she said. "What are you doing here?"

Her sister leapt off the sidewalk and pointed at Charlotte's feet. "Are those Billy Martins?"

"Here we go." Charlotte rolled her eyes. "Yes, Charlene. These are, in fact, Billy Martin cowboy boots. They cost fifty-five hundred dollars. I intend to wear them every day for the next ten years, which brings the cost to..." She looked off for a second doing the math. "Roughly a buck-fifty a day. Do you have anything fashion-oriented to add to that?"

For once, Charlene was mum on the subject of footwear.

"How long have you guys been here?" Charlotte asked incredulously.

Mr. Nightingale was in no mood. His rump was numb from sitting on the concrete, and his back hurt. "We've been here all night," he griped. "Where have you been?" He clenched and unclenched his butt cheeks to regain some feeling.

"Las Vegas. Nevada."

"I know where Las Vegas is, you fool. It was your mother's idea to wait for you. Where is Charlene's doctor?"

Charlotte had been called an idiot, a terrorist, a loser, and a fool so often that one would have thought the words no longer held any weight. The time had finally come to tell them all that she was not having any more of it.

"Good for you, Dad. I'm pleased that my family's as on top of their geography as their current events." This was not at all the sort of response any of the Nightingales anticipated, and for an instant they were all speechless, which provided Charlotte with the perfect opportunity to more fully answer her father's question.

"Dirk and I drove to Las Vegas last night. We checked into a suite at the Flamingo hotel, did a little shopping, went to dinner and a show. He asked me to marry him, I said no, and he's now seeing a torch singer named Carla. That's about it. I'm exhausted, and I am going to go to bed."

The horrified Nightingales stood on the sidewalk in front of Charlotte's building, looking helplessly at one another as Charlotte walked away.

By mid-afternoon, Charlotte's apartment was spotless and she had brokered a deal with her next door neighbor to use his bathroom when the need arose. She got the cleaning bug and organized her closet, her dresser drawers, her books, and her life. She lugged two huge garbage bags to the door and was surprised to find a team of plumbers and handymen in the hallway with a shiny new sink resting on the floor between them.

"We're here to fix your bathroom," one said.

Charlotte happily swung the door wide open. "You can't miss it!"

They picked up the sink and headed inside. "There's another guy bringing up some PVC," said a man wearing a T-shirt that read, "Don't sleep with a drip. Call a plumber."

Although very little could have shocked Charlotte at the time, the unexpected plumbing development came as close to a jolt as possible. She was thinking about Mr. Shirley and what could possibly have caused him to break down and finally fix the plumbing, when there was a knock at the door. She opened it, fully expecting to find another hefty man in a T-shirt with a catchy slogan, but was pleasantly surprised to see Kwan with a paper bag in his hands.

"That was fast," she said. "It seems like I just ordered. How much is Emperor's cashew chicken today?" She reached for the bag, but he pulled it away.

"It's not on the menu. I was going to tell you that if you want to order it, you have to ask for Number 7, hold the..."

"I ordered Emperor's Cashew Chicken five minutes ago and the man who answered the phone asked me if I wanted it spicy or mild."

Kwan was confused.

"Yes, I actually ordered this time," she said, grinning, "and I have the money to pay for it. If that isn't cashew chicken in the bag, what is it?"

"I just came to see how things were. I wasn't at the restaurant. I didn't know you ordered anything." He shifted his weight.

"Would you like to come in?" She noticed his eyes for the first time. They were dark as a bottomless well, with flecks of gold that seemed to sparkle. She showed him to the sofa, kicking Phyllis's overnight bag underneath the cocktail table.

There was another knock at the door. "That's either PVC or cashew chicken for two. I'll be right back."

"Did you say for two? Perhaps I should leave. I don't want to interrupt anything."

"What? No, I didn't say two." Charlotte opened the door for a man with arms full of pipe.

"Through there," she told him, pointing toward the bathroom. She returned to the sofa and wondered how she had overlooked Kwan's high, smooth cheekbones in the past. Did he always have those broad, powerful shoulders?

"It's good that they're fixing the water. If you believe in that sort of stuff."

"Well, I believe in plumbing. On that issue, I am willing to take a stand. Why, what's your position on water?"

"Some people believe that certain elements are auspicious," he stated, wondering where Charlotte came by her lovely skin and whose expressive mouth she had inherited.

She was as confused by what he was saying as by an almost irresistible urge to reach out and touch his silky black hair. *Did I order cashew chicken...for two?*

"Water is life. When you have plumbing problems, everything falls apart." He gestured around the apartment. "Many things were done to bring you good fortune, and I wanted to see whether, well, whether they worked. I have to know."

"Good fortune can mean a great many things," she answered, pushing the bag of money farther under the table with her foot. "Did you have anything specific in mind?"

"You said your car broke down. Has it been repaired?"

"Abandoned, more like it. It was a piece of crap anyway. I've been riding buses and taking cabs, meeting some strange people along the way. Oh, yeah. I drove to Las Vegas in a Rolls Royce. I'm actually better off without my old Jetta. It caused me more problems than it was worth."

Kwan smiled.

"So? What does that prove?" she asked.

He sat back, more relaxed. "What else?"

"Else?"

He looked down at his feet. "You told me you lost your boyfriend. How's that going?"

His downcast gaze was almost demure, and Charlotte wanted more than anything to caress his cheek. "I didn't exactly lose him. I know where he is." She closed her eyes for a moment and could almost taste their good-bye kiss.

"It was the best break-up in the history of break-ups," she went on to say. "We wished each other well. And actually meant it."

"And that isn't how your break-ups usually go?"

"Uh, usually at least one shoe is thrown in the direction of the guy's head, but this time he was a gentleman and for that I am grateful. So that's a good thing, right?"

He nodded, avoiding her eyes.

"Can you explain what this has to do with my plumbing?"

"It's not just the plumbing. I adjusted the furniture, the wind chimes, rearranged a few items, and knocked some dust off." He looked around the room. "I can see you've done some housecleaning yourself."

"You cleaned my house?" It was a touching gesture, but weird. Her scalp tingled.

"I didn't clean your house. I made the arrangement of certain items more conducive to the flow of chi." He said it offhandedly, as if it were the most natural thing in the world. His own scalp was beginning to tingle as he felt the positive energy of the surroundings, and possibly Charlotte, flowing through him.

"I am completely confused," she said. "What is chi?"

"Before I finish, I have one last question. You told me you lost your job. This is unlucky for anyone. Tell me, do you have anything on the horizon?"

She pictured the stacks of cash under the cocktail table and suddenly feared that the tightening of her scalp was perhaps a warning. Did he somehow know about the money? Was he in cahoots with Don Stanton? He looked as innocent as a lamb, but she had been fooled by wolves in the past. This was the new and improved Charlotte Nightingale, after all.

"Why don't you say what's on your mind, Kwan."

He closed his eyes and understood her concern.

She must think I'm insane, he thought. *Maybe I am.*

"I should go," he said, getting up from the sofa. "I didn't mean to pry."

Without thinking, she grabbed his hand and in that moment, knew deep in her heart that he was no wolf. His hand was soft, but had seen work in its day. It was a hand that never struck out in anger, but that could hold its own if push came to shove. She felt the good and decent and kind blood coursing through his veins.

"Don't go. Please stay."

He sat down and held the paper bag on his lap. He appeared content to sit and wait until the conversation resumed.

At first, Charlotte thought the silence between them odd, but then she realized there was nothing awkward in it. As a matter of fact, she had never communicated as well with another person as she and Kwan were doing at that very moment. She looked at him and felt like the universe was unfolding before her very eyes.

It occurred to her, right at that moment, that she could do anything she wanted to. Perhaps she'd write a book, or maybe start her own business. She smiled and again took his hand in hers.

"Yes, I lost my job, but I found myself. Is that chi?"

He gently removed his hand from hers and opened the bag on his lap. He took out his most prized possession—the venerable Feng Shui text—and handed it to her.

"It is the ancient book of Feng Shui," he said solemnly.

She opened the book and marveled at the intricate drawings and elegant calligraphy inside. She knew instinctively that it was rare, and probably worth a fortune. Gauging the look on Kwan's face and how gingerly he had handed it to her, she knew that to him it was priceless.

"I want you to have it." He looked into her eyes. "A gift."

She was speechless.

"Feng Shui creates harmony, opens doors to good relationships, and invites health and prosperity. Four thousand years ago, it brought good fortune to my ancestors." He pointed to various objects around the room. "I moved the plant from there to there to bring you health. I hung the chiming bells for your prosperity. I placed the ducks in the hallway so you would..." He stopped abruptly.

"You placed the ducks so I would...?"

"The ducks aren't important. Here's the thing..."

Leafing through the antique manuscript, Charlotte came across a page that featured an illustration of Mandarin ducks next to a drawing of a man and woman locked in a passionate embrace. Clearly, the water fowl symbolized boom-shaka-laka and Charlotte was again aware of Kwan's hands-—strong hands with long, graceful fingers like an artist's—hands that could save the day if the day needed saving.

"At first I felt sorry for you. All that bad chi," he continued, shuddering at the thought. "Then I saw something else."

"What?"

"You," he said softly.

She bit her lip and looked away. No one had ever said anything so wonderful to her.

"Now I need to know, has your fortune improved, become auspicious?"

She reflected on the events that occurred since he showed up and moved things around in her apartment.

The first time he delivered cashew chicken she had not ordered, he interrupted a possible hair removal/suicide attempt with Joey's razor, which caused her to find the Polaroid of Joey and the stripper, which coincided with her discovery of the twenty-dollar bill in the trash.

The next day, she was summarily fired, accidentally bought a thirty-five-hundred-dollar outfit and broke up her sister's engagement to a plastic surgeon from Beverly Hills. Auspicious? She laughed at the thought, but her mind was racing.

After the second delivery of food that she had not ordered, things seemed to go from bad to worse, but then, that had been the baseline for her entire life. Perhaps good fortune was what one made of it, she thought. Was it so awful to be fired from Eebner City, or did it present her with the opportunity of doing something she had always wanted to do? Namely, help the swindled customers and gain back her self-respect at the same time?

Had her car not broken down and she been fired, Charlotte never would have been on the bus with the lady who forgot half her Nordstrom's shopping bags. Were it not for the lady, she would never have discovered Nordstrom's nor purchased an exorbitantly expensive dress that was the catalyst for Charlene's betrothed to take Charlotte's side in a family squabble.

Were it not for the dress, the doctor, and the trip to Las Vegas, Charlotte might have lived out her days never realizing the strength and beauty inside of herself. Then, of course, there was the suitcase of money that fell rather fortuitously into her lap. Things were definitely looking up.

"Yes," she said finally. "My fortune has improved. And come to think of it, so has my entire outlook."

He looked very wise as he took both of Charlotte's hands in his and pressed them to his heart. "It is the same thing, Charlotte."

Without any further thought, she leaned over, closed her eyes and kissed him. She saw golden rays of sunshine falling on a lush garden. In the garden were fat hibiscuses that glowed in dappled light. The vivid hue of the flowers and the warmth of the sun shimmered off a lovely fountain with a reflecting pool. There was a woman in the garden, framed by the blossoms, standing beside the fountain with light dancing over her face. She was beautiful and happy.

Kwan had the exact same vision at that moment. From the very first time he ever saw Charlotte Nightingale, it was always the same vision.

風
水

CHAPTER TWENTY-ONE

To anyone who saw Charlotte Nightingale only a few months later, she was the epitome of self-confidence, radiant beauty, health, and success. Her shiny, thick hair bounced with each lively step, her wardrobe of a crisp white shirt, faded jeans and Billy Martin cowboy boots suited her athletic build and easy style. Her heart was light, her eyes were bright, and she had the world on a string, wrapped around her finger.

Charlotte turned the corner of her block and strode purpose-fully into the lobby of her apartment building, where Mr. Shirley was busy polishing the brass mailboxes into a rich luster.

"Hey, Mr. Shirley," she said cheerfully. "How are those cacti of yours?"

"Happy as a pig in shit," he replied with a typical, vivid simile. "How are you finding things on the fifth floor?"

She rang for the elevator, the doors opened, and she stepped inside. "Couldn't be better. We are loving it," she said, pressing the button for the charmed floor.

The elevator opened directly onto the lobby of a beautiful suite of offices, where Charlene sat behind a magnificent lacquered desk, underarms stained with sweat. She handed a stack of messages to Charlotte.

"I can't handle this," she whined. "About a million people phoned while you were out, and Mom's been calling every five minutes. When are you going to have a chance to go over there?"

"You have my calendar, Charlene. When am I available?" Charlotte picked up a container of fish food and shook a little out over an exotic koi pond in the center of the room. A small fountain burbled in the corner, surrounded by exquisite Chinese pottery and lush jade plants.

Charlene paged through a thick leather-bound date book. "Next July?! Mom'll have a fit!"

Kwan stepped out of an adjoining office, breaking into an irresistible grin the instant he laid eyes on Charlotte. She couldn't remember a time when he wasn't the most incredible man she'd ever met, and he was equally certain he was the luckiest man on earth. As they stood facing one another, an entire conversation seemed to pass wordlessly between them. Charlene looked from Charlotte to Kwan, then back to Charlotte, and she groaned. *Charlotte has all the luck.*

"We have a special delivery to make," Kwan informed Charlotte. "Washington D.C."

She whistled. "Are we talking the Big Kahuna?"

He nodded.

"I figured it would happen sooner or later," Charlotte remarked.

Snapping into action, Charlene flipped open a three-ring binder and picked up a pen. "Crystals?"

"Check," Kwan said, and Charlene ticked off an item on the page.

"Fishbowl, wind chimes, stones, portable fountain..." Charlene read from a list.

"Check, check, check," Kwan laughed. "I'll grab the bags and we'll go." He kissed Charlotte before going to his office for the luggage.

When he had gone, Charlotte took the thick leather date book from Charlene's desk and ran her fingertips over the embossed printing on the cover. She smiled the smile of the just and prosperous.

It read:

FENG SHUI KITCHEN
CHARLOTTE NIGHTINGALE & KWAN,
PROPRIETORS

Seven hours later, Charlotte and Kwan pulled up to the guard station at the entrance to the White House and were immediately escorted into the West Wing, where they placed Feng Shui enhancers in the appropriate sectors so as to activate chi and bring good fortune in all its manifestations to whomever set foot inside. Confident that they had done everything possible to create a favorable environment in the Oval Office, they spent three days taking in the sights of the nation's capitol, never letting go of one another's hand.

THE END

風
水

EPILOGUE

Although peace in the Middle East remained elusive, the President of the United States was subsequently re-elected to a second term and would go down in the history books as one of the great leaders of all time. She completed her tenure as President with unprecedented popularity and would be forever known as a progressive woman who initiated the reforms that restored America to its glorious status as a nation with a good heart.

風
水

ACKNOWLEDGMENTS

My amazingly wonderful and quirky mom and pops, who've supported me in every way there is to support someone. When a dream comes true, they're behind it.

Kira Henschel—a wonderful co-conspirator and beautiful soul without whom this wouldn't resemble an actual book, or me an actual author.

Samantha Stoeger, whose ability to do the work of 20 men while editing the book was a feat of perseverance and grace.

Cindy Guidry, brilliant writer, true friend, dog rescuer and my champion.

John LaViolette, my gladiator.

Laura Pursell Byrnes, the embodiment of the Golden Rule, and a damn fine torch singer.

Marta B, beloved second mom who encouraged me and laughed at my stories since always.

Melanie Roach-Bekos, my hero.

Colleen Anderson, dear heart, avid reader, angel.

Kevin Roach, encourager, believer, rocker, lawyer.

Kyle Roach, kindred spirit, political ally. Brad Bekos, an even keel always, and le chef de la famille, without whom I would have gone hungry many times.

Luz Sorany Machado, ever there with a smile, sleeves rolled up and an encouraging word.

Simone Van Kempen, my sister, confidante, my heart and soul.

Deborah Tyszka, for her unflagging perfectionism, razor-sharp design eye, sense of humor, and loyal friendship.

Sheryl Bernstein, baroness bedazzler with a heart of gold and a great knack for literary detail.

Ashami Kerr, my eternal partner in crime.

Foxy Susan Brown, travel companion and international agitatore.

Ingrid Walters, Soraya Sepahpour-Ulrich, Kathleen Campbell, Myra Morris, Mina Osheroff, Stephanie Osheroff, Bernadette Kelly—goddesses each and every one, who've made my journey sweet.

Lauren Anderson, Ava Anderson, Carly Anderson, Jamila Kerr, Charlotte Gourley—fiery, ambitious, and beautiful young women, basically everything that is right with the world.

Tyler Anderson, Elliot Anderson, Jack Bekos—my brave, handsome, and wonderful young men who are changing the world.

Greg Friedman, the most supportive, loving, big-hearted dude I know.

James O'Malley, whose cinematic eye is surpassed only by his generosity.

Howard Leu, without whose patience, enthusiasm, and good humor I'd still be corresponding via smoke signals.

Samantha Verant—esteemed author, generous advisor, and world's most romantic girl.

Julie Tarney, champion of all that is just, my sunshine.

And Bella Bekos—the best legs in the business, with the biggest, warmest, lovingest heart.

Special thanks to Brigette Breitenbach, Black Sheep, Company B, Tim Dixon, the Iron Horse Hotel, Michael Falkenstein, TC Badalato, Kate Davies, Anne E. Schwartz, Patti Zager, Marissa Schultz, Lori Bergen, Alexandra Bonesho, Neda Stevic, Chris and Sia Jifas, Veronica Ashworth, Robyn Pearce-Betlzer, Gladys Bullis, Katie Bullis, Giancarlo Sini, Scott Lockwood, and my very own personal physician, Dr. Kathleen Kornafel.

Always in my heart: Zelda, Rookie, Thelma Lou, Señor Delgado, Zimmerman, and Zuzu. And Bob Dylan, who made me want to be a writer.

You have all contributed to this book, and my life, in unique and wonderful ways. I'm lucky to know you!

Author Pam Ferderbar (Photo © by Tom Ferderbar)

風
水

About the Author

Pamelja Ruja Konvalinkova Ferderbar was born and raised in Wisconsin, the only child of two loving but quirky parents (Did you see the name?) After graduating Marquette University with a degree in journalism, Pam, the name which is easiest to remember and spell, worked in the family advertising photography business until deciding to try life in the big city (and winters that didn't require the use of electric underpants in order to survive going outside in January).

Pam moved to Los Angeles, where she married the first man who saw her fall off the turnip truck, and she began simultaneously collecting stray dogs, which was probably more than just a coincidence. In L.A., she directed TV commercials, wrote screenplays and the novella Feng Shui and Charlotte Nightingale, which would spark a Hollywood bidding war over the movie rights. New Line Cinema outbid the rest of the universe for the right to bring Charlotte Nightingale to the silver screen and in that capricious way the universe has of unraveling life's pretty little knit sweaters, all of Pam's executives at New Line were fired and the project was put on hold. (Classic #CharlotteMoment)

After a few years of marriage, the blush was off the proverbial rose, which ultimately spawned a lot of funny stories, a gazillion hashtags, one massive heartache, and the beginning of Pam's personal Act II.

After completing her first novel (based on the novella *Feng Shui and Charlotte Nightingale*), Pam returned to Wisconsin in 2013. Pam's father Tom, a student of the great Ansel Adams and a master photographer himself, has been tutoring Pam in the art of photography, for which she seems to have a knack. Pam is working on a second Charlotte Nightingale novel, a companion book to the Charlotte Nightingale series—*Charlotte Moments* from readers, making photographs, and occasionally rescuing stray dogs. Of the canine variety only.

For more information about the author, upcoming events, delightful *Charlotte Moments*, Charlotte Army Street Team news and Pam's blog, please visit www.pamferderbar.com.

twitter.com/pamelja
facebook.com/pferderbar
Linkedin.com Pam Ferderbar
pinterest.com/pamferderbar/
instagram.com/pamferderbar/

Please visit Pam's photography websites. Beware, however,
Pamela Portraits is a teeny bit racy!
www.pamelaphoto.com
www.pamelaportraits.com

CPSIA information can be obtained at www.ICGtesting.com
Printed in the USA
LVOW08*0016110615

441987LV00001B/1/P